STAR-CROSSED

STAR-CROSSED

MCKENZIE BURNS

ISBN: 979-8-9902658-3-7

FANTASY WORKS BY MCKENZIE BURNS

From the Shadows

Through the Flames

Legacy of the Night

Rise of the Dragon

ROMANCE WORKS BY MCKENZIE BURNS

Starstruck

Love on Tour

WORKS WITH APPEARANCES BY MCKENZIE BURNS

Magic & Moons: A Fantasy Anthology

Chaos & Curses: A Collection of Unfortunate Tales

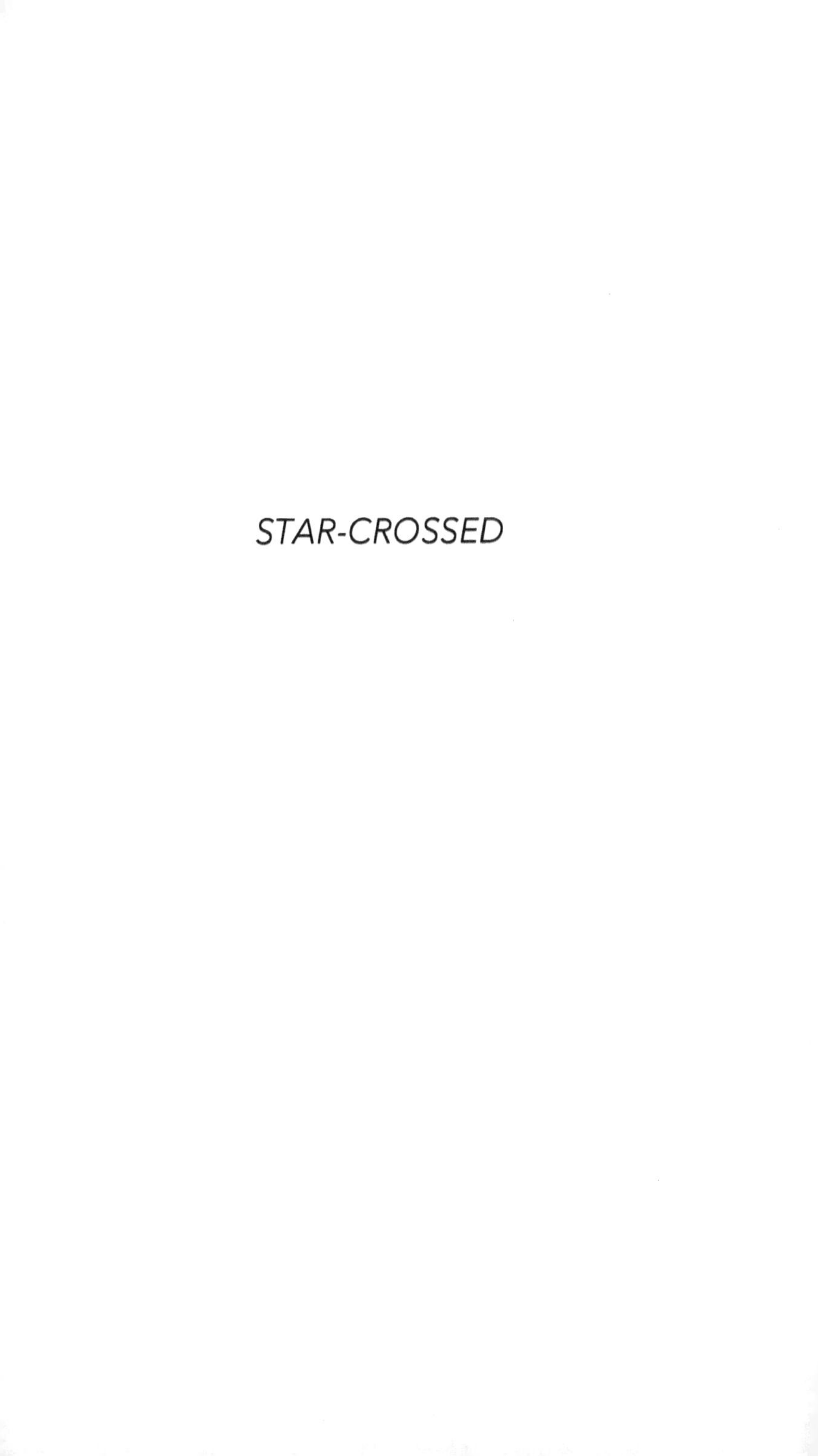

STAR-CROSSED

TEN MONTHS EARLIER

I GRUNTED AS my back hit the wall just inside the hotel room door. Hands grasped my hips as a warm, hard body pressed against me, letting me know that my companion was already just as into this as I was.

Why, exactly, I was into this was a whole different can of worms I didn't want to open just yet.

At this point, I would have been as content as a middle-school boy with some over-the-shirt titty groping. This kissing—this touching—was much more than I ever thought I'd get, given my current sexual drought.

I guess when your work bestie—slash partner in crime for the current promotional book tour you've been assigned to—

starts frequently ditching you in favor of her sexy new beau, it becomes more obvious how loveless your life is.

Or sexless, at the very least.

I was happy for Jordi, don't get me wrong, but something about hearing how wonderful her boy toy was in bed… it was becoming draining.

I'm not saying the current situation was a result of that. But I'm not *not* saying it either.

My hands worked blindly at undoing the buttons of my partner's shirt, and as soon as I finished, he shrugged it off, never breaking away from me. That was until he decided he wanted my shirt to hit the floor, too.

And damn, this over-the-bra fondling—which exceeded my over-the-shirt expectations—was definitely doing something to me.

My back arched off the wall, and I moaned when hungry lips made their way to my jaw, then to my neck.

"*Fuck*," I said through a breath when my partner sucked. I hadn't had a hickey since high school, and even though make-up had improved significantly since then, I wasn't about to allow any evidence.

Jordi would never let me hear the end of it if she saw any unwanted marks on my neck. *She* was the one dating a vampire—or rather, a man who'd played a vampire on TV for eight seasons. I had no excuses.

"Should we take this to the bed?" I rasped.

My chest rose and fell with heavy breaths, and I couldn't deny the ache that was growing between my legs. It had been my suggestion, but the mere thought of taking this any further than it had already gone…

A chill replaced where hot breath had just been on my neck, and I was met with a glasses-rimmed stare.

Apparently, my partner was just as surprised as I was that I wanted this to keep going.

"Yeah," Jackson panted. "Yeah, let's do that."

CHAPTER ONE

"IF NO ONE has any other questions, I think we can consider this meeting adjourned."

Muffled conversation and the squeaking of office chairs filled the conference room as the marketing and events team for Starr Publishing and Media pushed back from the long table to go about the rest of their days.

I lingered, shuffling papers and straightening my notebook, until everyone filed out. I'd learned that sometimes people felt more comfortable coming to ask me questions when I was alone. I wanted to be as approachable as my predecessor, Lynn, had been, but knew I was a bit more… intense, for lack of a better word. A mental filter was still something I was working on since coming into my new role.

When silence filled the room, I knew I was in the clear to head out too.

My muscle memory still sometimes brought me to my old cubicle, which a new team member had taken over after I received a career upgrade. Now, I needed to remind myself to take a right out of the conference room, instead of a left. Toward the part of the office space reserved for management and executives. Those intimidating private offices that I never thought in a million years I'd call my own.

But sure as shit—that was my name on the plaque outside one of the doors, letting everyone know who they'd find inside. *Victoria Wilson, Senior Director of Marketing.*

I smiled, the same as I always did, at the shimmering gold crown sticker that had been placed on the wall above my name. Jordi had only been gone a few months, but I still missed her. It was probably for the better of the company—and our careers—that she was gone, though. There was no telling what chaos we'd get into now that I had an office. Our vortexes—otherwise known as the conversation rabbit holes we'd often gotten ourselves into—would have been much easier to hide in there versus out in the open at one of our cubicles.

Yes, it was *definitely* for the better. She was off living a life most women would die for. At least in our world, anyway. Dating a mega-hot actor. Freshly signed with a literary agent—who just so happened to be our old boss. Traveling back and forth between Chicago and London, and everywhere in-between to join said actor boyfriend at various events.

It was every fangirl's dream.

While many people wouldn't necessarily think of me as a

nerd, I was. At least of the book variety. It was why I'd gotten into this career in the first place. It was like the best of both worlds: I got to satisfy my bookish appetite while also traveling around the country. Plus, everyone thought I was smart because I worked with books.

I was, in fact, very smart, which was another thing most people didn't assume at first glance. Why would they? In high school, I'd been the loud cheerleader. I went to all the parties that then continued into college. But I'd always been at the top of my class despite that. Now, in my career, I was climbing just as high.

It wasn't without a little help, of course. I knew I'd only been considered for my new role because Lynn had thrown my name into the bucket. Then basically told the hiring committee the bucket was full. Thus, landing me a pretty easy promotion.

Even knowing that, though, I'd still been excited. Lynn thought *I* was the best person for the role, despite what others—namely my *new* boss—might think of the change. It was that filter thing. I knew I spoke out and offered opinions that were sometimes hard to swallow. I'd grown up that way. No bullshit. No beating around the bush. Tell it how it is. That carried over into life.

Unfortunately, not everyone could handle it the same way I'd been raised to handle it.

The filter might have time to develop at work, but I imagined it was too little too late in life.

"Alexa, play Boss Bitch playlist at volume two," I called out to the device on my file cabinet after I closed the door.

"You've got it," the robotic female replied. "Now playing Boss Bitch playlist from your music library."

The opening notes of an Ariana Grande song started to play, and my mind immediately eased. I could always count on my girl Ari to get me out of a mental spiral.

"I want it, I got it," I muttered along with her as I set myself up at my desk.

I owed Rahm Singh a report, then I needed to schedule some performance reviews. There was the meeting with the team for one of our newer authors to work on a promotion plan for the trilogy she'd been signed on for. Then with our romance imprint's marketing manager to make sure the latest campaign was in a good spot. Then there was always the inevitable meeting with—

My head popped up when someone knocked on my door.

"Alexa, pause," I said, then called out, "Come in," when she listened.

My heart just about jumped out of my chest when Jackson S. Albrecht came into view. He gave me a shy wave before he slithered his way through the crack he'd created, then closed the door promptly behind himself.

If there ever was a man that no one in the Starr office wanted to see, it was this one. Not because he was foul to look at. The opposite, actually. Jackson was plain as they came when looks were considered—a little skinny, just shy of six-feet, well-groomed—but not unattractive by any means.

No, it was because he'd made quite the name for himself around these parts. Around the publishing world as a whole, I was sure, at this point. But we lucky souls at Starr were the ones who got to deal with his diva attitude and borderline-absurd requests.

I mean, none of our other authors came with demands to make sure their favorite brand of Costa Rican coffee beans had been stocked in the break room for their visit. Or that the office thermostat be set to exactly seventy-two degrees. Or that he be allowed an office—not a spare cubicle—so he could write in peace between meetings.

And, as always, he'd found his way into *my* office.

"You look guilty," I said by way of greeting.

His brows furrowed as he made his way further into the space. "I do?"

"Very." I stood from my chair and met him in front of my desk, my arms crossed over my chest. "Any reason for that, Mr. Albrecht?"

By this point, I expected it—when his hands found their way onto my hips. I didn't budge, but he used his hold to pull himself closer to me.

"I suppose I've been thinking a lot," he whispered.

"About anything in particular?"

His hands began to roam, clutching my blouse and untucking it from my pencil skirt. "About what you might be wearing today for our meeting."

"It's not *our* meeting," I reminded him as my hands snaked

up his chest then latched around his neck. "It's a meeting for *your* contract extension."

"Then even more reason for me to think about this," he said. His hands were now working at my buttons, undoing them painstakingly slow. "I need all the distractions I can get. Keep my mind off it."

"You worried?"

"What will happen if I say yes?"

I couldn't help but grin. If there was one thing Jackson S. Albrecht wasn't lacking, it was confidence. Especially when it came to his writing career. He'd earned his contract with flying colors, just as he had the other two times Starr decided to give him extensions for his best-selling series.

Still, I could play along.

"I bet I could think of a few ways to keep your mind off everything," I teased.

A new sparkle lit his glasses-rimmed brown eyes, as he said, "Care to enlighten me?"

I made a face, playing hard to get, before I finally shrugged and hopped onto my desk. My hands found their way back down his chest until they latched onto his tie and pulled him between my legs. Then, I tugged again to bring his lips down to mine.

Okay, so maybe it didn't matter that Jordi wasn't here to engage in vortexes with me anymore. My office was serving other purposes instead.

My blouse was open in a matter of seconds, revealing the lacy black bra I'd chosen for the day. I might have planned it. I might have planned my whole outfit, actually, knowing what my schedule for the day entailed. The moment I'd seen the meeting with Jackson's team on my calendar, I'd known what I could expect, as I'd come to expect it from time to time over the last ten months.

That one night was meant to have been just that. One lust-filled night to let out any pent-up sexual frustration.

But then the next stop on Jackson's book tour had come around, and as much as I'd tried to act normal, it had been awful.

His penis had been inside me, for fuck's sake. How did someone continue working with someone knowing what the other party's penis looked like? What it felt like? What absolute orgasmic magic it could cause?

Because there was no other word for what Jackson had done. He'd dickmatized me. And I hated to admit, but I'd been chasing the same high ever since.

Hence, what we were currently getting up to in my office.

I still had no idea why he'd continued to entertain me. As far as I'd ever been able to tell, I was leading the polls for Most Annoying Human Being in Jackson's eyes. It definitely used to be worse; our bickering wasn't nearly what it had been before we started having sex. But there were still the days we got under each other's skin.

Thank god we'd learned to ignore those days, though. Otherwise, I wasn't sure I'd get these periodic sexual reprieves.

His lips left mine to kiss my jaw, my neck, before he continued lower on my chest, until eventually he kissed each of the ample swells of my breasts.

"I like this," he commented, as he sometimes did in references to the surprises I left for him under my clothes. It hadn't taken long to learn Jackson liked lacy little things—just as much as I liked teasing him with them. I dressed for conventions knowing I'd get to watch him suffer as he stared at me, wondering what he might find underneath my outfit for the day.

My evilness didn't stop me from eventually letting him see, though.

It was just another level of what we already did with one another. The playfulness—previously limited to banter—that got us through whatever time we were forced to spend together.

I didn't bother replying to his compliment before he pushed the fabric away, one of his hands finding a breast while his mouth found the other. I dragged my bottom lip between my teeth to keep from moaning as he sucked my nipple, his tongue flicking over the peaked bud.

One of my palms fell flat on the top of my desk, keeping me upright. The other fisted his hair, searching for something— anything—to keep me grounded.

Fuck, I was already so turned on, and we'd just gotten started.

Along with my lack of filter, patience was definitely not a virtue I possessed. As much as I loved what he was doing to my tits, I'd need him to satisfy that ache between my legs very, very—

We both startled at the knock on my door.

"Shit," I muttered and used my hold on Jackson's hair to push him away. "Just a minute. Finishing a meeting," I called out as I re-adjusted my bra and began to hastily button my shirt back up.

"But if we don't push that on social, don't you think it would be a waste of time?" Jackson said out of nowhere, like he always did on the rare occasions we were interrupted.

"My team is already stretched too thin, Albrecht," I replied, trying to make sure my voice remained even. Calm. Not at all as flustered as I felt.

From the looks of it, Jackson was just as bad, if that bulge in the front of his pants was any indication.

He adjusted himself as he went on, "Can't you get someone from the events team to step in? I'm sure they're bored without any conventions scheduled at the moment."

"Just because there aren't conventions, doesn't mean there aren't other events," I countered, finishing up my blouse then reaching out to smooth down his normally impeccable light brown hair.

"Okay, then what about—"

"This can be discussed later at our actual meeting," I interrupted before, in a louder voice, I said, "Come in."

The door cracked open as timidly as it had when Jackson stood on the other side and, ironically, Alexis from Social

Media—who had been promoted to Alexis from Event Management with Jordi's departure—peeked in.

"I can come back later," she said, her eyes darting to Jackson who'd strategically angled himself away from her.

I tried to silently convey the message to think about dead puppies before I said to Alexis, "No, now's fine. I'm in meetings all afternoon, anyway." To Jackson, I said, "I'll talk to you later, Mr. Albrecht."

He cleared his throat, clearly still a tad uncomfortable, but there was nothing I could do. He was on his own now to handle his boner.

"Right, I'll, uh—we'll chat later. Pick up where we left off?"

I nodded once, willing my face into neutrality. "Definitely."

CHAPTER TWO

JACKSON STRODE INTO the room with all the confidence of a man who was about to have his publishing contract extended.

I pressed my legs together under the conference room table. Even though a few hours had passed, the feel of his hands on me hadn't. I knew that if I looked up, his eyes would find mine, a subtle grin would curl his lips, and I'd start thinking of any excuse to get this meeting over with and get him back in my office to pick up where we'd left off, just like he'd promised.

We all knew how this meeting was going to go anyway. After the success Jackson's books had seen this past year, it would be stupid for one of Starr's editors not to buy his new book series. Granted, Jordi's boyfriend was partially to thank for that, but I didn't have a single doubt it would have happened regardless. His first series had been extended from three books to six, and from what I'd heard through the grapevine, he might try to sell something new for that as well.

This was the meeting where we would see how much of that would actually happen, and what our editors wanted to keep the same and what they wanted to change.

"Alright, folks," said Rahm Singh, my boss and Starr's Publishing Board Director, as he bounded into the room, giving Jackson a run for his money. "Let's get started, shall we?"

Rahm made his way to his unofficial-official seat at the head of the conference table. I plastered a smile on my face as he nodded my way in greeting, same as everyone else, feigning respect for the man that I was pretty sure rivaled Jackson for most everyone's general distaste as well.

As soon as he passed, I finally took my chance and lifted my eyes to Jackson. He didn't notice me the way I thought he would. Instead, he was leaned toward his agent, listening intently to a whispered conversation I couldn't pick up.

"So, we all know why we're here," Rahm said as he sat down with a sigh. He gestured to his left. "Jackson S. Albrecht would like to publish more books with Starr."

A proud grin split Jackson's face as everyone's eyes fell on him.

Yup, this wouldn't take long at all.

"I sent around the updated catalog for *The Bandits of the Forsaken* series that includes the spin-off novella collection," Marcus said. "You'll also find the catalog for Jackson's new series we hoped we could discuss, which we're currently calling—"

Marcus went quiet when Rahm held up his hand. My attention strayed from my laptop to him, same as everyone else, curiosity written on all our faces, none more so than Jackson.

"I read the catalog. It's quite ambitious, if I do say so myself—and I'm sure the editors in the room will agree. And while I saw your vision, I also wanted to make sure we addressed some… issues that I would hate to see continue with any additional titles for Mr. Albrecht."

"Which are?" Marcus pressed.

My eyes slid to Jackson again. His lips were pressed into a tight line. It was clear that whatever *issues* Rahm had, they hadn't been brought up before this meeting.

This was the first time since I'd known him I was seeing this sort of reaction from Jackson.

Worry.

Rahm shrugged before he put his elbows on the table and steepled his fingers. "Recent events have given me more of a keen eye for certain nuances of your genre, Jackson," he began. "And in this modern era, we have to be especially careful what we're putting out. Any insensitive subjects would reflect poorly on Starr."

"I'm sorry," Jackson managed. I noted the tightness of his words, as though he was actually struggling to get them out. "But what insensitive subjects are you suggesting I'm writing?"

I was glad he'd asked it because, honestly, I was curious too. I'd only just started to pick up his books, but I hadn't caught anything particularly offensive.

"It's more how they're presented," Rahm clarified. "The cover art is a tad… out of touch, don't you think?"

I curled my lips in, finding something on my computer to make sure my opinions stayed to myself.

At the time the series had first been released, having scantily clad warrior women on the cover had been the style. The same way having shirtless Fabio on the covers of romance books had been the style.

Now, though…

"Okay, then we do a cover redesign," Marcus retorted. His eyes slid over to me. "I'm sure Tori has some ideas of what would be more favorable with the current market—"

"Too expensive." I'd never seen Rahm shoot down an idea so quickly. "We sought external designers, didn't we? Because your client wasn't happy with the covers we created in-house?"

All eyes slid to Jackson, who suddenly found his pen very interesting.

I mean, Rahm wasn't wrong—about either of his points. Designers were definitely skewing more towards a graphic-heavy style. People had all but been erased from covers of fantasy books.

But even if that wasn't the case, a mid-series redesign was out of the question. Jackson had made that very clear—on more than one occasion when I'd pestered him about the covers at various conventions. Nothing caused more uproar in the dedicated reader community than when their editions suddenly didn't match because of a redesign.

I couldn't say I disagreed on that front, but the part of me that had hackled him about it really wanted to get up and shout, "Ha! Told you so!" right in the middle of the meeting.

But I was a mature—and horribly horny adult—so I refrained.

Men were way too fragile to give orgasms to women who proved them wrong.

After a few seconds of pointed silence, Rahm crossed his arms on the top of the conference table, earning back everyone's attention.

"I think it's a simple, yet very frank point that needs to be addressed here," he announced. "Jackson isn't worth the investment anymore, especially when he is unwilling to cater to the market."

My heart dropped all the way to the floor.

What the actual—

"Whoa, whoa, whoa," Marcus stepped in, holding his hand up to stop anyone else from speaking. It didn't look like that would happen, regardless, though. Even Jackson was sitting silently beside his agent, his face like that of a deer in headlights. "You've seen the revenue Jackson's books have brought in this year, haven't you?"

"I have," Rahm said, nodding. "But have *you* seen the reports lately?"

"Of course, I have." Marcus's tone didn't match the determination on his face.

"Then you know we've seen a significant decline in sales over the last six months?"

Marcus appeared ready to give his rebuttal until his lips curled in and he regarded Rahm in silence. It was clear the man at the head of the table knew how to win these sorts of battles. There was space to argue with a lot of things in publishing—font choices, release timeline viability, marketing plans—but actual, numeric data was not one of them.

"Let's face it," Rahm continued. "What happened over the last year was a fluke. This series has been in a decline for years, and if not for the current contract stipulations, would have been concluded three books ago."

A pin could have dropped and it would have sounded like an airhorn. Not a single face in the room was anything short of stunned.

Fluke wasn't necessarily the correct word to use when it came to Jackson S. Albrecht. I would have considered words like *luck* or *happy accident* more appropriate, because that's what it had been. It wasn't every day a B-list celebrity strolled past a booth where your books were being sold and decided to share them on social media. It obviously helped when said B-list celebrity had a personal connection to said booth.

It also *didn't* help when said personal connection got offered her own book deal, left the company, and took the B-list celebrity endorsement with her.

Tori from ten months ago would have stood up and applauded the fact that Starr was set on the path of dropping one of the most pretentious authors I'd ever had the displeasure of working with. Ten-Months-Ago Tori would have ordered a glitter bomb, gotten it delivered to Jackson's residence, and, after it exploded, have it reveal the big, bold GOOD RIDDANCE note left behind.

Present-day Tori, however? She was a little nervous.

"Hold on," Marcus interjected. Oh, he was *pissed* now. "That's only accurate for *The Bandits of the Forsaken*. We came here to talk about a *new* idea and a *new* contract that *you* already verbally agreed to."

Rahm gave a noncommittal shrug. "Until it's in writing, things can change."

Holy. Shit.

I hadn't worked with Rahm this closely until I'd come into my new role, but now I understood the snide side comments Lynn sometimes made much more.

This guy was *brutal.* Zero fucks given if they didn't pertain to the success of Starr. Which, I suppose I couldn't blame him; man had to have gotten to his position of power somehow.

But verbally lambasting an author—to his face!—in the process was a lot.

"So, what?" Marcus challenged. "You're just dropping Jackson cold-turkey?"

Jackson's face visibly paled at that suggestion, that worry from before no longer able to be disguised as anything but what it was. There was no way Rahm would actually—

"We're true to our word at Starr Publishing and Media," Rahm said. "If we signed Jackson for seven books, then we will help him produce seven books. But, as I see it, any further partnerships between Jackson S. Albrecht and Starr can't be justified."

Double shit. He'd actually said it.

"There has to be some way we can continue to make this work," Marcus tried on his client's behalf. "A little bit of an extra push or something. What kind of marketing is lined up for the next release?"

That's when every head swiveled in my direction.

I wasn't normally a nervous person. Actually, I thrived with attention. But that was usually during times that involved off-pitch karaoke being sung too confidently or when the whole bar started singing 'Happy Birthday' to me (yeah, I was one of those people who actually enjoyed that).

Work meetings were different. Here, I couldn't sarcasm my way out of it, or suggest we take another tequila shot to defuse the tension.

Here, I needed to provide a solution that didn't involve any of my usual tactics and would (ideally) end with me still having a job.

"Well, we just came off that tour for the last release," I reminded them, which in hindsight probably didn't help Jackson's case. All that money spent on promotion and no long-term success to show for it. "And, uh, the next book's marketing plan is still in the air. Since we have other titles we need to prioritize before it."

"Such as?"

I turned on Jackson, one brow raised at the audacity of his tone. This was *not* the same man who, a few hours earlier, I'd wanted to bend me over my desk and have his way with me.

"Such as every title that has a release date scheduled within the next one to two quarters," I said flatly. It did nothing to shake him, make him feel guilty for speaking to me as if I were below him.

Being *beneath* him was one thing. At least I got something out of that, too. But there was no way in hell I was going to stand his better-than-you attitude.

"A lack of pre-release buzz could be part of the issue, don't you think?" he continued. Nothing had changed in the way he addressed me. "What if it's not so much a problem with the books as it is with the marketing of them?"

Oh, *hell* no. He was *not* coming for my ability to do my job.

I closed my laptop and crossed my arms on the table, head cocked to the side. "Do you know how many authors get dedicated attention after the release of their first book, Mr. Albrecht?"

Jackson's throat bobbed, and I'd be damned—was his hairline starting to glisten?

"Not many," I continued, answering my own question. "That promotional tour you just enjoyed was a rarity, even for our best-selling authors. So, don't tell me we aren't doing our absolute best to promote your work."

"Then, perhaps, do you have any other insights into why these books have lost their appeal?" Rahm asked.

I swallowed as I watched my boss sidelong. This was one-thousand percent a test.

"I don't think you're wrong about needing to make certain aesthetic changes to meet the standards of modern feminism." I paused, waiting for the usual defensiveness I'd gotten so used to over the years whenever I commented on Jackson's cover art, but it never came. "I do, however, think we might still have a chance here."

"Oh?" Rahm's surprise over my statement was evident. But it was nothing compared to Jackson's.

Clearly, he hadn't expected me to still go into defense mode. Unfortunately, he'd given me one too many orgasms to make me completely root against him.

I nodded, then turned to Jackson. "You said you came prepared with a new series?"

For a moment, he sat frozen, staring at me, until suddenly, he must have realized everyone in the room was waiting for his answer.

Jackson cleared his throat and sat up straighter in his chair. "I did."

"What can you tell us about it?"

"Well, it's still in the works but—"

"But it doesn't matter, because as I've already explained, Victoria, Starr has no plans to expand Jackson S. Albrecht's oeuvre at this time."

The finality in Rahm's tone shut me up immediately. My attempt at salvaging his deal had been a long-shot anyway. Our budget was locked tight after the tour put us over at the end of last year, so increasing the plan for Jackson again? Lynn had barely given the green light. Rahm? There was no chance. The only reason I'd brought up the next series was in the hopes an editor would speak up and claim it was bound to be a hit. Rahm squashed that plan like a bug.

Tension radiated around the room. No one seemed sure of what to do or say next. Shifty eyes looked left, right, everyone trying to gauge what the other meeting attendees might be thinking.

From what I could tell, no one—not even Marcus or Jackson—was going to say anything after Rahm had made his point very, very clear.

This was the end of Jackson S. Albrecht's career with Starr Publishing and Media.

CHAPTER THREE

THERE WASN'T ENOUGH ibuprofen in the world to cure the headache I battled.

What a fucking disaster that had been.

I'd been in lots of meetings over my career, both good and bad, but none had been as awkward as that one, when Rahm declared the meeting adjourned and *no one* spoke.

Especially not after Jackson shot out of his chair and darted from the room, Marcus on his heels.

He sure as hell hadn't returned to my office, even though when I'd gotten back, I'd opened the door slowly, almost expecting to be ambushed when I entered.

Apparently, he wasn't a stress-sex kinda guy. Couldn't say I blamed him, given the circumstances. This went a bit beyond *I forgot my mom's birthday* or *Will I have enough money to pay rent this month?* stress.

The man's whole career had just gone vamoose.

It wasn't to say another publisher wouldn't pick him up; authors switched more frequently than most people probably realized. But it wasn't to say another publisher *would*, either.

A steady knock sounded on my office door. My chin lifted as much as it could with my head between my hands, as if I'd expected to see who'd arrived. I hadn't opened that thing since I'd gotten back from the meeting nearly an hour ago.

"Come in," I called, and regretted it instantly.

Marcus peeked his head in and offered me a shy smile. I tried my best to return it, but my headache won this battle.

I didn't work with a ton of agents directly. There was minor communication here and there as we got ready to really push a book to market, but otherwise, my team and I were pretty hands-off.

Given how much press Jackson had gotten lately—and over the years in general—Marcus's name had become a regular one in my inbox. He'd also been a regular face at the office, since he was local to the Chicago area. Jackson, I believed, lived somewhere in Iowa? Missouri? Indiana? I'd never committed it to memory, honestly. But it was close enough to Illinois where he didn't mind driving in and handling a lot of his meetings in-person.

Bet he regretted that today.

It didn't seem like Marcus necessarily did, though, as he came the rest of my way into the office and groaned, taking a seat in one of the two chairs opposite me.

"Having a good day?" he asked me.

"Probably better than yours," I retorted.

Thankfully, he huffed a laugh. "I'm getting too old for this shit. I'm going to fail my next blood pressure reading."

"And people say *I'm* dramatic." I'd never asked, but I couldn't imagine he was much older than forty. Even that guess was only based on the few pictures he'd shown me of his tween-looking children. "You guys weren't given any prior warning about today?"

Marcus shook his head. "Not at all. I mean, we saw the numbers, and we knew the books weren't selling like they used to. But they aren't *that* bad. I've had clients get offered deals with less."

"Yeah, but did those authors have to deal with Rahm Singh to get them?"

To that, Marcus didn't reply. He ran his fingers back through his lightly salt-and-peppered hair and sighed instead.

"I've known you for a few years now, Tori. You don't strike me as a bullshitter," he said next, and not incorrectly. He lifted his eyes from where he'd been staring blankly at something on my desk to meet my waiting, curious stare. "Can I ask you to be honest with me?"

"Of course."

I didn't know why people in this office saw me as their personal therapist, but it was definitely a common occurrence. Though, I couldn't say many visiting agents had sought me out for help with their problems.

Marcus must be desperate.

"I mean it," he warned, eyes stern like he was scolding one of his children.

"Your no bullshit assessment happened to be correct." I leaned back in my chair. "Shoot."

Given all the pomp and circumstance, Marcus sure seemed hesitant now that the moment had finally come to divulge his deep, dark secret. The silence stretched until I was near bursting from anticipation. Then he asked, "Do you think they didn't want to re-sign Jackson because he's… well, because he's Jackson?"

"What does that mean?"

Marcus cocked his head. His expression asked *Really?* but aloud he said, "You know what I mean, Tori."

Ah. So, he'd gone with the polite way of asking, "Do you think they didn't re-sign Jackson because they're sick of dealing with his diva tendencies?"

Nothing of the sort had been mentioned during the meeting. Rahm spoke his mind, but he was also a professional. Just like Marcus had avoided it with me now, so did everyone else. Nothing about Jackson's attitude was ever said outright, but everyone knew about it.

There was a sort of unspoken agreement between everyone in the office: if you don't deal with him on a daily basis, you can't complain. Yet everyone suddenly became very interested in their job duties every time he visited the office. Or outright pivoted and fled when they heard him coming their way in the halls. Or faked a fainting spell to get him to stop bothering them.

Okay that last one was me, but I was coming off a two-day hangover and was absolutely *not* in the mood to listen to him babble.

Besides, no one on the Starr team knew Jackson better than I did—both the good and the bad. Though the good was really only limited to when we were naked. Or about to be naked.

"I don't—" I started, then Marcus's stare intensified. No bullshit. He was expecting no bullshit. "Maybe?"

Marcus groaned and doubled over, his face going into his waiting palms.

Perhaps it would have been better if I'd lied.

"I mean, no one said anything about it *directly*," I amended. "But he's built up a bit of a reputation."

"I know," Marcus mumbled into his hands. He sat up. "I *know*," he repeated. "Do you know how hard it was to land him his original contract with Starr? That was before anyone had gotten to know him. If we lose this, there's no way another deal will come easily."

I swallowed. "Well, you know there's another option, right?"

"I'm not dropping him," Marcus stated matter-of-factly. "There's been too much time and effort put into him. Besides, he truly is a genius. I've read hundreds, if not thousands, of queries, and Jackson's still lands in the top five I've ever seen. To lose a client like that would be the dumbest move I could make."

Didn't blame him there. Whether Jackson was a pain in the

ass or not, the man still had to eat. Hopefully, he'd negotiated a good cut of Jackson's royalties.

My following silence gave Marcus the chance to groan as he leaned back in the chair. It took approximately two seconds for him to slip into a very casual slouch.

"You sure there's nothing you can do on your end?" he asked. "No magic marketing?"

I shook my head. "I really wish I could give you a positive answer, but after that tour, our budget's been sliced. Not to mention the fits the other authors and their teams would throw if they hear Jackson's getting more special treatment."

"Then do you have any other tricks up your sleeve?" Marcus tried. "You know how to deal with him probably just as well as I do at this point."

Oh, there were definitely lots of ways I knew how to handle Jackson. None of which were appropriate to bring up in this conversation, however.

Thank god my desk was there to cover me as I pressed my legs together, trying to ward off the thoughts that kept wanting to slip through to the forefront of my mind.

People needed to stop saying things that were so easily twisted. Not that they knew my brain spent ninety-five percent of the time in the gutter.

"I'm sorry, Marcus," I said. "Outside of switching personalities with the guy, I'm not sure how much help I can be here."

Marcus huffed a laugh. "Yeah, wouldn't that be some—"

My brow lifted the moment Marcus sat up in his chair, eyes wide, staring at me like he'd just seen a ghost.

"Some…?" I prompted after a few seconds. Silence was even less my thing when it was weird. And this was definitely weird.

"That's it," was all he muttered in reply.

"What's it?"

Marcus stood, the sudden movement startling me. The despair he'd been suffering through for the last ten minutes appeared to have vanished entirely, replaced by this renewed sense of hope. *It* was apparently a monumental game-changer.

"I knew you were the right person to come talk to." Marcus waggled his index finger at me. "I absolutely knew it."

"You're welcome?" I tried. "But I'm not exactly sure what I did."

"You've come up with a potential solution to my problem," Marcus explained. He dipped around the chair, nearly tripping himself on one of the legs. "I'll explain more later. I need to go speak to a few people first, but I believe you're onto something here, Tori."

I still had no idea what I'd said to inspire such an epiphany, but it was enough to have Marcus scurrying towards the door. He flung it open and rushed into the hall. It closed behind him with a solidifying bang.

What—and I could not stress this enough—the actual fuck.

THE WORLD'S LONGEST day of work just kept getting longer.

Try as I might, I couldn't think of a single reason why Rahm would want to see me again after the shit show of a meeting earlier. I'd figured everyone involved would have wanted to sulk much like Marcus.

Maybe Rahm needed some good old-fashioned Tori therapy, too. Though he didn't really strike me as the spill-his-guts-to-a-colleague type. As far as I knew, he steered very clear of the office gossip whenever possible.

But for as much of a ghost town as the office had become since we'd left that cursed meeting room, it seemed Rahm's office hadn't suffered the same fate.

I slowed, trying to pick out as many of the voices as I could from my place a few feet away. The door was cracked, but even that wasn't enough to distinguish the mumbled tones that accompanied Rahm's softly accented one.

Within two more strides, I was able to see who they belonged to. It appeared as though Marcus had found a new home, and he was now joined by Jackson's publicist, Delaney, as well as Starr's very own Senior Publicist, Iris.

One thing I'd learned? Conversations where a publicist was brought in were never fun.

Conversations where *two* publicists were brought in? Downright nightmare-inducing. Especially for the person who was in charge of all promotion of authors.

Also known as me.

I was just about to turn and run for the hills—fake an illness or four—when Rahm looked past Marcus and met my half-panicked eyes.

"Ah, Victoria. There you are."

Every head turned. Caught.

Dammit.

Ever the professional, I plastered on my best customer-service smile. That time as a bartender in college then as a booth consultant at author events these last few years had really paid off.

"Hi, everyone." Yup. Bubbly and totally not internally freaking out. "Looks like I'm late for the party."

"On the contrary. It's just getting started." For someone who'd crushed another person's dreams a few hours ago, Rahm didn't sound like anything less than his usual corporate-cheery self. "Come in. Come in."

Hesitantly, I nudged the door open a little wider with my hip before I slid in and took a spot standing next to Delaney. She gave me a soft smile, which I returned. Then all attention was back on Rahm as the conversation picked up where it had left off.

"And you said it would take how long?" he asked.

Marcus, clearly understanding the question was intended for him, shrugged. "There's no way to tell. I'd say three weeks? Maybe four."

"A *month*?" Iris challenged. "You think this will take a whole month?"

"I can't have our Senior Director of Marketing out of office for an entire month, Marcus."

Senior Director of Marketing what now?

"Um…" All focus came my way. "Yeah, so I know I came in late, but what's this about me being out of office?"

"That's where everyone is confused," Marcus clarified. "You don't need to be out of office. You just need to work remotely."

"Victoria is needed here," Rahm argued. "She's a vital part of our day-to-day operations."

"Especially while that new Events Manager is transitioning," Iris said, rolling her eyes.

Poor Alexis. She'd get it eventually.

"What are you planning to do if Tori decides she wants to go on vacation?" Marcus challenged. "Think of this like that except she'll still be available to do her day-to-day tasks. In fact, I imagine she'll be even more productive. That's the whole point of this, after all. We're creating an environment that's conducive to producing a best-selling novel."

My eyes widened so quickly it was a miracle they didn't pop out of the sockets.

"I'm sorry," I said. "What?"

Marcus met me with a smile. "I'm taking you up on your offer." My confusion must have been obvious enough because he continued, "To switch personalities with Jackson."

"Hate to break it to you, Marcus, but this isn't *Freaky Friday*," I said. Delaney smiled beside me. "I said that sort of as a joke."

"And I took it sort of literally," he retorted. "Not in the switch-bodies way. More of an influential way."

"Huh?"

Iris turned in her chair just enough to face me. "I think you're the last person that needs to hear Jackson's attitude is part of the reason we decided not to extend his contract."

My eyes slid to Rahm who shrugged, unfazed. That part of the conversation must have happened after we'd left the conference room. Or at some point, in private, beforehand. Clearly with Iris.

So, Marcus had been spot-on with his guess.

The puzzle pieces were starting to fit together. But it still didn't answer my most burning question.

"So why do I have to work remotely for—you said a month?"

"No," Rahm cut in, face stern. "It won't be a month."

"Let's call it two weeks with the potential to extend," Marcus compromised and received no backlash.

"Okay, so what will I be doing during these two weeks with the potential to extend?" I repeated with air quotes.

"Fixing Jackson," Iris blurted.

Marcus leveled a stare at her. "He's not *that* bad."

"He's not great, Mark," Iris countered. After over twenty-five years in public relations, she no longer bothered beating around the bush. "Delaney and I speak more often than I speak with any other author's personal publicist."

The personal publicist in question shrank a little when everyone's eyes landed on her. "He's a bit much," she agreed. "But I don't mind doing the work. Honestly, it—"

"It shouldn't be as much of a problem as it is," Iris concluded. "And that's where our lovely, spirited Victoria Wilson comes into play."

"You know Jackson very well—"

"I wouldn't say *very*…"

"—so you'll know exactly what's needed in order to turn his attitude around," Marcus finished explaining. "His books are one thing, but an author is only as successful as his fans. And Jackson—well, he—"

"Doesn't have a whole lot of those," Iris finished.

"He's made the *New York Times* Best-Seller List," I reminded them. Not just anyone did that. Let alone someone without fans.

"People like his books for the most part," Delaney said. "He's been getting a few shaky reviews lately, which is part of what Mr. Singh was talking about in the meeting earlier." When she gestured to the man behind the desk, he gave a nod of acknowledgement. "But people don't generally like *him*. As a person."

"How do you know that?" I didn't imagine Delaney was going around interviewing every person who'd ever met Jackson at an event.

"A quick social media scan," she explained. She pulled out her phone and went to Jackson's tagged photos on Instagram. "There's not too many negative captions here. In fact, they're pretty neutral. But if you do a search of his name…"

She pulled her phone away to do just that, and when the

screen was in front of my face again, she started to pull up a few meet-and-greet photos.

"Then there are the ones like these."

Most of the pictures she'd found were from the tour we'd conducted, since that had been Jackson's last big chance to see readers. My eyes scanned the screen, trying to get as much of the caption in as I could before Delaney moved onto the next.

At least Alfie Fletcher was amazing. His book recs not so much!

Don't meet your heroes.

Superb series. Subpar author. But signed books are cool I guess.

Damn.

"That's not to mention what's happening or Twitter—or whatever the heck it's called these days," she continued, closing out of one app, ready to pull up another.

I waved my hand, letting her know it wasn't necessary. Those few comments had been more than enough to get the picture.

"And I'm supposed to change these people's minds?" I asked.

Marcus gave a one-shoulder shrug. "By default, I suppose that should happen. But what we're really looking for you to do is give Jackson a bit of an attitude adjustment."

"Basically, be yourself around him," Iris added. "Let some of that positive energy rub off on him."

"And this will be happening where?" Jackson lived in an entirely different state. It wasn't like either one of us could just pack a bag and show up for an impromptu, work-sanctioned sleepover.

Though if Jackson was involved, I wasn't sure there'd be much sleeping. Given our track record as of late, that was.

"Consider it Starr's last investment in Jackson S. Albrecht," Rahm said, clearly a bit annoyed.

"We'll book a rental house for you. Great Wi-Fi, of course, but far enough off the grid where Jackson will be able to focus."

Sometimes, I was the absolute best at keeping a poker face.

This was not one of those times.

A private house? With Jackson Albrecht as my only housemate? For multiple weeks?

Screw my office or three-star hotel rooms. Starr was literally setting my vagina up for the best-case scenario.

I'd need to go shopping. I didn't have nearly enough lingerie to satisfy him for multiple weeks' worth of sex.

There was no way, regardless of how we'd spoken to each other in that meeting, that he wouldn't be thrilled about this, too. He'd be pissed off about the premise of the trip, sure, but once we were there it would be nothing to stop us from absolutely—

"We know this isn't the ideal situation for you, Victoria."

I was startled from my fantasies when Rahm's voice cut through. He wasn't the only one watching me. It appeared as though everyone was waiting for some sort of verbal reaction on my end.

At least they'd mistaken my visible one.

"Yeah, it's—" I cleared my throat. "It's definitely not great."

Not great for my sleep schedule, maybe. But my libido was

doing a little happy dance.

"You don't know how beneficial this will be if it works out," Marcus added. "You'd be doing everyone in this room a favor. Of course, there's the obvious."

"But if this is successful—and this is very much the only reason why I'm humoring the idea in the first place," Rahm added. "We could see sales numbers from Jackson S. Albrecht like those when he was first signed. Or when he had that celebrity endorsement."

"Consider it as much a marketing campaign as anything else you do for this company." Marcus smiled at me. "Except this time, it's just you."

"Which means there's a lot more riding on this, Victoria." Rahm wasn't smiling. He stared me down like a parent scolding a child. "Prove to us why you were the right choice to take over when Lynn left."

Any fantasies that lingered had a bucket of ice water poured over them.

Point received.

CHAPTER FOUR

"WAIT, WAIT, WAIT—let me get this straight."

Laura turned completely away from the TV where her girlfriend and our (honorary) other roommate, Bianca, continued watching the latest episode of *Drag Race*. I, on the other hand, was frantically rushing around our modest two-bed, one-bath Oak Park apartment, trying to get my shit together before leaving for my upcoming excursion.

Apparently waiting a week then dropping the I'm-going-on-a-two-week-work-trip bomb on your little sister—who gave me a run for my money when it came to being a busybody—the night before you left wasn't a great idea.

I couldn't help it. I'd been busy. Work had been utter chaos, trying to figure out how things would run while I was essentially out of commission. I'd thought Alexis was going to faint when I told her I was going to be gone so long. The only reason she hadn't was because I reassured her I'd have my phone with me at all times; she could call whenever she needed.

In the end, we'd decided that Iris would be the stand-in me at the office. I was doing her a massive favor by trying to transform our most troublesome author, after all. The least she could do was handle my team. I'd be handling the real beast.

Who, speaking of, hadn't bothered to contact me at all about this little trip of ours. Not even when I sent him a picture of me in his favorite lingerie set—one of the many I planned to stash in my suitcase.

Maybe he was just as stressed. I knew writers had their routines. I'd worked with enough of them over the years and heard enough complaints about how hotel rooms just weren't the same as their usual creative spaces.

This was more extended than a few days of a promotional tour or a convention appearance. And with so much on the line, Jackson was probably panicking a little.

From the corner of my eye, I caught Laura following me with an extended index finger. "You mean to tell me you're going to be gone for two weeks?"

"Maybe three," I added, then snagged the sweater I'd been looking for from where it had been hanging on the back of one of our kitchen stools. How the hell had it gotten there?

"*Three weeks?*" Laura repeated, wide-eyed.

"Shouldn't you be thrilled? You two get to turn this place into your sex dungeon and don't have to worry about me coming home to interrupt."

"I'm not complaining," Bianca said from the couch, not

bothering to turn around. "Have fun on your business trip, Tor."

I grinned. "This apartment better smell like a bleach factory when I come back."

Bianca's shoulders shook with laughter, but Laura wasn't having it. She hit her girlfriend's arm with the back of her hand before she returned her attention to me.

"Did they just spring this on you or something?"

"No, I've known for a week."

"And you just never mentioned it?"

"I was a bit pre-occupied, Lo. You know—figuring out how to handle this long-term disruption with a week's notice."

Honestly, I'd thought it would take a bit longer for this all to come together. But when Marcus's email with the rental house information had hit my inbox, I'd jumped into action, making plans for my extended in-person absence.

Traveling wasn't a problem for me; I did it all the time. But I'd yet to do it with my new title.

My new title that was apparently under scrutiny based on the success of this little social experiment.

I *really* hoped Iris could handle everything else while I was away because I'd be focusing at least ninety-eight percent of my attention on Jackson to make sure I came back with positive news.

"Do you know where you're going?"

I shrugged. "Wisconsin, I think. Definitely somewhere north-er."

"Is that why you're packing the entirety of your closet?"

"Exactly," I confirmed as I flung open the closet door that hid our in-unit washer and dryer. A true blessing, especially in times like these.

I grabbed a few bras that I'd left hanging in there to dry, along with a flannel and a t-shirt I'd intended to wash. I'd only worn them once. It would be fine.

"Three weeks in the spring in the Midwest?" Bianca added. She gave a low whistle. "Good luck packing for that."

"Is the whole company going?" Laura asked.

"No, I'm going solo for this one. Well, with one of our authors."

"I thought you were done with all that author event stuff? With your big new promotion and all that."

"This is a bit different." I don't know why I bothered trying to fold all my clothes. They'd probably just end up being shoved in my suitcase. "It's a bit of a writer's retreat."

"And they thought *you'd* be a good companion for that?"

I paused what I was doing and poked my head around my bedroom doorframe. "Excuse me? I'll have you know I'm a fucking muse."

"Sure, but what about when the author actually needs to write?"

"What's that supposed to mean?"

"Being quiet doesn't exactly run in the Wilson gene pool," Bianca offered. Laura gave her another back-handed tap.

I snorted. "It'll be fine. Jackson is totally used to my—"

"Whoa, whoa, whoa, whoa, whoa!" The speed at which Laura spoke made the words basically come out as one.

Forget sitting on her knees. My little sister fought the couch cushions as she hopped up onto her feet, eyes wide and hands in the air as she frantically tried to keep her balance.

"Hold on," she finally said when she'd steadied herself. "*Jackson?* Did you say *Jackson?* As in that prick hole you went to all those comic cons with last year?"

And it was at that moment, I realized I'd fucked up.

Massively.

I ducked back behind the safety of my doorframe before I answered, "Nope."

"You liar."

The next thing I heard were Bianca's warnings to be careful and two hard footfalls on the floor. Before I could properly get into defense mode, Laura was sliding *Risky Business*-style into my room.

"You totally said Jackson," she accused, index finger aimed at me. Then she called back over her shoulder, "You heard her say Jackson, didn't you, B?"

"You said Jackson, Tor."

"Traitor!" I shouted back. When no further comment came from the living room, I returned my attention to my sister. "It seemed like a minor detail."

"Is that why you didn't mention the trip? Because you didn't want to mention that Jackson was going?"

"Why does it matter if Jackson is going?" I challenged, trying to act as nonchalant as possible.

Laura knew exactly zero details of what had actually been going on with Jackson and I for the last ten months, and I intended to keep it that way. I had, however, never refrained from bitching and moaning about every instance in which he gave me high blood pressure. Which was a lot.

As far as she knew, I was being sent on the work trip equivalent to visiting the fiery pits of hell. Actually, based on the stories I'd told her in the past, she might consider hell to be paradise compared to this. A straight-up, all-expense-paid trip complete with fruity drinks with little umbrellas.

"Oh, I don't know," Laura said, her voice dripping with sarcasm. "Maybe it matters because I like having a big sister."

"You'll still have a big sister when this trip is over."

"Sure, but I'd also like her to not be in an insane asylum. It's much more convenient to have you down the hall."

"Okay, first," I said as I folded some jeans. "Insane asylum is totally insensitive. Mental health is health."

"And yours will be in ruins if you spend three weeks with Jackson."

"And second," I continued, ignoring her quip. "I'll be fine. I'm a big girl. I can handle myself."

A large portion of my concentration was split between finishing my folding and mentally rehearsing responses to any and all of Laura's possible future arguments, so it took me a moment to realize she hadn't said anything at all.

Turning slowly, I cast her a suspicious, narrow-eyed stare

over my shoulder. "I don't like it when you're quiet."

As a Wilson woman myself, I knew silence was even more deadly than when our filter-less thoughts made it out into the wild. She was devising. Deducing.

Not that I'd given her any clues to deduce.

"I don't like when you're calm," Laura retorted, her expression mirroring my own. "Especially when asshats are involved." She leaned back against my desk and crossed her arms over her not-there chest—one of the only traits that would make people question if we were actually sisters. "We should be over here planning his demise. Plotting pranks like in *The Parent Trap*."

"Lo. Seriously?"

"You can't tell me you're above chocolate syrup and fan feathers, because I know you're not."

She was right. And at thirty-two-years old, that realization should have been cause for a life reevaluation.

But when my mind put Jackson and chocolate syrup in the same thought, it wasn't necessarily in a childish prank way anymore.

My eyes cut to my suitcase to make sure none of my lingerie was visible. That would have been all the ammo Laura needed. Thankfully, it was safely hidden beneath my sweatshirts.

I didn't care who my housemate was on this trip. I was going to be comfortable, dammit.

"Did you ever think I'm just trying to keep a positive attitude about this all?" I countered. "How would *you* react if you were told you had to spend two-to-three weeks with someone you didn't like?"

"I would've bought every bottle of cabernet at the nearest Binny's and drowned in my sorrows." I snorted. If anyone could compete with my theatrics, it was definitely Laura.

"But after that?"

She shrugged. "I'd still go."

"Exactly."

"Did they explain why it *had* to be you that went?"

"I'm apparently bubbly and personable."

This time, it was Laura that snorted. "They've clearly never seen you before you've had your morning coffee."

"Or if I stay up past ten."

"There's no way this trip is lasting the full two weeks. Jackson's going to jump ship before then." She paused then, "Over, under four days before he leaves?"

"Okay, I'm not *that* bad." When Laura leveled me with another look, I said, "Over. For sure."

She grinned and pushed off my desk. "You're just trying to prove your point," she said, then extended her hand so we could shake on the no-stakes bet. I accepted.

"You'd better be getting one hell of a bonus for this," she said a moment later as she made her way back towards my bedroom door. Bianca hadn't paused the show, and the faint sounds of Ru Paul's cackling laughter floated over to us. "I'll have my phone at all times. Feel free to call and vent whenever you need to."

"Love you, Lo, but like I said, I'll survive."

"If you say so…"

With that, she went to rejoin her girlfriend.

CHAPTER FIVE

MARCUS HAD PROMISED our location would be off-the-grid, but I hadn't thought it would be *this* off-the-grid.

My decade-old silver Camry was doing the closest thing to off-roading I'd ever put it through as I rolled up the gravel driveway to my home for the next two-to-three weeks.

It was cute. Exactly what someone would expect from a little getaway home. I'd always loved the *Little House on the Prairie* books growing up, though I couldn't say I'd ever thought I'd be staying in a home that was reminiscent of the log cabin the Ingles family had lived in.

Hopefully the inside had made it out of the nineteenth century. I could only live without streaming services for so long. And Jackson would panic if we didn't have the super-speed Wi-Fi Marcus said came with the place.

Honestly, so would Rahm.

My eyes roamed the surrounding forest as I exited my car.

When I shut the door, some birds took flight from the towering treetops above me. Once they were gone, there was nothing but the buzzing of random insects left.

Forget streaming services. I needed Wi-Fi to connect to my music. This silence was going to get really brutal, really fast.

This was one of those times I wished phones automatically allowed you to track your contacts. Jackson still hadn't replied to me, and when I opened up our text string—which showed admittedly more action on my side than his—I saw my ETA message had been left on read.

Damn.

Sure, the lingerie picture might have left him speechless, but the least he could have done is throw me a thumbs-up to let me know he'd seen it.

I thought I remembered Marcus saying Jackson would be flying in. Where to, I didn't know. Outside of Milwaukee and Green Bay, my knowledge of Wisconsin's cities was pretty limited.

Something told me, though, that Timberland Creek didn't have a commercial airport. If it had an airport at all.

I'd seen nothing but farmlands and woods for at least twenty miles before I'd arrived at the cabin. Lots of cows, complete with the wonderful manure scent that lingered much longer than it took me to drive past them. On occasion, there had been what I'd thought was a house, but it turned out to be a little shop of some sort. One in particular had stood out, selling pies, pickles, salsas, and jams.

That combo alone had clued me in that I was very, *very* far from the hustle and bustle I was used to.

Marcus had done his job, I supposed. A little too well, maybe.

I pulled up my camera and snapped a selfie in front of the cabin, which I then sent to Jackson with the message, made it! see you soon!

Deciding it wasn't worth waiting around to see if he'd finally honor me with a response, I stuffed my phone in my back pocket and sighed.

Might as well make use of my time.

THE MUSIC PLAYING from my phone speaker wasn't enough to block out the tires rolling up the gravel driveway thirty minutes later.

Perfect.

I dropped the stack of clothes I'd been unpacking and rushed over to my phone to hit pause. Then, I second-guessed myself and pulled up a new playlist: *Spicy time.*

A sultry Ariana Grande tune started playing. The woman truly had a song for everything.

I wasn't paying too much attention to it, though, as I rushed out of the first-floor bedroom. It was the first one I'd found after I'd decided I wasn't going to try to lug my suitcase up the narrow, curved, enclosed staircase. Wheeling it through the open living and kitchen space to the back of the house had been *much* easier.

Just like it would be much easier for Jackson and I to make our way there as soon as he walked through the front door.

His car shut off just as I positioned myself in the plaid armchair that allowed me to face him as he entered. Shit—this thing was small. I wiggled a bit as I tried to cross my legs, adopting a sexy yet casual pose.

Outside, Jackson's car door opened and shut. What was probably his trunk followed a few minutes later.

Oh—I should probably have some buttons undone. Nothing like a little boob action right when he came in. The man's eyes would be bugging the moment he saw me.

I'd gotten through four buttons on my flannel when the front door creaked open. Jackson cursed under his breath as he fought to drag his suitcase over the little lip in the doorframe that prevented it from rolling smoothly into the living room.

Cabins didn't give the luxury of foyers.

"Nice of you to join."

He gave his suitcase a particularly strong tug the same time I spoke, and the door's bad springs forced it shut with a *bang*. I didn't know if it was that or my state of half-undress that had his eyes widening.

The song changed as I pushed myself out of the chair—that I would *never* sit in again, thank you—and sauntered closer to my new housemate.

"Thought you might bail on me," I said. My hand brushed up over my chest, my collarbone, until it found the top of my flannel shirt, and I pushed it aside.

"Tori," was all Jackson said in reply.

"You've been playing hard to get these last few weeks," I continued, mirroring my actions with the other side of my shirt until my whole bra-covered chest was exposed.

"Tori," he said again through gritted teeth.

I reached out to him, aiming for the collar of his bomber jacket. "Lucky for you, it's only made me want you—"

"Fuck. Tori—stop."

He pushed my hands away before he fisted the handle of his suitcase and moved further into the house. I watched him, half-dumbstruck, but all frozen where he'd left me.

"Um, okay," I said when I finally regained my composure. "Work doesn't have to start right away, you know."

Jackson's knuckles were white from how tightly he was clutching the handle. He hadn't made it further than the end of the L-shaped counter that separated the kitchen from the living room.

"Fix your shirt," he practically snarled.

I did as he asked, unable to take my gaze from him as I worked on righting myself.

"You have a bad flight or something?"

His next movements were like something from a scene in a horror movie, when the creepy doll slowly turns to her victims and they realize they're fucked. Maybe it would have felt less threatening if we weren't in the middle of nowhere. Not that I thought anything was going to happen even now that we were.

But I had to admit, for a pretty lanky, coiffed-haired, glasses-wearing dude, Jackson could deliver a mean glare.

"Middle seat?" I joked, trying to lighten the mood.

The handle of the suitcase slammed down with a solidifying *click*. Jackson never took his eyes off me.

"No, Tori, I didn't have the middle seat," he said. "In fact, my flight was quite pleasant. Took advantage of my first-class cocktail and everything."

My lips pursed, eyes narrowed, as I tried to decipher why he might be in such a bad mood then. "So… traffic?"

Anger flared in his milk chocolate-hued eyes.

"I shouldn't have had to deal with a flight," he said. "I shouldn't have been worried about traffic. I. Shouldn't. Be. Here."

Oh.

"I—"

"That meeting was supposed to be the next big move in my career," he continued, taking slow steps my way. "Instead, when I'm set to pitch possibly the best idea I've ever come up with, I get roasted by the man in control of my future. And what's better is the one person in the room who I thought would vouch for me took the other man's side."

He was in my face now—well, as much as his near six-foot frame could be in comparison to my impressive five feet, three inches.

But if there was one thing Jackson Albrecht should have learned by now, it was that I might be small, but I sure as hell wasn't going to let that influence me to back down from a fight.

Especially a fight where I was being wrongly accused.

"Whoa, whoa, whoa," I started, jabbing my finger into his chest and pushing. It wasn't hard by any means, but it got him to back up a few steps. Which I then covered with furious stomps. "What happened in that meeting was *not* my fault. And for the record, I *did* try to give you the chance to pitch the new book."

"Maybe it wasn't entirely your fault, but you could have tried harder to prevent it from taking the turn that it did."

"How?" I demanded. "*How* would I have done that, Jackson? I'm not sure if you're aware of this, but *my* job is on the line in those meetings, too. Every decision I make is a reflection of how I'll perform in my new role."

"A new role where you have *influence*," he countered. "If you would have just said something—"

"What else could I have said? We've already used up most of our budget on you."

"You could have said anything other than whatever got us sent on this—this fucking writing retreat." I startled when he kicked his suitcase over then raked his fingers back through his perfectly styled hair.

"This is embarrassing," he continued. "My publisher—my *agent*—has so little faith in me that they sent me away. With a babysitter on top of that."

I bit my tongue to keep from explaining that the reason for my presence wasn't accountability. This temper tantrum would give me way too much ammo to use against him. Not that I was acting much better. At least I had an excuse, though. My Scorpio tendencies were making themselves known.

"Listen, you think I wanted to uproot my life for however many weeks, too?" I kept telling people three to play it safe, but if this was how things were going in the first ten minutes since he'd walked through the door, Marcus might need to contact the rental host. We could be moving in permanently.

This wasn't something we could just lie about. Either Jackson came back with a change of heart or he didn't. We couldn't sugar-coat it. And if it turned out to be the latter, we'd both be screwed.

Jackson's eyes slid my way again. "Please. You're getting a vacation. I'm the only one who really has to work here."

At this point, I'd be returning from this so-called vacation with no tongue. Or at least one that had been severed in half from how much I'd have to bite it.

I sighed, shutting my eyes. When I opened them again, Jackson wasn't even looking at me. He was taking in our surroundings: the outdated interior design, furniture that had probably survived four decades if the upholstery choices were any indication, wall decorations that looked like they'd been purchased at Camping World or somewhere like it.

The extent of my time with Jackson was limited to signing events, convention halls, hotel rooms, and the Starr office. I had no idea what his decorating preferences were like. Probably something sterile, if I were to wager a guess. Neat. Clean. As meticulously prepared as his hair.

This place was not that.

It wasn't a pigsty, by any means. Clearly the hosts had tried their best to bring it into the current century with the addition of a big, wall-mounted smart TV in the living room and stainless-steel appliances. But otherwise, it was very much giving Lumberjack Couture.

"How about this," I started when it was clear he was planning to give me just as much attention in-person as he had over the phone. That was to say, none. "There's a room upstairs that you can have. The whole floor can be yours if you want it. That way, you can concentrate, especially when I'm working." I'd already decided the kitchen counter would most-likely become my desk. "You go settle in. Unpack. Do whatever it is you need to do. Then we can figure out how this is going to work, because this"—I gestured between the two of us—"is not it."

"You're right about that," he mumbled. I wondered if he'd wanted me to hear him at all.

"It's been a long day for the both of us," I continued. "Let's separate, cool off a bit, then maybe we can go get some food?"

I had no idea where, but this town couldn't be without restaurants, right?

Jackson's chiseled jaw worked, like he was grinding his molars, as he regarded me. So, apparently, we were back to square one. Colleagues with some level of animosity. It was like this whole trip, from its inception to this argument, had erased everything that had happened between us over the last ten months.

For him, at least.

Finally, his hand latched back onto his suitcase handle and he yanked it up again.

"We'll see," he said, his tone bland. "I'm not sure I'm allowed to partake in such frivolous activities like going out to eat. I'm supposed to be writing the world's best novel."

I had nothing to say to that, and when it became apparent I wasn't going to answer, he walked away, suitcase rolling behind him, and made his way up the stairs.

He cussed the whole way up as he struggled with the tight turns.

Laura had been right.

This trip was going to be hell.

CHAPTER SIX

JACKSON COULDN'T HAVE been gone for more than five minutes before I heard him crashing back down the stairs, this time not bothering to keep his cussing under his breath.

I tried my best to ignore it, focusing instead on my unpacking. I'd made it nearly to the bottom of my suitcase where my lingerie was hidden. Wouldn't be needing that, I supposed. At least I'd also decided to pack my vibrator at the last minute. If Jackson couldn't satisfy me on this trip, I'd take matters into my own hands.

Thankfully, none of the above were visible when Jackson bounded into the bedroom.

"Is this some sort of joke?" he demanded.

"What?"

"There's no bedroom up there."

"What?" I repeated, this time more panicked than confused.

"It's a game loft or something," Jackson explained. "There's a desk, some chairs, and a bookshelf of board games. No bed."

"No way," I said, even though I believed him. What did he get out of lying about it? "The listing Marcus sent said this place slept four."

My phone was in my hand in an instant, my thumb swiping through hundreds of emails to find the one Marcus had forwarded with the information about the house.

"Christ."

My eyes lifted from my phone screen to find Jackson running his hands down his face. When they fell away, he pointed in my direction.

"Don't you dare blame this on me. Marcus said—"

"No, I'm pointing to the beds," Jackson grumbled. "One, two," he counted, shifting his finger to point to each of the white-framed antique twin beds in the room. Then he used his other hand to point outside the room. "Three. And four, technically."

I leaned, trying to see around him. As far as I remembered, there hadn't been another bed out there. But then it came to me.

The couch. It probably had a pull-out bed.

Now it was my turn to grumble. "Did he not look at freaking pictures of this place before he booked it?"

"I can't sleep on the couch. I won't be able to walk. Back problems."

This was the first I was hearing about any sort of back problems, and we'd been in plenty of situations where they would potentially be put to the test. And while I might have normally argued that it was the gentlemanly thing to do—to take the less comfortable sleeping arrangement—I didn't blame him for being so definitive here.

One look at that couch told me there would be nothing but springs on that thing. Sleeping on it for a night would be brutal, but for multiple weeks? Neither one of us would bode well after that, back problems or no.

I tossed my phone back onto the bed that housed my half-emptied suitcase and crossed my arms over my chest. "I guess there's only one option then."

Jackson stared at me for a moment before his eyes widened. "You can't be serious."

"We've slept in the same bed before," I reminded him with a shrug. "We won't even have to share any covers here. There's a solid three feet separating us."

"But we'll be in the same room."

"Good work, Sherlock."

His eyes strayed to the back of the room, where a single door resided. "If this is the only bedroom… do you think…?"

My attention shifted, immediately picking up what he was throwing down. "It's probably the only full bath, yes."

"Well." Jackson threw his hands up in exasperation before they crashed back down at his sides. "What are we supposed to do?"

I rolled my eyes. "First, we're going to stop acting like we've never seen each other naked. And second, we're going to start acting like fucking grownups. Or at least you are."

"Me?" He said it with so much incredulity, it was almost laughable.

"Yes, you, Mr. I Can't Share A Room With A Girl. What are we? Twelve?"

"This is a work trip. It's totally inappropriate."

"Oh? And how would you categorize all our hotel rendezvous?"

His cheeks turned redder than the plaid of the room's bedding.

I sighed. "Listen, I know you're pissed as hell at me right now, but it's like I said before. I'm not thrilled about this either." Or I wasn't now that I knew Jackson had developed a strict hands-off policy. "But it sounds like we're both going to have to make some sacrifices here, alright? Starting with you coming to terms that I'll be your roommate."

"And what's your sacrifice?" Jackson challenged. "I don't see you bending over backwards."

"I'm here, aren't I?" I retorted. "And I have to deal with your dramatic ass the whole time, so quit your bitching, unpack, and just deal with it the same way I am."

I knew my tone had been harsh, but I hadn't expected it to completely silence Jackson. That was one thing I could always count on with him: he'd have some sort of response for me.

That was how it had always worked between us. The banter

kept it interesting, and, honestly, he was one of the few people who could keep up with me. It was only when I got particularly vulgar that he removed himself from the conversation, his cheeks heated much like they'd been a few minutes ago.

This? This was different. We were having real fights now, not just the playful kinds we knew would be settled when a new reader came to greet him or I had to deal with some behind-the-scenes issue.

There was no one here to diffuse the tension. It was completely up to us.

Just like earlier, he took matters into his own hands.

"Where are you going?" I asked when he pivoted and exited the room.

"I'm taking the couch."

THE FIRST NIGHT in a new place was always jarring. There were, of course, the basic adjustments like trying to figure out how to turn the shower on, but then there were the bigger ones.

I considered finding out how many animals and insects I could hear outside the tiny window above my bedframe part of the latter category.

I pulled the covers tighter around me, but it did no good. They were cheap. And the quilt that came with the bed had probably been stitched together decades ago. Years of use had made it thin and not nearly comforting enough to make me believe it could protect me if a bat or bear or giant man-eating spider somehow made it inside.

And I didn't doubt there were at least five of those man-eaters in the surrounding woods.

I'd done a bit of exploring once Jackson had made his stance clear. Absolutely no interaction, even if it meant permanent spine damage. Got it. Message received, loud and clear.

That meant no invitations as I tried to figure out what, exactly, this little town had to offer.

Turned out, it wasn't much.

I'd walked probably half a mile before I came to the end of the cabin-lined road—though that was probably even a generous over exaggeration for how many other houses I'd passed on my afternoon adventure.

Four. That was how many other households were within walkable proximity to our cabin. Given the size of the town I'd stumbled upon, it checked out.

A tavern dating back to 1847. A grocer. A house that had been turned into a coffee shop. Some knick-knack stores. A couple boutiques. A supper club. A confectionary and fudge shop.

Those were the only businesses I could find in Timberland Creek.

They didn't even have a bookstore. What kind of town didn't have a bookstore? Some cardinal rule of small towns had to have been broken with its lack of existence.

My distress over that fact kept me distracted for a little bit—

until the owl screeched from what sounded like three inches away.

"Jesus," I cussed, pulling the quilt up to my chin.

I was pretty sure I'd once said I'd be able to camp for a week; how hard could it be?

I wanted to take it back. Here, I had four stable walls, some drafty windows, and creaky floors to keep me safe(ish). Out there in nothing but a flimsy tent, there was nothing stopping the owl from capturing me in its talons and taking me back to its lair.

I turned off my back and onto my side, facing the bed that had been left vacated. Earlier, I would have bet an obscene amount of money on Jackson's inability to stick to his word. But my lack of company proved me wrong. Every now and then, I heard the couch squeak as he turned, trying his best to get comfortable on the hide-a-bed that had seen better days.

My bed wasn't much better, to be honest, but I was sure it felt a lot closer to what I had at home than what he was sleeping on.

Try as I might, I still couldn't figure it out. Sure, I got why he was pissed off. This whole trip *was* sort of a slam on his ability to do the one thing he believed he was best at. And he was brilliant. Now that I'd read his books, I could never deny him that. But why was it *my* fault?

Maybe it was because I'd been the one sent to join him. Because Rahm and Marcus and everyone else even remotely involved were back in Chicago or wherever else they came from. I was the most easily accessible target for his anger.

It just sucked. There was no other word for it.

All the hope I'd had for this trip had dissolved as soon as he'd pushed me away. To think… I'd believed what I'd said to Laura. I could handle this. It would be fine.

The owl screeched again, simultaneously with another poor creature letting out its own pained noise.

I wrapped the quilt around my head as best as I could and stared at the empty bed.

CHAPTER SEVEN

JACKSON WASN'T IN the kitchen or the living room when I came out of the bedroom in the morning. In fact, aside from his suitcase tucked in the corner—because of course he could go on a trip and not make it look like a tornado had come through whatever room he inhabited within fifteen minutes of arriving—there were no signs I even had a housemate.

Birds chirped outside and the sun cast golden rays down. They just barely made it through the treetops, thin strips of the light streaming in through the four-panel window above the kitchen sink and the long one that spanned most of the width of the wall behind my plaid chair enemy and its twin.

It was peaceful. No one would have ever guessed this was the same place where I'd spent the whole night listening to woodland rodents getting eaten.

I made my way further into the kitchen. The coffee scent hit me harder once I was closer to the pot, in which I found at least three cups still available for me to consume.

So, Jackson was here. Or he had been. Maybe the owls had snatched him up, too. I would maybe forgive them for my nightmares if they had.

I searched through the ample number of cabinets available until I found a mug. It was filled with steaming coffee within seconds, and it wasn't until that point I realized my mistake.

One quick peek in the fridge told me I was correct. No creamer.

No anything, actually. Except for some ketchup that, upon further inspection, had expired three years ago.

I didn't know how much Jackson made from his books, but my salary—even with the raise that came with my new title— wouldn't be able to support eating out every night. My expenses wouldn't be reimbursed fast enough.

My eyes lifted to the ceiling, half in annoyance and half because that's where I guessed my housemate was actually hiding.

One of us had to be the bigger person.

I climbed up to the supposed loft, one rickety, creaking stair at a time. If Jackson had managed to make it up here without me noticing, he was more dangerous than I'd originally thought. Maybe he was a spy on top of being an author or something.

Sure enough, he'd found a spot at the desk. And he'd been very right in his brief description of the space to me the day before. There was hardly anything up here. At least I knew I'd never get bored. There were enough board games to last an entire year—without playing any of them twice.

It would have been impossible not to hear me approach, but Jackson didn't bother to look up. He remained still as stone, hands on the side of his head as he stared at his laptop.

"I'm gonna head into town," I announced. "I don't know if I can survive without my coffee creamer."

Silence.

"Do you want anything?" I continued. "Like, what do you eat for breakfast?"

To that, his response came in the form of lifting his coffee mug off the side table then immediately setting it back down.

I chewed the inside of my cheek.

Bigger person, Tor. Be the bigger person.

"It's a cute little town." I moved a few more steps toward him. "Did you see it when you drove in?"

More silence.

I inhaled deep through my nose, then silently exhaled through my mouth.

"If you wanted to come with, I could use a companion. I just need to get changed, but then maybe we could—"

I didn't finish the sentence. Jackson lifted his head, and I was met with red, dark-circle-rimmed eyes. He looked absolutely miserable.

"I'm trying to work," he grumbled.

It was Saturday, which meant I didn't need to do anything for my job; I was free to explore to my heart's content. Relax a little bit by the lake that bordered the town. But I felt like the standard five-day work week didn't apply to authors.

Still, if I was going to succeed on my own secret mission, I needed to get him out. Socializing. Interacting with people in a generally pleasing way.

Not cooped up in a windowless loft with only his coffee and board game pieces for company.

"You have the whole day ahead of you for that," I argued, trying to sound more upbeat than I felt. "It should only take an hour to—"

"Please leave," he said. His tone was like a punch to the gut. "I need to concentrate."

His head lowered again and he took up the same position I'd originally found him in. I watched as his eyes darted back and forth, seemingly speed-reading whatever was on the screen. Over and over and over again.

I counted to sixty, waiting to see if he'd give me anymore time. He never did.

AS IT TURNED out, the grocer in town was more of a bakery than anything else. And a liquor store, which thank god for that. Not even twenty-four hours in and I knew I'd be making frequent visits to their wine aisle. Or the tequila section. Jackson liked margaritas. Maybe that's how we could bond.

It was a funny thought, considering how much more intimate

bonding we'd done in the past. Went to show how desperate I was to make this work.

I'd needed the walk into town more than I'd thought. Try as I might to drown my thoughts with my Boss Bitch playlist playing at nearly full volume in my earbuds, I couldn't stop thinking about the way Jackson had looked at me. Or rather, the way he hadn't.

It was hard to believe that this was the same man who, only a week ago, had had his hands on my body. Who over the course of ten months, would whisper sweet nothings in my ear while he was inside of me, bringing me some of the greatest pleasure I'd received from any sort of partner in a very long time. How those eyes that had stared so coldly used to look at me in a way that made me feel like… like maybe I wasn't the second choice for once. The stand-in. The good-enough-until-something-better-came-along.

I almost dropped my carton of eggs as I thought about his eyes. In that moment, I'd put a circus clown to shame with the way I juggled everything in my arms, trying to save it all from splattering on the tiled floor. I might as well have screamed, "Hey! I'm the new hot mess in town!"

I hadn't gotten much more control of my groceries, now in bags, thankfully, as I made my way into the one place in town I needed most.

The smell of coffee beans hit me with a vengeance as soon as I opened the red front door of the white-house-turned-shop at Sunrise Brews. Compared to the stale, half-burnt scent of the coffee Jackson had made at the cabin, this was heaven. Or maybe it was just the shop itself, which was a perfect blend of eclectic and chic. Right up my alley.

I shifted the hold of my bags on my arm and lifted my sunglasses onto my head with a sigh. It was enough to earn the attention of the short, brown-skinned woman behind the counter, who grinned as she finished helping the customer ahead of me.

"Got everything?" she asked by way of greeting when I made my way up to the front of the line.

"Hardly," I admitted, earning a wider smile and a soft chuckle. "But I also haven't had coffee yet."

"Miracles happen once caffeine hits."

"I've never felt so understood."

She chuckled again. "What can I get for you?"

"Um…" I panicked, the same way I always did in a new coffeeshop, even though I knew they would all have my order. "Large caramel latte with oat milk, if you have it."

"That I do," the woman confirmed as she typed the order into her tablet. "Anything else?"

My eyes strayed to the array of pastries to my left. "What do you think of the cinnamon rolls?"

"They're the best in town."

"Are you saying that only so I buy it or is it an undisputed truth?"

The woman leaned back, head cocked to the side as she regarded me with a smirk. "You're a spitfire."

"I take cinnamon rolls very seriously."

"How about you get this one, try a few others—even though I don't know that there are many more sold around here—and if it's not the best, your next one is free?"

And she'd called *me* a spitfire. "Sold."

"And a name for the order?"

"Tori."

"Hemdeep," she replied as she flipped the tablet my way so I could pay. "But you can call me Hemi."

I tapped my card against the reader before I took the hand she offered to me to shake. "Nice to meet you, Hemi."

"Are you new around here?"

"That obvious?" I asked.

She shrugged. "We get a lot of tourists in the summer, but we're still a few months out from our usual busy season. Something else bringing you here long enough to buy groceries?"

"Work." Kind of, but I wasn't about to unleash all my feelings about the last twenty-four hours on this poor woman. She was a barista, not my therapist. Although her coffee would probably work just as well when it came to brightening my mood, and at a fraction of the cost.

"Interesting location." She smiled and passed along a to-go cup filled with whatever brew was in one of the three large dispensers behind the counter to the woman who'd ordered before me.

I gave a nonchalant shrug as I slid over to take up the space the woman had vacated. My grocery bags clunked when I set them on the counter. I still had a half mile back to the cabin; my arms needed whatever breaks I could give them.

"I don't ask questions. I just go where the boss tells me."

"You're smart."

We fell into a comfortable silence as she finished making my drink, then passed it over to me. I took a sip as she returned to the pastries to retrieve my cinnamon roll. One touch of the latte on my tongue and my sour mood was already a little sweeter.

I just needed it to last for thirteen more days.

Hemi would be seeing me around *a lot*.

"And one of Timberland Creek's best cinnamon rolls," she announced as she handed me the pastry to-go box. "Enjoy."

"I'm sure I will," I said as I took it and stacked it on top of the egg carton. "I'm holding you to your deal, though."

Hemi shrugged. "I'm not worried."

I grinned. If not for her coffee, then I'd be coming back here just to chat. It was a breath of fresh air after Jackson.

Hell, maybe she'd be able to help whip him into shape even better than I could.

With my cup raised in cheers, I pulled my sunglasses back down over my eyes, dragged my bags off the counter, and made my way out of the café.

JACKSON WAS DOWNSTAIRS when I finally clambered

through the front door of the cabin. He'd situated himself on the couch, and once again didn't bother looking up from his laptop—which he was actually typing on this time—as I made my way, struggling, through the room.

He did jump, however, when I hefted the bags onto the counter. Eggs be damned. This shit was heavy.

I leaned back against the counter and wiped the back of my hand across my forehead. Wisconsin was more north, so didn't that mean it was supposed to be colder than Chicago? Especially this time of year. I hadn't packed nearly enough warm-weather gear if this was what we'd be experiencing.

"Got some eggs," I announced. "And bacon because it's the superior breakfast meat, so sorry if you're a sausage guy. Oh, and coffee creamer. Flavored and plain, since I didn't know what you liked. But I figured—"

"Victoria." The sudden use of my full name, short and stern, made me tense.

The keyboard clacking had come to a stop. Jackson was staring at me with the same semi-crazed eyes as before. Somehow, even though the coffee pot was almost entirely empty now, he looked even more tired.

He sighed and ran his fingers back through his hair. I'd never seen him do it so much. Usually, Jackson was the epitome of polished. Now that I really got a good look at him, he was probably the most disheveled I'd ever seen him. Not that he was anything close to my current state of unkempt, but he was in joggers and a faded Purdue University t-shirt. That was the

Jackson Albrecht equivalent of wearing the same shirt for three days in a row—something I was a frequent culprit of.

"I understand you probably don't know how this works," he began, throat flexing as if he were physically fighting to get the words out. "But I need to present a novel at the end of this trip. In order to do that, I need quiet, which isn't something I'm sure you're capable of. I expressed this concern to Marcus before we left, and he seemed to think everything would be okay." He slammed his laptop shut and leaned back. "*Nothing* has gone okay if you ask me."

"I told you you could sleep in the other bed."

"It's not about the bed. It's about—" He shook his head, as if he'd thought better about what he'd been about to say. When he met my waiting gaze again, desperation shone in his eyes. "I need to succeed, Tori, and you being here isn't creating an environment to allow me to focus. It's doing exactly the opposite, actually. So, unless you learn how to be quiet and leave me alone, I'm going to have to ask Marcus to remove you from the setting."

I huffed a laugh and crossed my arms over my chest. "It doesn't matter what you say, because they won't send me away."

"They need a manuscript. A career-saving manuscript. That can't happen if you're here doing god-knows-what all the time and—"

"If you think this is strictly about your book then you're sadly mistaken, my guy."

Jackson's brows creased. "What?"

It took me two steps to make it to the protruding portion of the counter. I placed my palms flat against the surface and leaned forward, trying to come across as serious as possible in leggings, bright-pink athletic zip-up, and matching headband that was strictly being used to tame my mass of blonde curls.

It seemed to work. For the first time since we'd gotten to the cabin, I'd earned Jackson's undivided attention.

"I'm not here to babysit you while you write a book, Jackson," I said. "Trust me—there's nothing more I'd like than to leave. I want my mattress and grocery stores with more than two options of eggs and to fall asleep to the sound of traffic instead of cute little animals being murdered, but no. I'm here because your team has determined that you're a dick, and apparently, I'm the last hope they have of giving you an attitude adjustment. So, I'd get used to having me around real quick because I'm unfortunately not going anywhere."

To say my confession had stunned him into silence would have been an understatement. I didn't even think the man blinked the entire time I spoke. He definitely wasn't now, as he stared me down, his expression softened considerably since he'd given his little spiel.

Maybe I could have toned it down a notch. And maybe *dick* hadn't been the right choice of words. Too bad the only other ones I probably would have been able to come up with were asshat, schmuck, and—my personal favorite—douche canoe.

Pissed-off Tori had never really had a way with words.

Or maybe this was exactly what had needed to happen. Hearing the brutal truth had a way of changing people. Obviously, the man wasn't about to become an angel overnight, but perhaps he'd at least concede to some of my civil requests.

A girl could dream.

And it, unfortunately, didn't look like it was going to come true any time soon.

"Good talk," I said when Jackson continued to remain silent. I tapped my hands on the counter twice then pushed off. "I'll let you unpack these," I added, gesturing to the grocery bags. "Partly because I bought them, and partly because I feel like you're the kind of person who'll throw a fit if the eggs are on the middle shelf off to the right or some shit."

He blinked.

Well, it was something.

When nothing else followed, I snatched my coffee off the counter. "If you need me, I'll be very out of your space, quietly taking a shower."

My gym shoes squeaked on the wood floors as I pivoted, only to turn right back round again.

"Oh, and by the way." Jackson's eyes were on me immediately, making me wonder if he'd ever looked away. "There's a coffee shop in town. Seems pretty low-key. You know, if you ever need to get away from me."

I didn't give him a chance to respond before I walked into the bedroom and shut the door behind me.

CHAPTER EIGHT

JACKSON DIDN'T TALK to me the rest of the day, and went as far as to extend the silent treatment into Sunday. The most I'd heard from him were his little comments he made to himself. Sometimes it was normal things, like muttering about the nonsensical organization of the kitchen. But other times he sounded like he was speaking complete gibberish.

It took me much longer than it should have to realize he was reading parts of his book out loud, going over lines repeatedly, a few of the words changing each time, until he worked out whatever it was he'd been stuck on.

In all the years I'd worked for a publisher, I'd never once actually seen an author at work. Not this up-close, anyway. They talked about their processes all the time. What worked. What didn't. Seeing it—or hearing it, I supposed—actually play out was a whole different experience. It was like being inside Jackson's head.

Normally, that would have scared me. In these cases, though, I couldn't deny I was fascinated.

He probably had no idea I was even paying attention, but it was hard not to. Especially with the thin walls of the house. I'd mostly stayed cooped up in the bedroom, and when he migrated back to the loft, I'd ventured onto the couch to read.

Take that for being quiet.

That's where I was when, suddenly, the beautiful natural light I'd been using to see the pages of my book darkened.

I tilted my head up to find Jackson looming over me.

"Yes?" I drawled.

Considering he was the one that had approached me, he seemed very unsure of what to say. Maybe he'd expected me to give him the same cold shoulder I'd been on the receiving end of. Or he'd just wanted to toy with me. Marcus might not send me home, but maybe Jackson thought I'd go of my own accord if he tried hard enough to piss me off.

Joke was on him. I was already pissed off, and my ass was staying right where it was on this awful couch.

He'd learn soon enough I wasn't so easy to crack.

"If you have nothing to say, I'd like to continue with my book."

"I'm sorry."

I'll take Things I Never Expected Jackson To Say for two-thousand, Alex.

I shut my book. "Excuse me?"

"I'm sorry," he repeated. "For… for what I said. Or did? I'm sure it's a bit of both."

"Who, what, when, where, why," I rattled off.

He didn't seem impressed. In fact, if the look on his face was any indication, I'd guess he was contemplating walking away.

"I think a few of those answers are obvious," he said instead. "But as for why?" He shrugged. "We're going to be here for however many weeks together. I figure it might be more pleasant if we were amicable."

My eyes narrowed. "Who are you and what have you done with Jackson Stephen Albrecht?"

"What do you mean?" His brow furrowed. "That's also not my middle name."

Jackson's eyes traced my book as I tossed it to the other side of the couch, flinching when it landed, as if my carelessness had physically wounded him.

It distracted him enough that he apparently hadn't noticed me approach. For someone nearly a foot taller than me, he sure reared back when I showed up in front of him, lifted onto my tiptoes in an attempt to appear bigger, eyes still narrowed as I inspected him.

"What are you doing?" he asked, his voice half an octave higher than usual.

My head cocked to the side.

"Tori, you're really starting to—*gah*!" He pulled back his hand almost as soon as my acrylic nails pinched his wrist. "You know I *need* that hand to write, don't you?"

"Dammit, you *are* the real Jackson."

"Have you gone insane?"

"Have *you*?" I retorted. "The Jackson I know doesn't apologize."

"This is my first attempt at that attitude adjustment you mentioned," he explained, massaging the spot I'd pinched with the index finger of the opposite hand. "Apologizing feels like an easy start."

"It does," I agreed, but my expression hadn't changed.

Jackson struggled to keep eye contact, not that I was giving him much of an option at the moment. His eyes darted between my discarded book to just about any other part of me. It took all my strength to keep my composure when, sometimes, his gaze landed on my chest, my lips.

His hand went to the back of his neck. "What, uh, are you reading?"

"Smut."

"Sounds… interesting." If I'd thought the treatment of my book had pained him, it was nothing like what crossed his face the moment that adjective left his mouth.

"Liar," I accused. "You love to make fun of me for reading stuff like this."

Jackson's lips pursed, and I realized he was biting the inside of his cheek, likely trying to hold back whatever retort he wanted to fire my way. If there was one thing Jackson hated, it was books he deemed held no literary value.

It just so happened that those same books were often my favorite. Made for great entertainment when I really got him going about it.

This didn't seem like one of those times he would bite, though.

Finally, he sighed. "I'm trying," he said. "I need to concentrate and—"

"I've kept to myself all day. I haven't even put anything on the TV. I've been listening to everything through my headphones."

"I noticed. And I appreciate it. But—" He shook his head, hand rubbing at the back of his neck. "I think that's the problem."

"Huh?"

"I can't concentrate because I can't stop thinking about how I've been—to use your own words—treating you like a dick."

"Ah, so you did notice."

At that, Jackson took his turn to narrow his eyes at me. "I don't like it, but sometimes you leave me no choice."

A million responses ran through my head, *I* sometimes *like it rough* and *There are other ways you could apologize* among them. I kept my mouth shut, though. Even if the idea of making him squirm had my toes curling in my fuzzy socks, Jackson had made his new stance on that part of our relationship clear the moment he'd arrived at the cabin. I couldn't risk whatever olive branch he was finally offering by bringing that into the mix.

Him admitting his guilt was enough to make me finally soften.

"I appreciate you saying that," I said. "Thank you."

He must have thought I'd reply with some sort of snarky response, because Jackson's tension eased too, like a soldier who realized the battle had been won. His hand flopped back down at his side where his thumb hooked in the pocket of his jeans.

"I'll let you get back to your reading, then."

"Wait."

I'd never been good at sports, primarily because my aim wasn't that great. Case in point, I'd intended to grab Jackson's wrist as he'd turned away, ready to retreat back to wherever he'd been before he came to see me.

Instead, my hand wrapped around his fingers.

The tension returned as quickly as it had disappeared, and along with it, a jolt that started in my chest and ran all the way down to my toes.

I stared at where we touched. My hand had been wrapped around much more indecent parts of Jackson once upon a time, yet this was what made heat creep into my cheeks. When I dropped my hold and looked up at Jackson, I found his own were colored pink, too.

"I, um," I tried. "I just—you know what, never mind."

"No, it's, uh—it's alright." Jackson shifted, and when my eyes naturally lowered to watch the movement, I couldn't help but notice the slight bulge in his pants.

Dear god almighty, save the woodland rodents. Let the owls take me instead.

"It's not important. I'm just gonna—" I continued, then

gestured with both my thumbs toward the couch.

Jackson nodded too quickly. "Right. And I'll just—" He pointed at the stairs to the loft. Apparently neither one of us was capable of speaking. At least I didn't have to suffer in my embarrassment alone.

"Good talk."

"Glad we had it."

We stared at each other a moment longer before Jackson cleared his throat. "I'll be upstairs if you need me. Not that you'll need me. I'm sure you'll be plenty entertained with your—"

One glance at my book, and I swore his bulge grew even more. Both our minds were now in the gutter, and knowing the contents of what I'd been reading didn't help the matter.

His tongue wetted his lips, and my own parted as I stared unabashedly, waiting for him to make a move, though the *sort* of move, I wasn't sure about. He'd likely go back to the loft, as he'd said he planned to. But now, a part of me was wondering if he'd linger. If he'd grab me and push me back onto the couch. If those same lips and tongue would work me in ways I knew were magical. Life altering. Orgasmic.

But Jackson, ever the annoying man of his word, shook himself out of his trance, gave me a tight-lipped smile, and rushed up the stairs.

Silence filled the cabin.

I DIDN'T SEE or hear Jackson again for another few hours. And good thing, too, since his absence gave me plenty of time to relax. Not with my book. No—there was no way I would have been able to enjoy it now that my own body was aching for the same kind of release I knew the main characters would be partaking in.

I chose to relax in the shower.

It had started innocently enough, but soon my thoughts began to wander. I'd run my soapy hands over the curves of my ample hips, the swell of my stomach, my breasts, between my legs, unable to shake the desire. Unable to stop imagining they belonged to someone else. *Wishing* they'd been someone else's.

Still, that didn't stop me from making myself come. Twice.

Some relief was better than no relief at all.

The humidity from the shower steam and the scent of my shampoo followed me out of the bedroom once I was dressed again, my honeyed curls in a towel.

I'd hoped I'd have a few minutes sans-Jackson to decompress a bit more, but instead I found him at the fridge, the door flung wide open while he surveyed the contents.

"I haven't moved anything," I said by way of greeting. "Everything's where you put it."

"We don't have many options."

"There's two creamers. And I got—"

"Not for coffee," he clarified. "For food."

"I didn't know you ate. I was beginning to think you survived on caffeine and angst alone."

He cast me a narrow-eyed sideways glance, and I smirked. That shower had truly done wonders for my mood. And having him be the one to initiate the conversation for a change wasn't too bad either.

"Har-har," Jackson fake-laughed as he shut the door.

I pulled the towel off my head, letting my hair fall free. "No, I didn't get much food. I figured, if anything, we could—what's wrong?"

Jackson's eyes widened, and I paused squeeze-drying the ends of my hair.

"Huh?" he asked.

"Your face is all scrunchy. What's wrong?"

"Nothing's wrong," he replied. Then he leaned in closer. "Is that… coconut?"

I nodded. "Why? Is it bad?"

"No, I—it's nice. Is it new?"

It took a moment to realize that yes—Jackson would have reason to notice if I'd started using new products. Or at least question why I smelled different than he was probably used to. Hotel shampoo just didn't have the same scent appeal as my normal hair and skincare products.

"I've been using it a few years now. Helps tame the mane," I said in reference to the damp mass of curls that, in a matter of hours, would go back to their full, bouncy volume. "But getting back to the food."

Jackson straightened. "Right. You were saying?"

"While I enjoy granola bars and scrambled eggs as much as the next girl, maybe we could go into town for dinner?"

"You said there was a coffee shop?" When I smirked again, he amended, "For food, not coffee."

"There is," I said. "But there's a tavern too. Probably has burgers and stuff." Jackson's brow quirked when I narrowed my eyes at him. "You aren't going to complain that the floor is sticky or anything, are you?"

"*Is* the floor sticky?"

"I have no idea. Probably."

His lips pursed again, then, "Depends how sticky."

I grinned. "Let me go blow-dry my hair."

CHAPTER NINE

THE FLOOR OF Ziggy's Tavern wasn't bad when it was compared to the bar. Despite the barbacks that glided by, wiping a rag over it each time one of the patrons got up, my crossed arms still stuck when I rested them in front of me. The rag was probably part of the problem, honestly. I would have bet big money on its last wash being over thirty days ago, if the black spots on it were any indication.

Jackson shifted on his barstool and removed a small packet from his back pocket.

"Shut up. You did *not* actually pack sanitary wipes."

He tilted his head toward me and paused his wiping of the counter. "I did, and for this exact reason."

A smart remark sat at the back of my throat, but I shook my head and returned my attention to the menu instead of letting it free.

"Oh, thank you for that, darlin'," a gray-haired woman

probably in her early sixties said as she appeared in front of us. "I can't pay you for the service, but I can give you a half-priced beer."

"He's okay," I said. "No payment necessary. He's just a priss."

Jackson's glare bore into the side of my head. I didn't bother looking up from the menu to witness it.

The woman chuckled. "Ah, young love. I miss those days."

My internal debate between ordering the patty melt or chicken tenders suddenly became less interesting. "Oh, we're not together."

"Far from it," Jackson added. I nodded my confirmation.

"Sorry 'bout that. I just assumed, given how close you're sitting to one another."

My head tilted downward the same time Jackson's did, only to notice that the woman was right. One little shift to my right and my thigh would be pressed up against Jackson's.

I cleared my throat as I angled myself away.

"What can I get you two started with then?" the woman asked, thankfully changing the subject.

"I'll have a vodka soda," Jackson declared.

"And I'll have…" I stared at the draft list. "Spotted Cow. Oh—and can we put in an order of cheese curds?"

"Wow, really going for the full Wisconsin experience, are we?" the woman asked with a wink, then turned to go put the order into the system.

"I'm lactose intolerant," Jackson muttered.

I shrugged. "More for me then. Also, you should have reminded Marcus of that before he set us up in America's Dairyland for weeks on end."

"You got one more joining you?" the woman asked, her eavesdropping surprising Jackson more than it surprised me. He'd clearly never worked in a bar before.

I shook my head. "No. Just someone we work with."

"More me than her." Oh, here we go. "I'm an author. *New York Times* best-seller, actually. Marcus is my agent."

The woman gave a low whistle. "You don't say. What's your name?"

"Jackson S. Albrecht," he said, putting on the smile I'd learned so well from the various conventions and bookstore signing events. The woman took the hand he extended across the bar and shook it.

"Well, Jackson S. Albrecht, it's very nice to meet you. I'm Rosie A. Donahue."

She turned her attention on me, one brow quirked.

"Victoria E. Wilson," I greeted with the quickest wave known to mankind.

"It's a pleasure to meet you both," Rosie smiled, clearly satisfied. "And now that we're all acquainted, I'll go ahead and get your drinks ready."

I watched from the corner of my eye as she wandered away, only to get pulled into a conversation with two men with long gray beards and hair, each with a pint of beer in front of them. Their exact conversation was hard to hear over the classic rock song that had just started playing, but Rosie's animated reactions were enough for me to assume it would be a little while before she returned.

"You've got to be kidding me, Jackson Samuel Albrecht," I said.

"Still not right." He was doing a rather wonderful job of not looking at me while he got back to cleaning the counter.

"But how fun would it be if it was? Like Samuel Jackson but backwards."

Jackson sighed. "What are you going to chastise me about now?"

"*I'm a* New York Times *best-seller*," I mocked in my best attempt at Jackson's deeper voice.

Now, he did look up. "Huh?"

I flipped my tri-fold menu shut. "Okay, rule number one— well, actually rule two since you mastered apologizing on your own."

"What's that?"

"Congrats on all your success. Truly. But no one cares about your accolades when you're first being introduced."

"Some people do."

"Like who?"

"Marcus."

"Is Marcus here?"

The same pink tint that had colored Jackson's cheeks earlier returned. "No…"

I shifted so I could face him, all the while paying very close attention to making sure our legs didn't touch. "Like, how do you not know after thirty-two—"

"I'm thirty-four," he corrected. I didn't know why I'd assumed we were the same age.

"Okay, thirty-four years—even though that kinda makes your case worse."

"What case?"

"Your case of extreme pretentiousness."

"Is that even a word?"

"Is now. And I'm diagnosing you with it."

"Why shouldn't I tell people I'm an author?" Jackson sat back as much as his backless stool would allow him without toppling over and crossed his arms. "That's something I'm proud of."

"You're allowed to tell people you're an author. That's cool as shit. Do you know how many people actually get to say that?"

I'd meant it hypothetically, but Jackson answered, "About three out of every hundred people." The more you know.

"See? You're a rarity. So, tell people about it by all means. But there's a way to go about it that doesn't sound so…"

"Prissy?" Jackson finished when I trailed off.

I grinned at his use of my word from earlier. "There's a time and place. You're not trying to sell anything here, so there's no need to be Jackson from press events. In settings like this you should be just… Jackson."

"Would you be able to tell if I was Just Jackson?"

I shrugged. "Maybe. Probably. We've spent a lot of time together. I'm sure I've seen him once or twice."

His jaw tightened, highlighting a sharpness that was only visible when he was thinking hard. I'd noticed it a few times at various events when we needed to problem solve, then again over the last day when we'd crossed paths in the cabin.

His cogs were turning, digesting, thinking of everything I'd told him.

But instead of arguing against the advice, he gave me a curt nod and said, "I'll work on it," before he returned to his menu.

That was that. I waited, thinking he might eventually have questions—about our conversation or the menu he was so intently analyzing—but nothing came.

Alright then.

"ORDER'S UP, FRIENDS."

My mouth was practically watering by the time Rosie set down our cheese curds and entrees. Apparently there had been a back-up in the kitchen, which meant food was served twenty minutes later than I'd anticipated. Jackson, too, if the glow in his eyes as he stared down his hamburger was any indication.

"Eat up," Rosie said with a smile. "And let me know if you need anything else. Refill for you, sweetheart?"

I nodded, my hand already in the basket of curds. "Thank you."

She left us with one more well-wish to enjoy the first bites of our meal, then was back on her way to help another set of customers.

Jackson moaned beside me, and when I glanced to see what had elicited that sort of reaction, I found him with his burger in his hands.

"I've never been so excited for food in all my life," he said, then proceeded to take the world's largest bite.

It fell, half-chewed back into the paper-lined red-plastic basket the burger had been served in seconds later.

"What's wrong with it?" I asked as Jackson chugged what was left of his vodka soda.

"I don't know what that was," he said, half-pained. Holy shit, he was *sweating*. There was actual moisture by his hairline. "But it wasn't a burger."

"Rookie move."

We both turned halfway in our seats to find the bearded men from down the bar standing behind us. One—who I'd heard Rosie call Gus—clapped his hand on Jackson's shoulder.

"Never order the burger," he informed and his unnamed companion nodded. No Name, in all his muscular, biker-esque might was actually looking at Jackson like my companion had just learned he had two weeks to live. "Everything else is completely edible, but the burger—" Gus shook his head. "I don't know what Ro does to it, but it's... something."

"It's like rubber," Jackson added. "But it tastes like Play-Doh."

The men nodded, lips turned in, faces somber. "Now you know for next time, right? In the meantime, can't go wrong with the fries."

Gus squeezed Jackson's shoulder twice then saluted me as he and No Name made their way to the door.

"See you kids around," he called out, waving to us without turning around.

"Oh boy." Jackson and I both faced forward again, eyes wide with guilt, when Rosie spoke. She set down my fresh beer, then her hands found her hips while she stared toward the front door of the tavern. "Were Gus and Marty bothering you?"

"Not at all," I said, hoping I didn't sound nervous. God, I hoped she hadn't heard what they'd said. Rosie had been in my life for all of thirty minutes, yet I felt the fierce desire to protect her with the same gusto I'd protect my mom or grandma. "Just giving us some town insights."

"They're nothing but trouble, those two," she said in return, but the soft curl of her lips told me she probably actually liked them. Then her face softened, lit with joy, as she asked, "How are the first few bites tasting?"

Considering Jackson's first bite was sitting half-chewed next to his pile of fries...

"Great!" I tried not to react at the too-loud compliment Jackson offered. "Just what I needed after a long day of writing."

I gawked in wide-eyed astonishment as he picked the burger back up, brought it to his mouth, and took a bite that put the first one to shame.

"Hmmm," he hummed, closing his eyes. To anyone else, it probably looked like he was in bar-food-induced bliss. *I*, however, knew he was probably trying to hold back his tears.

"Oh, isn't that just wonderful to hear!" My heart melted when Rosie's lower lip jutted out in a slight pout, her folded hands resting under her chin. "I figured those boys were just being dramatic about the burgers. No one else has ever complained."

So maybe she *had* heard us. Or at least, she'd heard Gus. But something told me everyone else who unwittingly ordered the menu item went into it just as clueless as Jackson. Then what else were they supposed to say when the literal reincarnation of Golden Girls-era Betty White asked for their opinion?

It was physically impossible to make Rosie sad. Even if she was essentially a total stranger.

Case in point, the usually too-blunt Jackson was lying his ass off like a pro right now.

"I'll leave you to your meals then." Rosie's grin widened. "Holler if you need anything else."

She'd had her back turned to us for no more than three seconds before Jackson's jaw opened and the unchewed bite of burger toppled into the basket.

My lips curled in as I tried to keep my laughter at bay. But the moment Jackson turned to me, I broke.

"It's not funny," he said. He eyed the basket of food sidelong, scowling. "I'd take the electric chair before I took another bite of that thing."

A fresh laugh burst forth, my shoulders curling inward, as I leaned toward the bar.

"Yeah, keep laughing. I'll wait."

My abs still trembled as I fought to tame myself. My eyes were watering a little bit, but nowhere near as badly as Jackson's, which was the reason one more snort escaped.

"I'm sorry," I half-wheezed. "Seriously. It's just—you did well. Really."

"Uh huh," Jackson said. "Keep going."

"Huh?"

"Go on. Laugh," he said. "I know you aren't done yet."

He was right. I wasn't even close to being done. My stomach physically hurt from how hard I was trying to keep my laughter contained. My lips were twitching with the desire to curl up into a smile.

"Here lies Jackson Simon Albrecht," I said through a wheeze. "Cause of death? Ziggy's Tavern Hamburger."

He didn't respond, and the silence excited me enough that I aimed a lifted brow at him.

"Not Simon either," he confirmed, much to my dismay.

"Dammit!"

He rolled his eyes. I didn't miss the slight curl of his lips, though. Like he might actually be enjoying this all. "Carry on with your jokes."

"No, really, I'm done," I assured him. "But, god, that was hilarious."

"To you, sure." He shook his head and grimaced at the food in front of him. "I was getting flashbacks."

"To what?"

"My Memaw made me a pot pie for my tenth birthday, and it was one of the vilest experiences of my life." He looked at me. "I used to love pot pie. I used to love burgers, too." I grinned when he nudged the basket away.

"What did you tell your Memaw?"

"Same thing I told Rosie." He shrugged. "Hurting Rosie's feelings felt like hurting Memaw's."

Wow. Turns out Jackson Something Albrecht did have a heart after all.

I sat there smiling, and wasn't even fully aware how long I'd let the silence drag out until he turned to me.

"Why do you look like that?" he asked.

"It's just… that was sweet."

He huffed a laugh. "Now there's three words I never thought I'd hear you say."

"I say things are sweet all the time."

"I meant in reference to me."

Oh.

My smile fell, the joy from earlier shifting with his admission. Jackson wasn't even looking at me. He hadn't been for some time, I realized. Since he'd begun to talk about his pot pie incident. Since he'd… opened up.

I'd spent more time with Jackson than any other author on Starr's roster, which made it hard to see him as anything other than that. An author. A client. A means to an end for the company I worked for—the end being revenue.

I'd been preached to, day in and day out, to make our authors happy. To give them attention. To make sure their books sold. So, for all this time that's what I'd focused on.

The authors were a business.

But this man sitting beside me… even if we had developed a rather complicated relationship over the last few months, he'd never been what he was now.

A person. With a past and a family and digestive issues.

"You like tater tots?" I asked. He tilted his head to face me. Not fully, but it was something. I pointed at my basket, where my still-untouched patty melt and tots sat. "I've got more cheese curds than I know what to do with. You can have some of the tater tots. To make up for the burger."

He regarded me silently, and for a moment, I thought I'd get the same response as always when I tried to mend the bridge between us. The cold-shoulder. A standoffish remark. The silent treatment. Hell, I wouldn't have been surprised if he up and left Ziggy's.

Instead, he nodded and said, "Sure."

That little curl in his lips grew as I transferred the food into his basket.

It wasn't much, but us sitting here, behaving amicably—if not awkwardly—was a start.

That was all I needed.

CHAPTER TEN

"HOW ARE THINGS with the he-devil?" Laura asked.

Truthfully, I was shocked it had taken her four days to finally call me. As sisters and roommates, we were on a talk-daily basis. But between my spotty signal—the Wi-Fi was great; cell service not as much—and Laura's work schedule, it had been nearly impossible to find a time that worked for both of us.

I'd found a spot outside the back door of the cabin on a wood Adirondack chair that creaked a little too much under my weight to give me much comfort, but it was the only seat available if I wanted to give Jackson some peace. I could have sat on the ground, I supposed, but with the number of gnats buzzing around my head, I wasn't going to risk figuring out what I'd find crawling around.

"Things are… good," I answered, and it was the truth.

I didn't know why, exactly, but one bad burger and some shared tater tots later and Jackson's mood had taken… well, I didn't want to say a one-eighty. Even I wasn't *that* good at influencing, both good and bad. But he was improving. Much less snark at my expense. Same with the glowering when I interrupted his writing time to ask if he wanted something to eat—this was mostly for his health since I noticed he seemed to neglect that in favor of working on his manuscript—or if he wanted to join me in town. He'd only accepted the latter once, under the pretense he wanted to see this coffee shop I'd told him about. We'd sipped our drinks and dabbled in semi-awkward small talk on the walk to and from. At least it was something.

The days where we spoke to each other normally—not with ceaseless banter or half-assed attempts to get to know each other—were upon us. I could feel it. But we weren't there quite yet.

I'd take this, though. Partly because it made the whole living situation a little more bearable, and partly because it had allowed me to give a semi-positive report to Rahm and Marcus on our progress call this morning, too.

"I don't believe you."

Funny. Rahm and Marcus's faces had told me the same thing. They hadn't been as bold as my sister to voice it aloud, however.

"Why would I lie to you, Lo?"

"I don't know. Maybe so I don't drive up there and feed the he-devil to the bears or something?"

"Can you stop calling him the he-devil?" I asked with a glance up at the circular window above me, beyond which I knew Jackson was writing. Or at least that's where he'd been when I first stepped outside.

He could never again tell me I didn't put his process into consideration. I made myself scarce more often than not.

"Is there another term you prefer?" In the background, I could hear cabinets shutting, dishes clattering. "Prickhole? Asshat? Dickwad?"

Wilson women clearly had a penchant for inventive insults.

"Don't forget twat-fuck," Bianca called from somewhere in the background.

Okay, so Wilson women *and* women dating Wilson women.

I hummed contemplatively. "Maybe asshat. Diva also still qualifies." I didn't think I'd ever forget the feeling of secondhand embarrassment when Jackson complained to Hemi that his extra hot latte wasn't extra hot enough.

"Phew. I was getting scared for a second."

"About what?"

"That you were developing a soft spot for him."

I blew out of *pft* of air. "Please. Never."

But even as I said it, I felt heat making its way into my cheeks—between my legs.

The latter was something I *desperately* needed to get a grip on. But alas, once a woman masturbated to the fantasy of her temporary housemate touching her—or fucking her like she knew he was very much capable of—it was hard not to notice every little movement.

And I meant every. Little. Movement.

The way he sucked peanut butter off his finger when we made sandwiches. The way his tongue snuck out to wet his lips when he was deep in concentration. The way his hands grasped his coffee cup, for god's sake.

I'd never been so jealous of a tater tot as I had the night at Ziggy's, knowing they got to experience what it was like to have Jackson's lips on them.

Those little deep-fried bastards.

"Just making sure," Laura sing-songed. "Small towns make romantics of even the biggest hardasses."

"Whoa, whoa, whoa—hardass, I am not," I defended and Laura chuckled. "Also, how do you know I'm in a small town?"

"Please. Do you not think I tracked your location then Googled every detail about the place in case I need to rescue you?"

I smiled. I would expect nothing less of my baby sister. "What did you find?"

"Population of nine-hundred and ninety-seven. The biggest attraction is the lighthouse off the bay. It's supposedly haunted. But other than ghosts, you'll be happy to know the last major crime to take place was in 1995 when a guy was stabbed over a stolen fishing rod dispute."

Something told me Gus and Marty would know something

about that. "Sounds like I've landed in the Disney World of the Midwest."

"More like Cape Cod. The Hamptons maybe."

"*The Hamptons?*" I repeated, unable to hide my shock. At that moment, the chair decided to creak for no reason again.

"I take it Starr didn't put you up in one of the mansions I saw on Zillow?"

"No, they did not…" Damn, Rahm hadn't been kidding about sacrificing no more budget towards Jackson.

"That sucks," Laura sympathized. "Nothing like an all-expense-paid trip on the company dime. Is your place nice at least?"

"During the day, sure."

"What happens at night? The ghosts visit from the lighthouse?"

"Have you ever heard a squirrel being eaten by an owl?"

"I don't think so?"

"Consider yourself lucky." When a laugh came through the phone so loud I had to pull the device away from my ear, I added, "It's not funny! Those sounds are going to haunt me forever."

"Is it every night?"

"Yes!" Laura laughed again. "You aren't allowed to get entertainment from my misery. I'm your only sibling. If I lose my sanity, you have no one."

"Guess again, hardass," Bianca called from the background.

"Do you have me on speaker or something?" I asked.

"You just talk loud," Laura said, but I didn't know if I believed it. If I was on speaker, that made her laugh even more impressive. But it wasn't any breaking news that loudness ran in the Wilson family genes, too.

"Hey, B, since you're listening, you have any advice for how to handle ghosts?"

"I practice witchcraft. I'm not a medium."

"Isn't it basically the same thing?"

"I'm not listening to this blasphemy."

"Just think, Tor," Laura cut in, changing the subject. "You're almost a whole week in. Only two more until you're done."

I grumbled as I pulled my feet up onto the chair, my knees hugged to my chest. "Come rescue me if you don't hear anything by the end of week two?"

"Obviously," Laura assured me, and I'd never loved my little sister more.

We hung up after she caught me up on the latest drama of the restaurant she managed, and I made my way back inside. It didn't matter that I was in leggings, a lightweight sweatshirt, and gym shoes. There was still a solid chance I was covered in bug bites.

Turned out I hadn't needed to be too worried about Jackson listening in from the loft because he was in the living room when I re-entered the cabin. There wasn't a laptop in sight, but instead a book and a fresh cup of coffee were on the table beside him. His phone was in his hand.

It seemed even he wasn't invincible when it came to a good doom scroll.

"Break time?" I asked by way of greeting.

He turned over his shoulder, as if confirming it was me, then shrugged as he went back to his phone. "Just not in it at the moment. I needed to find some inspiration."

"Ah, yes. Because whenever I need inspiration I go straight to"—I glanced at his screen as I passed—"donkeys playing soccer."

"This isn't what I normally watch…" he mumbled in return.

"Mhm. *Sure*, Jackson Sebastian Albrecht," I teased.

He shook his head—the usual reaction as I continued my guessing game; I'd found out Sean and Spencer were also duds—but his lips were curled up a little more than before.

My laptop was still waiting for me as I made my way over to the kitchen and resituated myself in one of the counter stools. I'd been on the phone with Laura for forty-five minutes, and I was dreading the number of emails I'd received in that time. Alexis had sent me at least fifty on her own over the last two days. The girl really needed to—

"Is it really that bad?"

My head popped up from my email. Could Jackson read minds?

"Is what that bad?" I replied.

"The animals," he clarified.

So, he *had* been able to hear.

"Um, yeah," I said, then shrugged. "It is what it is."

"Is it happening all night?"

"Pretty much."

His eyes widened at that. "Are you sleeping?"

It was such an innocent question, and his face showed so much concern that, for a moment, I had a difficult time forming a response.

"As well as someone can on a twin bed with a mattress from 1980." I nodded in his direction. "Probably still have it better than you. Sounds of dying critters and all."

His lips pursed, his brow scrunched, in a way I'd come to learn he was thinking. Not in the same way he did when he was writing. This was him. Just Jackson. The cogs turning with some notion he was either too shy or too embarrassed to say aloud.

He gave a little hum of acknowledgement—more than I normally got when he lost himself in his thoughts—before he asked, "Who was on the phone with you?"

"My little sister. And her girlfriend, by default."

"Is she your only sibling?"

"Sure is," I replied with a nod. "I'd charge into a zombie apocalypse to save that girl."

He nodded slowly, but didn't ask anything else.

I filled the silence instead. "Do, uh, you have any siblings?"

"I had a foster brother. Haven't seen him in years, though.

Once he was out of the system, he up and left."

"I'm sorry."

Jackson shrugged. "I've gotten used to it."

I had a feeling he hadn't actually, but I could have been misinterpreting his tone. It wasn't like we'd gotten much more in-depth about our lives than this… ever. Even our pillow talk had been way more superficial, filled with the same banter we always used with one another.

Jackson had gone quiet again. This time, I didn't think I'd have as much luck getting him to continue, so I went back to my laptop. I sighed when I realized my inbox had loaded. Sixty-two unread emails, and at least half were from Alexis. A few from Iris. It looked like a chain had started between Marcus, Rahm and I, where I'd yet to participate. Then there were a few other agents of authors with upcoming releases. And—

"What does the E stand for?"

My head popped up again. "Huh?"

"The E," Jackson clarified. "Victoria *E.* Wilson."

For a moment, I still didn't understand how he knew my middle initial. Then I remembered the dinner at Ziggy's. Rosie's introduction. We'd all used our middle initials to introduce ourselves.

There wasn't a doubt in my mind that Jackson had been sitting on that question for the last two and a half days since, especially given all my pestering about his mysterious middle initial.

"It's Elizabeth," I answered.

"Victoria Elizabeth Wilson?" he asked, and I nodded. "You're named after *two* queens of England?"

A grin grew on my lips, and I winked. "Obviously."

He nodded slowly, expectantly.

"What?" I asked when he didn't stop staring.

Jackson shrugged. "I guess I assumed you'd ask me outright what the S stood for."

My grin widened. "Are you kidding me? I'm not stopping until I get it right. And don't you dare tell me, Jackson Sheldon Albrecht!" I added when he opened his mouth to say something.

His jaw shut quickly, and only due to the quiet of the house was I able to hear the light chuckle he emitted.

"Incorrect once again, Wilson," he said.

"But I'm one name closer to figuring it out."

That time when Jackson went back to watching videos on his phone, he was grinning too.

IT WAS OFFICIAL. Owls? Easily a top-three scariest flying thing right behind pterodactyls and giant bats.

Hedwig had us fooled. Big time.

My heart raced, my stomach twisted in a knot as I listened to the latest victim being taken outside the window. Seriously—

how many critters were left for the taking at this point?

It didn't help that the wind had picked up after nightfall. I hadn't seen rain in the forecast, but that didn't mean anything. This was the Midwest, after all. It could be sunny and seventy-five in the afternoon then snow overnight.

The owls didn't seem to be bothered by it, surprisingly. I'd have thought flying would have been harder with the heavy gusts, but what did I know?

Apparently, nothing as the horror film continued to play out on the other side of the cabin's wall.

My eyes popped open and my body froze when the wind howled. Or, at least I hoped it was the wind. Call me crazy, but whatever I'd just heard sounded an awful lot like an *oooo* to me. A ghostly *oooo*.

Ho. Ly. Fuck.

I should have paid so much more attention to Bianca when she was doing her witchy things. Medium or not, that woman gave I-know-weird-facts-about-ghosts vibes, and I suddenly found myself really needing to know if ghosts could leave their designated haunting areas. Where the hell was the Timberland Creek Lighthouse anyway? For all I knew it was in my backyard. The ghost could have taken a wrong turn and made its way right into this creaky and easily penetrable cabin to—

I shot up in bed, screaming, when the door to the bedroom flew open and a silhouetted figure appeared.

For a moment, I might have believed my nightmarish

thoughts had come true—if the figure hadn't screamed too.

"Jackson!" I shouted and reached for one of the decorative bed pillows to hurl his direction. He dodged it, but just barely. "What the fuck are you doing?"

"You were scared!"

"Yeah, because I thought you were a ghost!"

"There's ghosts?" His head darted about the room, searching for a spooky guest.

"No, you idiot! I thought *you* were a ghost!"

"Well, I'm not!"

"Then I repeat: what *the fuck* are you doing in here?"

"I told you! You said you were scared!"

"I—"

My lips clamped shut when the realization of what he'd said slammed into me.

He wasn't talking about me being scared now. He was talking about earlier. When I'd told Laura that I hated hearing the sounds of the animals at night. Because he'd overheard me.

All the tension in my body eased. My shoulders slouched and the hand that had been holding the quilt up—as if *that* would shield against the paranormal—flopped onto my lap.

"So," I started, my voice much softer now. "You decided to… check on me or something?"

He took a step into the room, allowing the moon to cast its blue light onto his face rather than backlight him from the kitchen. He was in a pair of plaid pajama pants and a plain black t-shirt. It wasn't until this moment that I realized I'd never seen Jackson in his pajamas before. He changed and was up in the loft writing before I got up in the morning. And before… well, before we'd worn nothing while we slept together.

"I actually thought I'd take you up on your invitation," he said. "From the day we arrived."

"You… want to sleep in here?"

He nodded, and when he stepped to the side, I noticed he hadn't come alone. His body had blocked his suitcase.

"I meant to come in here earlier, but then I got caught up in a scene and didn't want to break my concentration. I honestly assumed you'd still be awake. You seem like a night owl—no pun intended."

I couldn't help but grin. "I was still awake, just not for the reasons you probably thought." Even in the moonlight, I caught the way his body went rigid. "You know, scrolling on my phone or something," I added hastily.

"Right. Yeah. Of course." Jackson cleared his throat. "So, is it okay if I…?"

"Um, yeah, sure. Come on in."

Remaining calm wasn't in my usual way of life, and it was even less present as Jackson offered me a small smile and rolled his suitcase into the room. He placed it on the side of the dresser closest to the bed he'd be sleeping in—which made me realize I should probably move my stuff out of those drawers so he could move into them if he wanted to—and slapped the handle down.

I was even more hyper-aware of his movements as he made his way over to the bed, pulled back the covers, and situated himself beneath them with a content sigh.

"Already so much better than the pull-out bed," he mused.

As much as I wanted to make some sort of smart remark about how he should have listened to me, I kept my mouth shut. No words would have come out—not coherently, anyway. They would have sounded as jumbled as my brain felt at the moment.

Because Jackson S. Albrecht was sleeping in the next bed over.

And for some reason that felt very, very wrong.

Mostly because part of me wished he was curled up beside me instead.

CHAPTER ELEVEN

MAYBE THE WIND had been the first sign of an incoming lousy weather, because I woke the next morning to the soothing sound of falling rain.

No, not rain.

A shower.

I sat up slowly in bed, still feeling half delirious—being woken up before an alarm should be a felony offense—to find the first bits of the day's sunlight streaming past the sheer white curtains. A mourning dove cooed somewhere in the distance, followed by the rapid chirp of a cardinal.

Everything sounded peaceful, and, for once, I could say I agreed.

Aside from the whole woken earlier than intended. And the confusion as to why the shower was running.

One glance at the unmade bed beside me gave me my answer.

Delirium and my short-term memory were not friends, clearly. But it didn't take Sherlock Holmes to deduce that it was Jackson locked in that bathroom. I hadn't even heard him get up, which given his entrance last night, shocked me.

Had he been doing this every morning? Come to think of it, I hadn't seen him shower once in the five days we'd been here, which *ew*. But I doubted that was actually the truth of it. The man was way too polished to neglect his personal hygiene.

The rush of water cut off and the sharp slide of the curtain rings on the metal pole that held them escaped past the door.

Sleeping in the next bed over was one thing. Knowing that behind that door, Jackson was buck-ass naked, was another.

I blamed my sleep-addled brain for the way my hand grazed up my body to my chest. My nipple was hard under the thin fabric of my camisole when I found it and pinched it between my index finger and thumb. I bit my lower lip into my mouth, suppressing a groan, my eyes never leaving that door. My thoughts never straying from the man behind it.

God, I wish he wouldn't have been so stubborn. If he hadn't made it so painfully clear he didn't want me anymore, I would have no qualms about walking into that bathroom and letting him—

I startled, eyes going wide and hand falling away from my breast, when the doorknob turned slowly, quietly, then the door creaked open. Jackson filled in the tiny sliver through which he was visible, and then his eyes found me—already staring at him like a creep.

Not that he left me much choice. Especially when he opened the door the rest of the way and greeted me with an embarrassed smile.

I'd be honest: Jackson wasn't the guy written about in romance novels. His physique wasn't toned. His muscles weren't particularly corded, but they *were* visible. Like he did just enough at the gym to stay in shape, but not bulk up. If I showed a picture of him to any of my friends and asked their honest opinion, most of them would say, "Swipe left." The few that would say, "Swipe right," would do so with the disclaimer that he, "Looks like a nice guy."

In other words, he was about as average of a dude as there ever was.

But in this moment, he could have been Adonis.

The steam from the shower trailed after him, leaving his skin glistening. I was witness to a lot of said skin, seeing as he was carrying his shirt in his fist, rather than wearing it. As a small blessing to my libido, he'd opted to put on his jeans. They hung on his hips like they'd been perfectly tailored for him. But I couldn't stop myself from tracing the happy trail that disappeared beneath the waistband with my eyes. Or the vee of muscles that I hadn't remembered being there before.

I shifted, pressing my legs together under the covers. My nipples tightened.

Under normal circumstances, I would have been totally fine seeing him like this. But considering I'd just been feeling myself up while imagining it had been *him* doing it…

"Sorry," Jackson said by way of greeting. "I'm, uh, not proving to be a great roommate."

I didn't say anything. I just continued to stare like a dumbass. *Pull it together, Tor.*

He held up his shirt. "This fell in the sink when I was brushing my teeth. Have to grab a new one."

To that, I managed a nod, which was his cue to move. Jackson practically sprinted over to his suitcase and dug through it until he found a replacement shirt.

When I realized I was staring at his back—seriously, when had he developed some of these muscles?—I decided I should probably say something.

I tugged the quilt a little higher, hiding my chest as I asked. "Did you like sleeping on an actual mattress?"

"I didn't realize how much I took such simple things for granted," he replied. "Still have to call my chiropractor, though. There's no way those first few nights didn't cause some lumbar damage."

Jackson rose with a new shirt in hand—a black polo—and slipped it over his head. I watched his arms as he pulled it down, then went back into his suitcase to retrieve a matching black belt.

"I'm not sure what your meetings look like for the day, but I was going to go into town. Write at Sunrise for a bit. If, uh—if you wanted to join."

This was the first time he'd been the one to extend an invitation.

"I'd love to," I said and meant it. "But, uh—" My lips curled in, and I slapped my hand down on the top of my quilt, giving him the best *dagnabbit* mannerisms I could muster. "I have an early morning meeting. At…" I glanced at the alarm clock on the bedside table. "At seven thirty. And I still have to get ready, so I can't."

"Why so early?"

"London division," I lied. "Six-hour time difference. It's a bitch."

God bless Jordi and her new boyfriend for giving me the knowledge to pull that excuse off.

"Got it. Well, next time maybe."

"Yeah. Totally. Love me some caffeine."

Jackson gave me a quick smile before he finished getting ready. Socks, shoes, glasses, the one final look at himself in the mirror above the dresser.

"I'll see you later then," he said. "Not sure when I'll be back."

"Go enjoy not having to hear me work," I attempted to joke, but it came out stiff. "I'm sure it'll be nice being away from my chaos."

A low chuckle rumbled out of him. "Yeah, for a bit," he agreed, then situated the brown leather messenger bag he'd carried with him during our last few trips into town, his laptop and notebooks inside, across his body. "See you later."

"Go write that best-seller," I called after him.

My eyes stayed trained on the doorway Jackson had just exited through, never straying, never blinking, until I heard the front screen door slam shut. The primary door followed after.

Finally.

My lips trilled as I laid back down, my gaze set on the ceiling, one arm draped casually over my forehead.

Where were the woodland creatures when I really needed them to distract me? Even the birds had gone silent, leaving me alone with my thoughts. And those were still set on Jackson.

Had I been so dickmatized in the past that I'd truly never noticed him the way I had today? Then again, we'd almost always been in the dark. Or I'd been the one to get half undressed for a quick rendezvous.

All I knew was I couldn't get the vision of him walking out of that bathroom out of my head. The way his skin had glistened from the humidity—and the way I knew how it would feel under my touch. The same as it did when we'd fucked, both of us coated in a layer of sweat as we clawed at each other, rough and hungry, chasing the release we both desperately craved.

The same release I wanted to experience now.

My eyes slid towards the door, as if Jackson would come back at any minute. The man was probably already in town at this point, given the pace at which he walked.

Which meant I had no problem when my arm left my forehead and my fingers trailed gingerly down my body, caressing it in a way that created goosebumps. They traveled all the way down until they disappeared beneath the band of my pajama pants and reached my slick core.

I moaned as I rubbed circles on my clit, feeling as if that might be all I needed to soar over the edge. Imagining this could be Jackson—knowing it once had *been* Jackson—with his callused hands and strong arms. My hands that were now between my legs or palming my own breast once scraping down his surprisingly muscular back, urging him to keep going. Harder. Faster. Deeper.

"Fuck this," I grumbled, and threw the covers off myself.

My hand wasn't going to be enough. Not this time.

I said quick thanks to past me as I dug through what remained in my suitcase and retrieved my vibrator. My pants were off, panties with them, by the time I made it back to the bed, which I didn't even bother using as a cover.

A soft hum filled the room, and my own joined a moment later when I placed the vibrator just where I needed it.

My head tilted back and my eyes closed as ecstasy overcame me. Yes. *Yes*—this was what I needed. It felt so good. Not nearly as good as Jackson, but *fuck*—it was better than nothing.

My free hand pushed my camisole down, and my breasts sprang free. I palmed one, then twisted my nipple between my fingers. The wetness between my legs intensified, and I desperately wished I had even more to satisfy the growing ache there.

But since this was all I had…

I ran the tip of the vibrator along my center then aligned it with my entrance. My hand grasped my breast, desperate to cling to something as the pink silicone disappeared within—

"Sorry—didn't think I'd come back so soon, but have you seen my—holy shit!"

I offered my own slew of inventive curses as I withdrew the vibrator and quickly tried to hide myself under the covers again. It was no use. I became a tangled mess. My breasts were still completely out of my camisole as it was, nipples peaked and pointing directly at Jackson.

"Wha… what are you doing here?" I asked, half breathless. Pathetically, I tried to shift so my camisole would go back up, but it was wishful thinking. Instead, I conceded to continuing my attempts at covering the greater of the two exposed evils.

"I realized I forgot my charger. I didn't put it in my bag when I switched rooms. I didn't… I'm sorry—I didn't realize you would be, uh, busy."

I shifted again, painfully aware of my vibrator still humming beside me on the bed. "You're good. It, uh, happens, I guess."

In bad pornos, maybe, but I needed to come up with *some* excuse to make this less excruciating. I'd never been so aware of my nakedness in all my life. Normally, it was something I tried my best to ignore when I was with a partner. I couldn't let myself begin to think about what they might see when I took off my clothes. How they judged the cellulite and love handles and rolls of my stomach.

But Jackson wasn't my partner here. No matter that he'd seen me naked at least a dozen times by now. This was different. So very different.

Yet, just like I'd taken him in earlier, he… was he gawking?

"I can, uh, just—" I cleared my throat. "I'll get dressed and help you look for your—"

"Finish."

Not many things could leave me at a loss for words, but those two syllables did.

"E-excuse me?"

"Finish," he repeated. "Please."

If I'd thought Jackson was gawking earlier, I'd been sadly mistaken. Because when I looked at him now—really looked at him—there was nothing but hunger in his brown eyes. I could barely tell where his pupils ended and his irises began, they were so dilated.

And when my eyes traveled down, I couldn't miss the bulge in his pants. The one his hand moved over, not to hide, but to stroke over his jeans.

Holy fuck.

The sight of that alone was enough to replace any embarrassment with a fresh wave of lust.

I didn't say a word as I reached blindly for my vibrator, never taking my eyes from him, and brought it back to my slick clit. I let out a soft moan at the contact, and I swore a growl escaped him in response. His grip tightened on his bulge, but he didn't do anything except continue to stroke himself. There was no way he wasn't in pain, the way his pants were straining.

My back arched off the bed when I hit a particularly good spot. Fuck, this was insane. I'd never done something like it before in my life, but there was no way I could stop. Saying no to Jackson's request had never even crossed my mind.

I didn't *need* to have my legs spread before him, pleasing myself.

I didn't *need* to watch as he eyed me with a hunger that both thrilled and scared me.

I definitely didn't need to moan, "*Jackson*," as my climax built and built and built until I was coming, right there on that shitty twin bed for my audience of one.

But I wanted to. I wanted it more than anything.

Because if this was the most he was going to allow me to have of him, I was going to take it, dammit.

The hum ceased when I turned off the vibrator, and the only sounds that filled the room afterward were Jackson and I's deep pants. I swore his were worse, even though he'd done nothing but stand there groping himself.

"I… I can help you finish too," I whispered.

Whatever trance he'd entered as he'd watched me snapped.

His gaze softened. His body loosened. His hand stilled on his crotch. But he still never looked away from me, making that vulnerability I probably should have felt for the duration of my little show creep up.

"No," Jackson replied, his voice gravelly. "No. We—I—"

He didn't say another word before he bolted from the room, pulling the door so it slammed shut behind him.

CHAPTER TWELVE

NOTE TO SELF: before masturbating in front of the man you're giving personality mentorship to, it's wise to consider how that man might look at you afterwards.

Because when it came to Jackson, he wasn't looking at me at all anymore.

All hope I'd started to develop that this convoluted plan of Marcus's—even though *he* would argue it was *my* plan—might work had vanished along with any smiles, chuckles, or even general eye contact that Jackson had finally started giving me.

We were back to square one.

And I was about three seconds from losing my shit if he ran from one more room when I entered it.

I scowled as his heavy footsteps pounded up the creaky loft stairs, my eyes tracking where he might be above me based on the noise. When he finally settled in what I assumed was the little desk up there, I groaned.

Had it been weird when he'd rushed out, leaving me half-naked, spent, and entirely confused on my bed? Yes. And had I expected everything to be completely normal again when he finally returned from Sunrise Brews, four-ish hours later? Of course not. But we'd never been normal. Not once. So being given the avoidance treatment left me with a cocktail of emotions I didn't even want to begin to decode.

At the very least, I'd hoped his insistence that I kept going meant he'd gotten over whatever weird funk he'd been in since we'd gotten here. The one where he just completely ignored the fact that we had been sporadically sleeping together for the last ten months.

Add that to the ever-growing list of things I might just never understand about Jackson Albrecht.

I slammed my laptop shut, calling it a day. I'd been useless as it was, completely distracted by just about everything other than work. The fact that Alexis had been able to formulate clearer answers than me during our team meeting today should have been the first sign I wasn't in the right mental space.

"I'm going out," I called out as I grabbed my jean jacket off the back of the kitchen stool I'd been sitting in. "Come if you want."

I cringed as soon as the words left my mouth. Asking Jackson to come probably wasn't the best thing to do at the moment—innocently intended or not.

I didn't wait for him to respond—he probably wouldn't have done so anyway—before I left the cabin.

I HADN'T BEEN in Ziggy's for more than two minutes when the freshly poured pint of beer was slammed down in front of me, the pale amber liquid sloshing over the sides a bit from the force.

When I looked up from where I'd been staring at the bar top, Rosie was waiting, an expectant brow raised.

"I didn't order yet," I said.

"I know," she replied. "This one's on the house. When you didn't stop staring at nothing for ten minutes, I figured you could use it."

Ten minutes? Shit, I really was out of it.

The middle-aged bartender leaned forward until her arms rested on the side of the bar top opposite me. "What's wrong, sugar?"

My hands wrapped around the pint glass. "Nothing."

She let out a *pft* of air. "I know we haven't known each other for very long, but this"—she gestured to my general being—"isn't nothing. Where's that high-spirited young woman who came in here a few nights ago?"

I was about to respond when a voice from behind me said, "If she's anything like her friend, those high spirits are long gone."

By the time I turned around, Hemi was already across the room and situating herself in the barstool beside me.

"You two know each other?" Rosie asked, her eyes darting between Hemi and me.

Hemi nodded. "Met this one last weekend," she said, pointing at me with her thumb like I wasn't right there. "Her and her friend come by almost every morning. Did you know he's an author?"

Rosie nodded once. "A *New York Times* best-seller."

Well, Jackson would be happy to know he'd left an impression. Too bad he wouldn't find out unless he allowed me to talk to him again.

Hemi turned on me then. "Where were you today? I had some of those cherry scones I wanted you to try."

After I'd confessed her cinnamon roll had been one of the best things I'd ever consumed in my lifetime, Hemi had been trying to pawn pastries off on me during each visit. So far, I'd had a lemon poppyseed muffin, slice of coffee cake, and an apple cider donut. All of them were just as delicious.

"I had to work," I half-lied. "Meetings and stuff."

That seemed to appease Hemi, who nodded slowly. "Probably for the better. Don't know how much you would have gotten done with your friend practically pulling his hair out all day."

"Poor guy," Rosie cut in. "I can't imagine writing is easy."

"No, no, no," Hemi replied. "He touched his keyboard maybe three times. He just kept staring at his screen or sitting there with his head in his hands." She aimed an inquisitive look my way. "You two said you were here for work?" When I nodded, she followed up with, "Big project or something?"

"He has to finish his manuscript by the end of the trip. Or most of it, anyway," I explained. Among other things I wasn't going to mention for the sake of Jackson's image.

Rosie's eyes widened. "They expect him to write a whole book in—how long did you say you'd be here?"

"A few weeks."

I didn't think it was possible, but her eyes widened even more. "No wonder the poor boy's stressed."

I shrugged. "It's his job."

Outwardly, I tried to match the nonchalance of my tone, but inwardly, my stomach was doing summersaults.

If there was one thing I knew Jackson was capable of, it was writing a good book. I'd seen him at it for the last few days, and there wasn't a doubt in my mind that once he got going, his inspiration well didn't run dry.

That's why he'd claimed he'd come into the bedroom so late the night before; he'd gotten hit with inspiration and couldn't stop. It was hard to believe that it would just disappear a few hours later. Then again, there was a reason I was part of the business side of Starr, not the talent side. An author's creative process was very far removed from my area of expertise.

"Well, if he's been making the kind of progress he made today—which is no progress, from the looks of it," Hemi said, "I'm not sure that'll happen."

"And he didn't want to come out with you tonight?" Rosie added.

I shook my head. "He's… in a bit of a mood."

Hopefully, given what Hemi had just said, they assumed it was related to something with Jackson's writer's block, and not anything to do with me.

"Too bad," Rosie replied. "Nothing a cold drink and a good burger couldn't fix."

I stifled a laugh when Hemi stared at Rosie in wide-eyed horror. "You fed that boy a burger?"

"And he lived to tell the tale?" came a voice from down the bar, followed by some chuckles. Unsurprisingly, it was Gus. Marty and a new friend with a long gray ponytail were with him, all three of them snickering.

"You hush!" Rosie scolded, taking her wiping rag off her shoulder and fake-whipping it in their direction. Then to Hemi, she added, "I'll have you know he told me he loved it."

"Sure he did," Hemi said. "And I'm the Queen of England."

That time I didn't bother hiding the smile that grew on my lips, my eyes sliding from the short, fiery woman beside me to the sweet, naïve woman behind the counter. Even with her hands on her hips and what I assumed was her best attempt at a stern glare, Rosie came across as nothing short of an angel on earth.

Hemi just shrugged, then her elbow nudged me. "You writing a book too?"

I snorted. "God, no. I'm not disciplined enough for that."

"Then what are you here for?" Rosie asked.

"Yeah, I sort of guessed you were both on some sort of forced writer's retreat once I learned what your friend did."

"No, not even close," I said. Then I pursed my lips and tilted my head from side to side before I amended, "Well, not for me. It is for Jackson, though. I'm still working, I just also have to make sure to—"

"Babysit him?" Hemi tried. Rosie nodded her agreement. "Because that's what it seems like."

It was hard not to make a face at that. It wasn't entirely what I was in Timberland Creek for, of course, but it would be hard to explain the strange assignment I'd been given. One needed to be exposed to Jackson a bit longer before they fully understood the necessity for my involvement.

Even if I was beginning to detest that involvement more and more as the days passed.

A woman could only take so much emotional whiplash.

Rosie scoffed. "Is that what this world has come to? Sending perfectly capable women away to make sure men do their jobs?"

"This world wouldn't run without us in it," Hemi added.

"Here, here," I mumbled and lifted my glass infinitesimally

in mock salute.

"That's right."

Rosie must have taken my half-assed actions to heart because she got straight to work, collecting bottles with her back turned to a very curious Hemi and me. It didn't take long to realize what she was doing, and when the two shot glasses filled with copper liquid were placed on the counter, I'd already mentally prepared myself. A third was in Rosie's hand.

"Oh, c'mon, Ro," Hemi complained. "I'm too old for this."

Hemi couldn't have been more than forty years old, but even at thirty-two, I was staring down at what I guessed was whiskey with the same sense of dread.

Shots had never been my friend. No story where shots were involved ever had a chill ending. Nope—they usually involved things like dancing on bars or making out with the guy you could have *sworn* was super-hot but was actually revealed to be the human embodiment of an earthworm when the lights turned on.

Given that the biker boys were the only other patrons at Ziggy's, I wasn't too worried. But the bar top was pretty nice. I could see Drunk Tori making it her runway if the circumstances allowed.

"I'm worse than you," the bartender argued. "But in the spirit of sisterhood, we're doing it." She lifted her shot glass. "Fuck men."

If I'd had a drink in my mouth, it would have been spit back out.

Well, I'd be damned. I'd been wondering if Rosie knew how to cuss. Though, the result of this attempt was a slightly embarrassed blush, as if she'd regretted it as soon as the word left her mouth.

Not wanting to leave her hanging, I grabbed my glass and lifted it. "Fuck men," I echoed.

Hemi followed. "I guess that makes three."

The whiskey burned just like I knew it would, and within seconds I could have sworn my head was spinning.

Nope. Shots were *not* my friend.

SOBER TORI HAD enough foresight to not drive into town. Drunk Tori was thankful for it. *Very* thankful for it.

Maybe walking alone on a forest path at night wasn't a good idea, though?

Nah. I'd be fine. It wasn't like I had any fishing poles to rob. No stabbings would be happening tonight. And if anyone tried, I'd just jab them with my quick reflexes. Like a mother-fucking *ninja.*

I practiced a few of said jabs on the air, just to be safe.

Oh yeah. Any attacker would be *screwed.*

Sadly, I never got to test out my strength before I was back at the front door of the cabin.

"Fuck men, fuck men, fuck men…" I mumble-chanted as I tried to finagle my key into the lock. It was so dark out here in the wilderness. Oh! I could use my phone flashlight and—

"Whoa!"

The front door flung open, and I stumbled into the living room. I might have made it all the way to that stupid plaid chair if a hand hadn't wrapped around my arm to jolt me back upright.

When I was sure my feet were no longer moving and I was standing relatively upright again, I turned. Jackson's confused stare was waiting for me.

"Oh, so *now* you want to touch me," I said.

His hand pulled back immediately and I swayed a little. Wow, I hadn't realized how wobbly I was. Maybe I was only steady when I needed to use my ninja moves.

My brain decided that was the moment to test out a hand-chop again. Jackson stepped back, the crease in his brow deepening. Wow, judgmental much? I knew who I wouldn't be saving…

"Where were you?" he asked.

"Out."

"Out where?"

"With my friends." Three shots later, Rosie and Hemi had definitely solidified themselves as such. We were bonded forever over whiskey and mutual distrust of the male species.

"What friends?" Jackson asked. "We're in a town of twenty

people."

"Nine-hundred and ninety-seven people, thank you very much," I recited with my index finger pointed at him. "I was with two of them. And Gus, Marty, and Ray."

"Who's Ray?"

"Gus and Marty's friend." I stepped closer so I could poke his chest with each word when I said, "Keep up, Jackson Sawyer Albrecht!"

I was apparently stronger than I thought because that last jab sent me careening forward. Two strong hands grabbed at my upper arms before I could fully fall into Jackson's chest, though. Too bad. I would have been able to figure out if it was actually as sturdy as I'd imagined it was this morning.

Jackson settled me back upright. "Tori, you need to go to bed."

"Oh, you *love* it when I'm in bed, don't you?"

His hands dropped away and a chill instantly replaced them. "What's that supposed to mean?"

I rolled my eyes and let out a *pft* of air. "Like you don't know." But even with three shots—four? I'd lost count—and just as many beers flowing through my system, I didn't miss his growing confusion.

"*Ugh*," I groaned, then got my hand out, ready to count. "You like me when you fuck me. Or when I fuck myself. Or when I'm scared of owls. But otherwise, you don't like me, Jackson. You don't like me. Not. One. Bit." He received three more punctuated chest pokes that thankfully didn't send me toppling.

Because given the look on his face, I wasn't sure Jackson would have caught me that time.

"Oh, no," I scolded, wagging the same finger that had just jabbed him. "No, no, no. You don't get to be upset because I'm telling the truth." I huffed out a sigh. "Why don't you like me, Jackson? I'm too loud. I'm too mean. I can't remember what shelf you like your coffee creamer on. It's not my fault you're so… so *complicated*."

I probably looked like a two-year-old throwing a tantrum when I threw my hands down at my sides and pouted, but I didn't care. I was so tired. So unbelievably tired of the back and forth.

So, when Jackson repeated, "Go to bed, Tori," that was the final straw.

"No—I will *not* go to bed. You know why?" I put my hands on my hips and gave him a very generous half a second to answer before I continued. "Because I'm *done* playing your games. This little hot and cold thing you've got going on isn't gonna work anymore. Nope—not with me, buddy. And you know what else?"

Maybe it was the memory of the toasts Rosie, Hemi, and I had shared, or maybe it was just all the emotions I'd suppressed while trying to be Happy Bubbly Tori. But everything was coming out now.

Honestly, given how our day had started, this likely wasn't in the top three craziest things to have happened in the last twenty-four hours.

Me shoving Jackson probably ranked, though.

He stumbled back, eyes wide with surprise as I shouted, "Fuck you!" à la my earlier feminist toasts at Ziggy's.

"Fuck you," I repeated. "Because I'm *great*, and you should consider yourself *lucky* that I've slept with you. And that I've agreed to be trapped here with you while you mope and tell me to be quiet and be subjected to all your stupid rules and—"

I grunted when my back hit the wall, and it took me a moment to realize that no—I hadn't fallen backwards. I was being held there, my hands above my head, and a warm, hard body in front of me. *Very* hard, given the pressure against my stomach.

Jackson held firm when I tried to squirm. For such a skinny man, he was surprisingly strong. Apparently, I hadn't been imaging those muscles during my lust-fog this morning because there was no way I was getting past him.

He took half a step closer, and his erection pushed into me. God, was this man *always* hard? But just the feel of him pressing against me—his body this close—had me aching too.

Then his lips were by my jaw, his breath hitting my skin in the most luxurious rush of heat. I bit my lower lip and squirmed again, this time to try and squeeze my thighs together.

He moved, slowly. Torturously slow. As if he was debating what he wanted to do with me like this. I could think of a few ideas, but I didn't dare say anything else. It was my ranting that had gotten us in this position, after all.

My heart stopped when he moved toward my ear, his breath caressing me as gentle as a feather, and whispered, "You have no idea how wrong you are."

I didn't know what to say. My mind had gone blank. All it could do was repeat those words over and over and over. The stimulation from his proximity was too much.

Thankfully, it didn't matter because Jackson dropped his hold on my hands. They fell down to my sides as he backed away. I never took my eyes off him, and he returned the challenge—up until he turned and rushed up the stairs to the loft, leaving me alone and feeling suddenly very sober.

CHAPTER THIRTEEN

I SHOULD HAVE known better than to let two middle-aged women in small-town Wisconsin make me believe I could handle taking shots on a random Wednesday night. Yet here I was, majorly suffering the consequences of believing I could hold my own.

Somehow, I'd made it into my bed. Making it into my pajamas was a different story, but hey—I'd take any win I could get.

Within two minutes of being awake, I'd already determined that making it into my bed might be my *only* win.

My hand flew up to my forehead, trying to apply pressure from the outside that might counteract the pressure within. The roiling in my stomach didn't help, but I couldn't actually place if that was nausea or hunger. Had I even eaten dinner yesterday? I could have sworn Rosie brought me a basket of something to munch on, but the details were definitely a little blurry after the third shot.

What wasn't blurry at all, however, was my interaction with Jackson. The tail end of it, at least.

I groaned and buried my face in my hands. There had been so much said, but I couldn't remember any of it verbatim. Whatever it was, though, had gotten me pinned against the wall like a heroine in a romance novel, which… now I understood. I *more* than understood the obsession with that.

I'd read enough romances to know that once the girl was pinned against the wall, she either A) brought a knife to her captor's throat or B) was kissed senseless by said captor.

Seeing as I hadn't brought any daggers with me, we would have probably ended up with option B—had Jackson not literally run away from me.

Some hero. He was the author here. Didn't he know how these things were supposed to play out?

My head lifted just enough where I could glance at the bed beside me. Unlike yesterday, it was made. The shower was off. Jackson's things weren't beside the dresser anymore. He'd moved out after only a single night.

Even if he couldn't stomach being roommates, I did know that he'd stopped me from falling—twice. He'd spoken to me. He'd even touched me. That was more than I thought I'd get, given how he'd treated me the rest of the day yesterday.

Creaking kitchen floor boards drew my attention in the

direction of the door, beyond which Jackson was probably refilling his coffee. Or getting his first cup. What the hell time was it anyway?

One look at my phone told me it was nearly nine. Shit.

Much to my head's dismay, I threw back the covers and bolted around the room, trying to get ready for the day as quickly as possible. I'd be expected to be online for work in the next three minutes.

Messy bun it was.

By the time I rushed out of the room, completely ignoring Jackson who stood by the kitchen sink, I'd managed to put on a pair of leggings and a respectable long-sleeve shirt. Remote work definitely had its perks when it came to waking up late.

Thankfully, when I opened my laptop—four minutes late; damn—there were no last-minute, early-morning meetings that had been added to my calendar. No fire drills. No tasks that needed to be handled immediately. Phew.

The sudden calm was what allowed me to notice the Sunrise Brews coffee cup and treat box beside my laptop.

"I thought you might want that," Jackson muttered, just loud enough to capture my attention, but not at a volume that would make my head pound any more than it already was.

I didn't reply as I read Hemi's writing on the side of the to-go cup. Large caramel latte with oat milk—just like I always ordered.

"And Hemdeep said you were supposed to try that scone,"

Jackson added. "Cherry, I think?"

I peeked through the clear top of the brown pastry box to see that it was, in fact, the cherry scone Hemi had chastised me about not getting. Unfortunately, with the way my stomach still hadn't made up its mind on how it wanted to feel, I didn't think I'd be eating it yet. But it looked delicious.

"How much do I owe you?" I asked, pulling out my phone in preparation to transfer money.

Jackson shook his head. "Nothing."

Bullshit. "Jackson Seamus Albrecht, I'm being serious. How much was the coffee?"

"You don't owe me anything," he reassured me. "I went there this morning anyway, and thought you might need it after all your… escapades last night."

I hadn't thought it was possible, but my head started to pound more.

Only the tittering birds outside and the tinkling of coffee as it filled the pot disturbed the otherwise silent kitchen, yet I wasn't sure Jackson could hear me when I said in hardly more than a breath, "I can't do this anymore, Jackson."

To his credit, he appeared worried. But it was clear he hadn't understood what I meant the moment he opened his mouth. "Hemi said you'd be expecting the pastry. I thought—"

"Not the pastry." I shut my eyes, hoping eliminating one of my senses might ease the pain in my head, the tension in my jaw. "The—this," I explained, gesturing between the two of us.

I opened my eyes again. "The back and forth. I'm literally terrified to step into a room with you because I don't know if I'll be given the silent treatment or if you'll bring me gifts."

"Technically the gift is from Hemi," he said. "She seemed to be apologetic for…"

He faded off, not bothering to finish his explanation when I leveled a glare at him.

Jackson cleared his throat. "Which would you prefer?"

"What?"

"The silence or the… the gifts. But I can't promise it will always be gifts."

Was he being serious?

I shook my head. "I don't *want* gifts, Jackson. I just… I want things to be *normal*. I don't want to have to wonder if I'm getting the Jackson who hates me or who tolerates me."

"I told you last night, I don't hate you."

It was a true tragedy that last night was as fuzzy as it was. "How else am I supposed to take the silent treatment, then? Because from my side, it sure seems like a big, neon Stay Away From Me sign."

Tension defined his jaw before his lips pursed. He was thinking, and I'd wait all damn day for him to find his answer if it meant getting mine.

Thankfully, it only took around a minute for him to say, "I need to do it for me."

"Do what?"

"Stay away from you," he admitted. "Draw some sort of line."

I hadn't realized how deep his breathing had gotten until that moment. It was like he was truly trying to keep some sort of tether on whatever was actually boiling beneath his skin, spinning around in his head.

"Why would you need to do that?"

His forearms flexed when he reached behind himself and grasped the edge of the counter.

"Do you know how hard it was for me that first day?" he ground out. "When I show up to this house and you're there waiting for me? You were inviting me to do the exact thing I'd been thinking about the entire *four-hour drive* from the airport. Four *hours*, Tori. And I had to tell you no."

Yeah, so my brain was officially broken.

He'd wanted it. He'd wanted *me*. He'd been thinking of the possibilities this little forced vacation of ours would present us with. And did that give me a bit more closure why he'd looked so damn hungry when he'd watched me touching myself the day before? Yes. Loads. From the sounds of it, the man had been dying to pleasure me himself—which, go at it, my friend. But it still didn't explain the rest of it.

"So…" I paused, shrugging. "So, we fuck—get it out of our system—then move on." It would have been nothing different than what we'd been doing the last ten months anyway.

Jackson shook his head. "I won't be able to do that. Once I

start touching you, I won't be able to stop."

Holy hell. And just like that, my headache was gone, replaced by a brand-new ache between my legs that had me pressing my thighs together.

"I was sent here to write a manuscript," Jackson continued. "A *best-selling* manuscript, at that. My entire career depends on the outcome of this trip. I can't have distractions. I know Marcus had no idea what he was doing when he sent you here with me. How could he have? And I tried so hard to convince him I could do this on my own, but he was so fucking insistent." Jackson ran his fingers back through his hair. "I didn't mean for you to feel like I hated you." His voice broke as he said it, making me believe he actually regretted it. "I needed to draw a line for my sake, and I'm seeing now that that was selfish and stupid and… I'm sorry."

I didn't say anything, half because I was stunned by Jackson's vulnerability and half because I was waiting for zombies to come through the door. I mean, getting two apologies from this man in less than a week was a sure sign of the apocalypse, wasn't it?

"So… you do want to talk to me," I concluded, finally speaking after the silence stretched to a point of discomfort. "You just… can't."

I'd been told a lot of reasons for why people needed to set boundaries with me. I was brash. I was loud. I was sometimes a bit overzealous. But never before had someone set a boundary because they literally didn't think they could operate properly while I was around.

It was equal parts flattering and confusing as hell.

Jackson nodded his reply. "Things between us became complicated a long time ago, Tori. I'm just doing what needs to be done to make this trip work."

"Yeah, and watching me masturbate really *un*complicated things, huh?"

Heat crept onto his cheeks, the tips of his ears, as he mumbled, "I never should have done that."

"I wanted it to be you, you know." He met my stare head-on upon hearing that. "If you'd have asked, I would have let you be the one to touch me."

The tension in his jaw returned, and his knuckles were practically white from how hard he was clutching the counter. That was all the proof I'd needed to know we were on the same page. He'd wanted to touch me too.

"You—" Jackson shook his head. "You can't just say things like that, Tori."

"Why not?" I challenged. "It's true."

"Because I can't handle it. I—"

He didn't even bother grabbing his coffee before he rushed away, past me and toward the stairs to the loft.

"No!" I called after him. "You don't get to keep running away from this, Jackson."

"Yes, I do." He paused on the stairs and whirled around to

face me one last time. "Because if I don't, then neither one of us is going to be able to deliver positive reports, and how will that look?"

Not great, but I couldn't admit that out loud. It would do nothing for my plight to finally get him to stop running. Stop hiding. His confession had given me so much hope that we were going to finally move past this, but here he was again, doing the same thing he always did.

Disappearing. Leaving me as the second choice to his career.

It wasn't like I'd expected Jackson to fall on his knees and beg to be with me. He wasn't that kind of guy. He'd always pick his writing over anything else.

But knowing he wanted me and discarded me anyway… it made the burn sting just a little stronger.

CHAPTER FOURTEEN

I WAS GOING to be fired at the end of this trip. Or demoted. Or heavily reprimanded, considering the lack of work I was getting done.

Focus was a myth. Maybe Jackson was onto something with his convoluted silent treatment idea, because it seemed like every time we spoke, I accomplished nothing afterward.

It might not have been such a massive issue if my literal reason for being here wasn't to spend time with him and fix his attitude.

His plan might work wonders for his progress on his manuscript, but me? At the rate we were going, whether we got the trip extension or not, I would have nothing positive to report back to Marcus or Rahm.

At least we didn't have another catch-up until next week. That gave me a few days at least to figure out how I wanted to handle everything.

I shut my laptop. The whole work day had passed and Jackson hadn't come down for anything other than to use the restroom and grab some lunch. The coffee pot still remained mostly full. Apparently, he'd only wasted time on what he deemed absolutely necessary. Wouldn't want to spend too much time around the horrible vixen he was forced to live with, after all.

It wasn't a matter of ignoring whatever was going on between us anymore. It was a matter of figuring out how we could both still come out successful and deal with the massive elephant in the room.

He was attracted to me, and I… well, he was becoming less annoying. I might even go as far as to say I found some of his comments a little charming. *Only* a little. And I was mature enough to admit that he wasn't *un*attractive to look at. Maybe even teetering on "swipe right," no outside opinions necessary.

I sighed, my eyes drifting to the bedroom door, beyond which I knew I'd packed the perfect solution to get Jackson to break.

IT WAS CLEAR Jackson hadn't expected me to show up in the loft, given the widening of his eyes as soon as I crested the staircase.

Or maybe it was because I'd shown up in the loft wearing a bathrobe I'd found in the linen closet.

Given our track record, it could have been either one, really.

"Hi," I greeted, kind of dumbly. So, I followed up with, "How many chapters did you get written today?"

"Three…" His hesitance was evident, his confusion even more so as he sat back in his chair, head tilted as he watched me.

"That's good."

His eyes narrowed. "Is that all you came up here for?"

I couldn't help but grin. He was learning so quickly.

"No, it's not," I confirmed. "I was thinking—about what you said earlier." I sauntered across the room until I stood by the desk, well aware that Jackson hadn't taken his eyes off me since I'd appeared in the loft. "You're going to drive yourself nuts if you don't take any breaks. The manuscript is important, yes, but you can't tell me you don't normally stop your entire life until you finish writing one, do you?"

Jackson shook his head. "Not usually," he admitted. "But I'm also not usually secluded in a cabin."

Fair enough.

"Well, we're going to take breaks here, too," I said. His eyes traced my movements as I reached for the tie of the robe, slowly undoing it. "You've been working hard all day. Three chapters, you said? I think that sort of progress calls for a break."

Never in all my life had a man looked at me the way Jackson did when the robe dropped to the floor at my feet, its removal fully displaying the black lingerie I'd hidden underneath. His favorite, so I'd been told. The same one I'd sent him a picture of me wearing before we'd gotten to the cabin.

I was beginning to realize his lack of response then might not have been all from anger, as I'd suspected. He might have simply been as speechless as he was right now.

He was still taking in the sight of me when I moved in front of him, close enough where I could place my index finger under his chin and tilt his head up so our eyes met.

"It's time you enjoyed yourself, Jackson," I whispered.

The heat of his hand was like fire when it found my hip, albeit hesitantly.

He swallowed, his Adam's apple bobbing with the movement. "I told you earlier I won't be able to stop," he said, his voice huskier than it had been just minutes ago.

I grinned. "You're assuming I'd want you to."

The hand tightened on my hip, but aside from that, Jackson didn't move. He didn't speak. He just sat there, staring up at me with conflict dancing across his face.

C'mon, dude. Just go for it. Accept the invitation…

Then his eyes darkened.

"Fuck distractions."

He was out of the chair, his hands on either side of my face and his lips pressed to mine seconds later.

This kiss was like the first bite of food after being starved. I was hungry as hell for anything he'd offer me, and boy was he offering me *everything*.

"Fuck," I breathed, head tilted back as he moved to my neck, kissing and sucking there the way I loved.

"On the desk," Jackson rasped between the ravishing.

I did as he instructed, making sure to move his laptop out of the way before. The last thing I wanted was for his entire novel to be erased by accident. That would be one hell of a mood-killer.

My hands tangled in the hair at the back of his head, and I brought his lips back to mine. I didn't think I would ever get tired of this—the way he kissed me like his life depended on it. All the frustration of the last week was finally being released, and it showed.

I sucked his bottom lip between my teeth and tugged as I pulled away, the action making a moan rumble out of him. Jackson's hands traveled down the curves at my sides, down my legs, until they hooked on my thighs, separating them just enough for him to step between.

The ache there only intensified the moment his erection pressed into me.

My legs spread wider, and my hips began to move, grinding against him over his jeans.

"You keep doing that and this won't last very long," he said.

"Touch me, Jackson," I begged. "I need you to touch me."

He obeyed, his lips once again finding my neck before he trailed them down the skin exposed by my barely-there outfit.

"So fucking stunning," he muttered against the skin of my breast.

His hand palmed one, slowly closing until my peaked nipple was pinched between his fingers. I gasped when he tugged, and my head fell back when he suckled the other into his mouth over the lace, his tongue circling the sensitive peak.

"Like that," I breathed. "Yes, just like that."

My hands unwound from Jackson's hair and moved between us, not to undo his jeans, but to ease the ache between my legs. My fingers had just barely brushed over the fabric of my panties when a hand wrapped around my wrist.

Jackson lifted his head from my breast.

"No, not today," he said. "Today, that's mine."

One thing I didn't think I'd ever get used to when sleeping with Jackson Albrecht?

The man *loved* dirty talk. And he was damn good at it too.

"Then hurry and take it."

He shucked his shirt over his head before he did anything more to me. Then, he thrusted his hips, pressing into me even harder than before.

The fucking tease.

"*Jackson*," I moaned.

The little shit had the audacity to grin. But he did finally listen to my pleas, falling to his knees before me.

"Do you remember on our first day here how I told you to be quiet?" he asked.

I sucked in a deep inhale when his finger ran over my soaked panties. "Mhm," I replied, my teeth tugging at my lower lip, my back arched as his thumb applied pressure right where I needed it.

"I don't want that anymore." His fingers curled into the seam of the fabric and pushed it to the side. "I want you telling me exactly what to do to make you come. And I want you shouting my name as you do it."

"*Yes.* Yes, anything—just start—"

Another gasp escaped me when Jackson slid a finger into me, a second following shortly after. And when his tongue started circling my clit, I wondered if they could hear my moan all the way in town.

My hand fisted his hair, making sure he stayed just where he was. Shit—it felt *so good.* My whole body was already tight and trembling, my release building faster than it ever did when I brought it on by myself.

"Fuck—Jackson. Don't stop. *Please* don't stop."

I was almost there. It couldn't have been more than a few minutes, but the way his fingers pumped, the way he sucked on my clit, it wouldn't take long before I broke.

"Yes. There. Right there. I'm gonna come. I'm—fuck. *Jackson.*"

The orgasm came over me like a tidal wave, my whole body

spasming. Jackson pulled away, and I had absolutely no strength at the moment to force him to stay. His sudden distance left a chill behind that, had my arms and legs not felt like gelatin, I would have remedied immediately.

But the moment he undid the button of his jeans and pulled them and his briefs down in one swift movement, I knew he had every intention of doing that himself.

I licked my lips at the first sight of his cock, and I swore it twitched in response.

"Stand up," Jackson commanded, as he stepped out of his pants.

I did as he asked, and he made his way back over to me. As soon as I was in reach, his hands found my hips. They turned me around before one urged me to bend forward, the other finding the band of my panties and tugging them down.

"I've wanted to fuck this pretty pussy since we got to this cabin," he said.

"Whose fault is it that you didn't?" I shot back.

That earned me a slap on my ass, and I might have said more had he not started to tease my folds with the tip of his cock.

"You okay if we don't use a condom?" Jackson asked.

I nodded. We hadn't been using one every time. I'd been on the pill for years, and we'd both confirmed we were clean.

My grip on the desk tightened when the head of his cock pressed into my entrance.

"Then we shouldn't wait any longer, should we?"

I bit my lip, stifling a moan, as he slid the rest of the way into me. It didn't matter how many times we did this. I'd never get over the feel of Jackson, the way he filled me so wonderfully.

His fingers dug into my hips, his hard thrusts lurching me forward, each one more luxurious than the last. Of all the men I'd slept with, there wasn't one that had ever satisfied me quite the way Jackson did. Even from the beginning, it was like he'd made it his personal mission to make sure I was pleased. Like he'd researched every inch of my body to make sure each time was better than the last.

I wouldn't have put it past him. He was a perfectionist, after all. But this was one instance in which I'd never bother him about it.

"Harder," I coaxed. "Hard—yes, like that. Fuck—*just* like that."

His thrusts became more hurried, more frenzied. His grip on my hips tightened to the point I knew he'd leave marks behind, but I didn't care. All I wanted was for him to keep going.

"Shit, I'm close," he muttered, then pulled out, leaving me feeling unbearably empty. "Turn around. I want to watch you when you come."

I'd never moved so fast, and when he pressed back into me, my desperation was immediately sated.

"I love the way you feel around me," he grunted. "God— watching you take my cock. You're gonna make me come, Tori."

"A little longer," I pleaded. "Please. I'm almost there."

A look of determination came over him then. Give Jackson a challenge, and he would fulfill it. This man was going to hold out until I finished, come hell or high water.

My fingers found my clit, rubbing circles to help him out.

"You're so fucking sexy when you touch yourself." Jackson sounded like he was in actual pain now.

"Harder," I said, following my own orders, the friction making me climb higher and higher toward another release. "I'm going to—fuck. I'm—"

Jackson thrust into me, and I clenched around his cock until he couldn't take it anymore. He pulled out, pumped himself with his hand, and spilled himself onto my lace-covered stomach, my breasts.

For the first time, the silence that fell between us wasn't tense. I truly believed neither of us could coherently form words at the moment. At least I knew I couldn't.

Then, he proved me wrong with one muttered, "Fuck."

I tilted my head back and laughed, a full-bodied sound that filled the whole room. When I found him again, Jackson was smiling, too.

"See?" I said. "That wasn't so bad, was it?"

"No, that was—" He shook his head and let out his own huffed laugh. "Fuck."

"Maybe take a break from writing the rest of the night if that's the best you can come up with, bud."

He chuckled in earnest that time, then bent down to retrieve the robe off the floor.

"What did you have in mind instead?" he asked, tossing it to me so I could clean myself off.

"Well, normally I would suggest round two, but I'm gonna need a break after that." The smile he wore was rightfully smug. "How do drinks and onion rings at Ziggy's sound?"

Jackson nodded slowly. "Almost a good enough substitute for more sex."

"Remind me who it was that didn't want to have sex in the first place?"

He stepped between my legs again, his hands running up my thighs, and I had half a mind to eat my words. Who needed breaks? Breaks were for the weak.

But then Jackson said, "I'll need fries, too, to consider it a suitable alternative."

I grinned. "Deal."

CHAPTER FIFTEEN

IT TOOK EVERY ounce of will-power I possessed not to touch Jackson.

I probably looked like I was in pain as we sat side by side at the bar at Ziggy's. He was so damn close to me. Had he always radiated this much body heat? I swore I hadn't noticed it the last time we'd come here together. And if I'd been worried about our thighs touching then, I was hyper-aware of it now. It was like one brush would set me off like an animal in heat.

Jackson, surprisingly, didn't seem any different than usual. Why should he be? We'd hooked up plenty of times before and gone about our lives like it had never happened. But those times, there were always other things that made it easy to stay away. Work. Conventions. Other people.

It was just the two of us now. No one but Rosie—who was taking a *very* long time to come chat with us—could save me this time.

I grabbed my menu and began to fan myself, which was mistake number one.

"You okay?" Jackson asked.

I nodded. "Yeah. Is it, like, really hot in here?"

He shrugged. "I guess. You could always take off your—"

Thank god his phone rang because Jackson saying I should take off anything only made the heat worse. I waved the menu harder. There had to be sweat on my brow.

"Shit," Jackson mumbled. He waved his phone at me. "Mind if I take this? It's my mom."

I was once again reminded that Jackson Albrecht was, in fact, an actual human being and not some robot planted in my life.

"Sure. Yeah." When he gave me a once-over, probably worried about my health—nothing else, surely—I added, "Don't want your mom thinking I went all serial killer on you and buried you in the forest behind the cabin."

That earned an eye roll and an amused grin. But it also did the job. Jackson was out of his seat and on his way out of Ziggy's with his phone to his ear within seconds.

"Don't tell me you're still getting hangover hot flashes."

Oh, sure. *Now* Rosie decided she wanted to show up. Just when I was finally in the clear.

"Are you kidding?" I replied. "I popped two ibuprofen, put a Liquid IV in my tumbler and went through my day like a champ."

Rosie grinned. "Atta girl."

"You feeling okay this morning?"

"Honey, if there's one thing you build up after working at a bar for thirty years, it's a tolerance."

"And you called *me* the champ." How was it that every time I visited Ziggy's I became more and more determined to become Rosie's friend?

She only shrugged, as if I shouldn't be impressed that someone probably double my age had recovered from a night out better than I had. But just as she looked ready to say something else, she closed her mouth, eyes narrowed and focused.

"Oh, sweetie. Do they not teach you how to hide a hickey in the big city?"

"*What?*"

The menu flopped down to the counter with a *smack*, replaced immediately with my phone. I thought I'd checked everywhere Jackson had put his lips on me.

Well, everywhere visible.

I swore if he hadn't told me I had a hickey—like some horny high schooler—I would—

My search came to an abrupt halt when Rosie started to chuckle.

"You made that way too easy," she said.

I locked my phone and placed it back on the bar, never taking my eyes off the sneaky woman across from me.

Oh yeah. We were going to be *great* friends. I'd make sure of it.

"I don't actually have a hickey?"

Rosie shook her head. "No. But *I* have my answer."

"And what's that?"

"That you and the author have a little thing going on."

A fresh heat that had nothing to do with my earlier problems spread through me. This time, I knew it was accompanied with a blush on my cheeks.

"How could you tell?" I asked.

"Honey, I knew from the moment you two walked in this bar that there was *something* going on. But tonight?" She huffed a laugh and her focus strayed past me, to where Jackson had disappeared out the door. "You could cut the tension with a knife."

"*Ugh.*" My arms crossed on the bar and my head fell into them.

Somehow, we'd managed to go months without anyone around us finding out about our little situationship, yet Rosie had caught on within a week. People really weren't kidding when they said there was no such thing as secrets in a small town. We weren't even locals and we'd made it into the gossip mill.

"It's not a bad thing," Rosie continued. "I think it's cute."

My head lifted. "Really?"

She nodded. "I don't really know the two of you all that well yet, but from what I can tell he's pretty smitten."

Now it was my turn to huff a laugh. There were a lot of words I could use to describe how Jackson felt about me. Lusty and frequently annoyed were definitely the top two. Not smitten. That sounded like such an old-school way of saying in love.

And Jackson was definitely *not* in love.

Still, Rosie's observation made me curious. "What makes you say that?"

"Doing this job has taught me to notice the little things people do. Like Gus." She nodded off towards the other end of the looping mahogany bar where the man in question sat among his usual trio. "Whenever he's about to take a drink, he rubs his hands together first."

As if he'd heard us, Gus did just that, his palms rapidly rubbing against each other before he let out a deep, body-sagging exhale and reached for his beer.

"And Marty scratches his head when he's confused by whatever Ray's ranting about today."

I couldn't hear what the men were talking about over the music, but the look on Marty's face told me he was, in fact, confused by whatever Ray was talking very animatedly about. It didn't take long before Rosie's second prediction came true.

"Okay, and what about Jackson?" I asked.

"He can't take his eyes off you," she said. "Every time you're not looking, he sneaks these little glances. It's sweet." Her brow furrowed then. "Are you *actually* colleagues or was that a front to throw me off?"

"No, we were telling the truth about that."

"I take it work doesn't know about your little… affair?"

I tilted my head. "Affair makes it sound so icky."

"Is it not icky?" I shook my head. "But it *is* secretive?"

"Kinda…"

"Because work doesn't allow colleagues to date?"

"Okay, I was telling the truth about that, too," I insisted. "We aren't dating. But it's… complicated. Mostly because Jackson isn't my usual type."

"And what's that?"

"Generally well-liked?" I answered with a shy smile.

"You *did* call him prissy the first time you two came in here," Rosie reminded me, nodding along.

"So… yeah. Complicated," I repeated.

Rosie's upper lip puffed out as she ran her tongue across her teeth, not once taking her eyes from me. When they darted from side to side, checking to see if anyone else was around, I knew whatever was coming would be interesting—even before she leaned forward, elbows on the counter.

"The sex is that good?"

"Rosie!" I took my turn to scan the space, trying to determine if anyone else had heard the question.

People—and by that I meant Gus, Marty, and Ray, since they were the only other patrons at the moment—were staring. But that probably had more to do with my outburst than what Rosie had asked.

I gave the gentlemen a shy wave and they all returned it in sync, wearing matching confusion.

I dipped down to Rosie's level, arms crossed on the bar, before I said, "You might have figured out what's going on, but not everyone needs to know."

"*Ach.*" She nodded towards the men and when I stole a sideways glance, found them still watching, but talking. Gossiping, more like it, probably. "They're clueless. Give it five minutes and they won't even remember."

I wasn't exactly convinced, but didn't have much time to dwell before Rosie tapped my arm with the back of her hand.

"So?" She wiggled her brows. "Is it?"

My whole face scrunched. "This feels too much like talking about my sex life with my grandma. No offense," I added hastily on the end. I didn't actually know how old Rosie was.

But she didn't seem to take offense at all, instead letting out a surprising chuckle. "Honey, how naïve do you think I am? I might be old, but I've been around the block," she assured me. "Besides, if he's not your type, he must be great in—"

The creak of the front door was like a siren when it opened.

Rosie straightened, pulling her wiping rag off her shoulder to begin rubbing what appeared to be a perfectly clean spot in the counter in front of me. I sat back in my chair, phone in hand to hopefully play it off like I'd been on it the whole time. Jackson didn't seem like he suspected anything as he retook his spot in the seat beside me.

"Sorry," he apologized. "Mom really got going. Apparently, she's a big fan of the blue-collar work going on up here. She kept talking about packers."

Rosie made a whimpering noise that sounded like someone had just pierced her straight through the heart.

"That's a football team, Jackson," I informed him. I wasn't very into sports, but I'd been to enough bars to name some teams that were regularly put on the TVs.

"That makes more sense why she kept telling me about the ones she thought were handsome." He shrugged. "It's all sportsball to me."

"Amen to that," I replied.

"Wow, would you look at that," Rosie chimed in. "You two have something in common."

"We'll take our regular drinks. Thanks, Rosie!"

I plastered on a toothy grin and aimed wide eyes that hopefully communicated my wish for her to be quiet and stop meddling. I'd come back first thing in the morning and give her all the answers she wanted if that's what it took. But I'd rather be struck by lightning than have Jackson find out Rosie had been asking about our sex life.

"Spotted Cow and vodka soda, coming right up," she recited. She didn't disappear without one final glance between Jackson and me.

He might not have caught onto us when he first came back into the bar, but he'd *definitely* caught that.

His brow furrowed. "What was that about?"

I desperately wished I had a drink to enjoy. It would save me from needing to respond.

"No idea," I said with a shrug.

Jackson stared at Rosie as she got to work preparing our drinks, his face set in that way that told me he was thinking.

Just when I was sure we'd fallen into another bout of companionable silence, his elbow nudged me—the first contact we'd made with each other since we'd left the house.

A wave of heat overcame me.

Now that I thought of it, Rosie could take all the time in the world bringing that drink over. Or at least until my blush faded. The last thing I needed was to supply more ammo for her interrogation.

"Have you tried the burger here?" Jackson asked. "It sounds good and was thinking I might—"

I nudged him back—harder—and was thrilled when it elicited an actual laugh. I hadn't gotten many of those out of Jackson before. In fact, I didn't think many people had, at least not while I was present.

Something about it made my heart leap. Knowing that I'd responded in a way that made him happy enough to let me hear it. Like I'd just been made privy to his most well-kept secret.

Jackson's laughter was definitely up there with things like apologies and smiles. He didn't give them out to just anyone.

Yet I'd gotten all three—within the last ten minutes, actually.

And if I was surprised by that, I was even more so by the kiss that Jackson leaned over and planted on the top of my head.

When I glanced at Rosie to see if she'd noticed, I found her finishing our drinks, smiling.

NEVER HAD I ever thought I'd use the word *funny* to describe Jackson Not-Sergio Albrecht, yet there I was—my head tilted back to the starry night sky as we walked down the road that led from downtown Timberland Creek to the cabin.

Before, I might have thought his story to be a bit on the eccentric side. Now, I couldn't see it as anything other than what it really was: a case of a grown man getting caught in a horribly embarrassing situation.

"Oh my god," I said through my fading laughter. "And what did you tell her?"

"The truth, obviously."

Yeah, should have expected that. The least-likely-to-sugar-coat-things superlative definitely belonged to Jackson.

"Which was…?" I prompted, wanting to hear him admit it out loud.

"That I had no idea the painting was an artistic interpretation of a penis when I bought it, and I thought it would look great in the living room, regardless."

"And did she actually hang it?"

He nodded. "Mom still tells me how popular it is with her book club."

Another laugh escaped me. I had to give it to him—he knew

how to tell a good story off the page, too. The whole time he'd talked, I'd been able to perfectly envision his mom's joy when she opened the present on her birthday. Having his foster brother, Sam, walk in and candidly claim, "That's a dick," was the icing on the cake, though.

I actually found myself upset when we reached the front door of the cabin, knowing that meant story time was probably over. It was nearing midnight, and two late nights in a row would not feel good in the morning. Granted, this one only involved a single drink before I switched over to pop. At least the drowsiness would come without a headache tomorrow.

Jackson ushered me inside first, the door he'd just unlocked held open by one arm. The other found its way to my lower back as he followed behind.

That touch alone reminded me of what we'd been doing just before we'd left the cabin for the evening.

It seemed it might have had the same effect on Jackson, because he removed it as soon as the front door shut behind us.

"I, um—" He cleared his throat. "I guess I'll see you in the morning? Unless…"

His eyes strayed to the couch, then his suitcase beside it.

"Unless…?" I prompted, curious where he was going with this.

"Unless you"—This time his focus went past the kitchen, straight to the bedroom door—"want a roommate?"

"Hmm…" I tapped my index fingers on my lips. "It

depends."

"On?"

"You *did* already ditch me once."

His worry visibly eased when he picked up on my teasing. "It was a horribly misguided judgement."

"Like the penis painting?"

"I still stand by that penis painting. It was a work of art."

I fought the urge to chuckle as I continued, "I was left alone. The owls could have broken in at any minute and eaten me. That's not so easily forgiven."

"Were the two orgasms not enough to earn forgiveness?"

Damn. He actually went there.

Good. It made my job easier.

I closed the distance between us in two steps. My hands ran up Jackson's white t-shirt-covered chest before they latched onto his long-sleeve overshirt.

"Well, you know what they say," I drawled, tugging a bit to get him to lower to my level.

When his lips were centimeters from mine, he asked in a breathy whisper, "What's that?"

I couldn't stop myself from grinning. "Third time's the charm," I said then brought his lips down to mine.

CHAPTER SIXTEEN

IF JACKSON HAD intended to sleep when he moved into the bedroom again, his plans had been gloriously foiled.

And writing? No way. Not an option after he'd surprised me in the shower this morning. I'd decided to surprise him at his desk to say thank you.

The metaphorical line had been crossed, and there was no way either of us could go back. The fantasies I'd dreamt of since this silly little retreat plan had been orchestrated were finally coming true, except now we had a week of pent-up sexual frustration to let out. Even passing each other in the kitchen had become impossible. Being anywhere near Jackson was like being struck by an electromagnetic shock.

I couldn't stay away, and he wasn't much better.

My toes tapped ceaselessly against the counter as I sat in my stool, trying my best to work. There was something that wasn't adding up in this spreadsheet, and I just needed to find out what. Our costs shouldn't be so high for the Local Author Summit. Had our sponsorship ended up being more than we'd originally discussed? Ugh. I really didn't feel like having to get on the phone with that sales rep again to—

The phone in question lit up, dancing across the kitchen counter as it vibrated. Iris's name showed up at the top.

"Hello, my savior," I said by way of greeting. She chuckled. "One week in. How's my team treating you?"

"They've been wonderful," my colleague assured me. "You have them very well-trained."

"And to think my mom never let me have a dog growing up for just that reason." That earned a hearty laugh. "What's up, though? If there's nothing wrong with them, I'm guessing it's something else?"

"You're correct." Some shuffling occurred in the background of the call, making me think Iris was settling in at her desk. "You know that one author? Romance. Gianna something?"

I grinned. "Iris, are you telling me you don't have Starr's entire author roster memorized?"

"Between all the fucking pen names and legal names I'm shuffling through, I can't keep anything straight anymore," she said through a tired sigh. "But do you know who I'm talking about?"

"I do."

"Yeah, well she was stupid on social media again," Iris announced. "I don't get why these people can't just shut up sometimes, but here we are."

"What did she say?"

"Fat-phobic stuff," Iris said with a twinge of worry in her normally steady tone. As if she was waiting for my negative reaction.

Yes, as a plus-sized woman this kind of shit definitely pissed me off, but I'd also spent many years learning to pick my battles. I wasn't going to let this one tidbit of information ruin my day.

"Not surprised," I replied. "I've read some of her books. I wanted to talk to our editors about it, actually." For the most part, the Starr editorial team was fantastic. But sometimes they didn't catch everything. Namely fat jokes or one-liners that could totally be played off as innocent, but, to people like me, had an underlying message.

That people like me—people with curves—didn't deserve the same kind of love as our thinner counterparts. That having a pant size with two numbers instead of one somehow made us less beautiful.

"Maybe do that sooner rather than later because her previous works are part of the problem."

I groaned, and placed my elbow on the counter. My cheek found a place to rest in my palm. "Readers doing their research?"

"Big time," Iris confirmed, then continued on her spiel of what she'd found out.

I listened to part of it until the stairs to the loft creaked. I turned just enough to catch Jackson appear in my peripheral, his mouth open like he was about to say something. The second he noticed I was on the phone, though, he shut it, his brow furrowing in question.

I rolled my eyes in response and mouthed, "Iris."

For a moment, he looked worried, and rightfully so. She was part of the reason we were here, after all. That grand Make Him A Good Person plan. But Jackson eased when I shook my head, letting him know it was something else.

That's when the most devilish grin spread across his lips.

Iris was nothing but background noise at this point as she continued on with what I assumed was a plan of how to handle our predicament. My full attention was now on Jackson as he crossed the living room into the kitchen, stopping when he got to where I was sitting.

The electromagnetic current was at full power when he grabbed the back of my stool and swiveled it just enough so I wasn't facing the counter anymore. Instead, I faced him.

It was my turn to show my confusion, as I said into the phone, "Yeah, uh huh," to let Iris know I was still there. God, I hoped she sent all this in a follow-up email.

Jackson's grin only widened as he lowered onto the floor and—

Oh. Oh no. No, no, no.

I waved my free hand frantically, trying to tell him to stop whatever he was doing. But the moment his hands found my thighs and spread them apart, it didn't matter. Desire overpowered any rational thought that remained in my brain.

To be honest, it wasn't much to begin with.

I pulled my lower lip between my teeth when he lifted my tennis skirt, eyes widening when he found me without panties. His eyes lifted to mine, and I shrugged.

This might not have been the plan for right now, but I'd certainly been hoping it would be later.

Jackson shook his head, a low chuckle rumbling out of him. The sound heated me even further, and when he ran his finger against my folds, my want was already very evident.

"So wet for me," he whispered, barely loud enough where I could hear him, let alone Iris through the phone.

I had to actually clamp a hand over my mouth to keep from whimpering when that same finger slid into me.

This was, by far, the hottest thing I'd ever done with a guy. Was there a level above turned on? Outrageously horny? Because I was that. Oh, I was very much that.

My lips curled in when he spread my legs further apart and eased another finger into me. I was trying so fucking hard to pay attention to what Iris was saying, but it was no use. Every single ounce of my concentration was now devoted to Jackson and the way his fingers pumped in and out, curled just enough to hit exactly where I needed them to.

When his tongue joined, I knew this entire call was a lost cause.

"So, what do you think?"

It was the first time I'd been directly addressed since Jackson had shown up, and I snapped to attention, my thighs tightening against the sides of his head. He whimpered a bit at the sudden force, but didn't stop.

"I, uh—*whoa*." My free hand found Jackson's hair, my body lurching forward when he sucked on my clit. "Wow, that's a lot to take in."

The vibration of Jackson's silent laugh was better than any toy I owned.

"But do you think you can do it?" Iris asked.

"Um, yeah. For sure." I had no idea what I was agreeing to, but hopefully I'd be able to pull something off to accomplish it.

My lips curled in to suppress a moan when Jackson slipped a third finger in. Holy hell. I was going to come just from the thrill of this. Not that Jackson was doing a poor job, by any means.

"I can get a call set up for us with the billing department, since I'm sure the invoice for the space already went through. But there's no way this event can happen before we make some sort of formal statement on behalf of—"

The noise, something between a moan and a whimper, escaped beyond my control, and there was no taking it back.

The whole room fell into silence. Jackson pulled back, his fingers sliding out of me, with a look of abject horror on his face. I probably didn't look much better because Iris had gone totally quiet too.

"Everything… okay over there?" she finally asked.

"Uh, yeah. There's just a—a bear! Right outside the window! I should probably go deal with that. I'll call you back, yeah?"

Before she could confirm or deny, I pulled the phone away from my ear and hit the end call button.

"Do you have secret bear wrestling talents that are common knowledge?" Jackson asked, smirking, before he sucked his fingers into his mouth, cleaning me off them.

I had half a mind to throw myself from the stool and into his lap to keep going after seeing that—especially since I'd been well on my way to having a mind-blowing orgasm.

Instead, I slammed my phone down on the counter. "It's time for ground rules."

His brow quirked. "That's something I thought I'd never hear you say."

Me neither, buddy. But when the sex was getting too distracting, something needed to be done. It was only day one of our sexcapades, after all. One more week like this and we could both prepare to present our failure speeches to our respective higher authorities.

I'd only suggested we let all the frustration out thinking it would help us concentrate less on sex and more on what we were actually here to do.

Apparently, we were way too horny for that logic.

"At this rate, neither one of us is going to get anything done," I said. "How much writing have you accomplished today?"

That confident smirk he'd been wearing faded into a straight line as his cheeks turned a nice shade of pink. "I came up with a title for a chapter."

"Congrats." I reached for him, encouraging him to get up off the floor and stand between my legs instead. "But I believe the assignment was to write a best-selling novel by the end of this. Or most of one."

Even sitting on a counter stool, it was hard to wrap my arms around Jackson's neck. His hands, however, had no issue finding my thighs, running up and down them in a soothing motion.

"You're here to help me out, right?" Jackson asked, and I nodded. "So, what do you propose I do to make sure I'm concentrating on my book and not on you?"

"As much as it pains me to say this, because I really, *really* like it when you concentrate on me," I began, earning another chuckle. "What do you think of a reward system?"

"Like a dog?"

"Well, when you put it that way it sounds horrible."

"That's what you're thinking, though, right?" he questioned. "I write a certain amount then get a treat?"

"I mean… yeah, basically."

"So, like a dog."

"Do you have any better ideas, smartass?"

"A few…" Jackson drawled. He leaned forward, his lips coming dangerously close to my neck. "The first one being mutually beneficial for the both of us."

"Ideas for progress on your book, Jackson Scott." I flicked the side of his head and he reared back. "We need results."

"And unless we suddenly start seeing as much success as you are guessing my middle name—which is none—we'll get them."

That earned him another forehead flick, and Jackson chuckled, stepping further into the space between my legs.

"I *did* warn you I wouldn't be able to stop once I got started."

He had a point there, and the fact that his claim was holding true made me clench my thighs a little tighter. His returned grin told me he noticed.

"Listen, I love sex as much as the next woman, but I also like having a job," I said, only half meaning it. It was more like I enjoyed having a steady flow of income than the actual work. "And I'm pretty sure you like being an author?" When he nodded, I continued, "So reward system or we're drawing your line again."

"Why is it *my* line?"

"Because I got to the cabin with the full intention of doing all this the moment you showed up," I reminded him. "You're the one who held back, and now we're paying the consequences. We could have gotten through this horny teenager phase right when we got here, but now we're halfway through the trip. It's crunch time."

The mention of our limited time in Timberland Creek was what finally seemed to resonate with him, his face going serious. And even though I'd been the one to bring it up, reminding myself that this *would* all come to an end—that we would have to go back to the same secretive routine as before—killed any mood Jackson had created.

"Okay," he finally said, nodding. His hands squeezed my thighs once. Twice. "I can deal with rewards. But I get to pick them."

"I would have expected nothing less," I said. "Always have to have your way."

"Speaking of…" His voice had gone low again. Seductive. "How soon did you have to call Iris back?"

I shrugged. "She's under the impression I'm fighting a bear right now, so that probably buys me a half hour."

"Perfect. I won't even need that," Jackson said, and I laughed as his arms wound around me and his lips came down to mine.

DESPITE HIS INITIAL arguing against the reward system, it turned out it actually worked.

Three hours and two chapters later, Jackson came down from the loft, victorious, and gave me his request for his first reward.

I guess after I'd let him have sex with me on the kitchen counter before I called Iris back—she was very upset I hadn't gotten any pictures of the supposed bear; apparently, she was a closet wildlife enthusiast—that wasn't something he wanted to use his request on anymore.

So instead, he'd gone with a home-cooked meal.

Which was how I'd ended up at the town market, trying my

best to find a pasta sauce that met all Jackson's requirements.

"How the fuck am I supposed to tell how chunky the tomatoes are?" I mumbled to myself, twisting the jars in each of my hands to see if I'd somehow find an answer.

"Go with this one."

I nearly dropped both the jars when a tattooed hand reached onto the shelf in front of me and removed one of the other pasta sauces. I trailed the artwork up the person's arm, until my eyes lifted to Marty's face.

"Wife isn't too keen on tomatoes," he explained. "She likes this one, though. We've been using it for years."

"Amazing," I said, taking the recommended sauce from him and placing it in my basket. "Your wife wouldn't happen to have a preferred"—I lifted my phone to read the note I'd typed out—"thinly sliced, well-trimmed chicken breast or dairy-free cheese, would she?"

Marty's brow furrowed. "You're going to have a hard time finding something like that around here."

"I figured," I said then sighed. "Lactose intolerance and Wisconsin, I'm learning, don't mesh well."

Marty chuckled, crow's feet forming at the corner of his corners of his ice-blue eyes when he smiled. I'd only ever really seen him from across the bar at Ziggy's, but up close I could guess that he'd been a handsome man when he was younger. Now, I assumed he was probably right around seventy-years-old. But he still dressed the same way he probably had in his youth, in a pair of semi-ripped jeans, an old KISS band tee, and silver chain necklaces.

But one more thing I noticed now that we were standing closer to one another was his obvious softness. From a distance, I had no reason not to believe this guy wasn't a badass—and I'm sure he was, to an extent. Now, that quiet nature I'd begun to pick up on from observing the usual trio at Ziggy's was really coming through.

Case in point, the only things in his grocery cart were a loaf of bread, some chocolate-chip cookies, and a bouquet of wildflowers.

"If you're set on using that sauce, Mary—my wife—makes pretty good Italian sausage and pepper sandwiches. No dairy necessary."

"Actually, that sounds amazing," I said, my mouth already watering at the idea. Jackson and I had decided on chicken parm because it was a relatively easy meal to make, but this didn't sound any harder. "Italian sausage, bell peppers, hoagie rolls, and marinara?"

Marty nodded at my correct list of ingredients. "And Mary's secret is a garlic butter spread on the hoagie roll before you add the rest in. It's—" He formed a circle with his thumb and index finger, his other three fingers still outstretched, to let me know the enhancement to the recipe was top-notch.

I smiled. "Sold. You literally just saved dinner, my friend."

"Take it you and your buddy won't be at Ziggy's tonight?"

I shook my head. "As much as we love the burgers there…" I tried to joke, and Marty chuckled again.

"Looks like Ro has no choice but to hang out with us tonight, then." He lifted a hand from the handle of his shopping cart and extended it to me. "I'm Marty, by the way. I'm not sure she's differentiated the three amigos to you, but figure you should know. You and your friend are giving us regulars a run for our money lately."

"Tori," I replied, accepting the hand shake. A whole week into this little retreat and I hadn't realized I'd never formally introduced myself to any of the guys at Ziggy's. "And my friend is Jackson."

"You guys new in town?"

"Just temporarily," I clarified. "Work."

"Oh yeah? Where you staying?"

"Um, some cabin?" I gestured vaguely in the direction I'd come from to get to the market. "About a half mile down the road? Very Little-House-On-The-Prairie?"

"One bedroom and a loft?"

There was no way I could have hidden my shock. Damn, did people in small towns know every nook and cranny? "Yeah, that one."

Pride shone through Marty's following smile. "That's one of my daughter's."

"Are you serious?"

He nodded. "Us Johnsons are pretty entrepreneurial. Mary and I own the art gallery up the way." Marty mimicked what I had just done, but in the opposite direction. "My eldest son owns a fishing supply store, and Quinn owns a few properties around the area that she rents out to tourists. Sounds like you landed in one of them."

"That's amazing. Well, hey—now I know who to go to if I'm ever looking to come back and need a place to stay."

"For the next few years at least."

My brow furrowed. "What do you mean?"

Marty shrugged. "Her and her husband both grew up in these parts," he started. "Now that they want to grow their family, they're talking about moving to a bigger city. Milwaukee, Madison, Green Bay—somewhere the kids will have a chance at making more friends. Most of the folks around these parts are older, with adult kids."

"So, she's getting rid of the properties?" I asked, and he nodded. "Can't she just throw them up on some rental site?"

"Quinny's not like that. She wants to be able to look after the property herself. Being away won't work for her. Trust me— Mary and I have tried to tell her the same thing."

Shit. Sounded like our temporary home might not be available much longer. Too bad, too. I was actually starting to find it a little comfortable—somewhere I'd maybe bring Laura or suggest to her and Briana as a little getaway. I mean, really, aside from the mattresses, the place wasn't *that* bad. Especially now that Jackson and I were sleeping in the same room and the nightly circle-of-life activities weren't as terrifying knowing I had some company. And a potential protector if the owl made it through the window.

"That's too bad," I said. "But who knows, right? Maybe she'll change her mind?" Marty and I might have been on a first-name basis for all of five minutes, but the guy was obviously sad about this. The least I could do was offer some positivity.

"Yeah, maybe," he said, but it sounded just as cordial as my comment had been. "But I won't bore you any longer with an old man's stories. You have some sandwiches to make."

"Oh, yeah, right," I'd almost forgotten about that, much like most things when I got caught in conversation with one of the townies. "I'll see you around at Ziggy's, I'm sure."

"I'd be upset if I didn't."

Marty gave me a half-hearted salute, before he continued on his way to the single register in the market. Looked like cookies, bread, and flowers were all he'd be getting. The idea that maybe he was bringing something back for someone at home made me smile.

Knowing that I was doing the same thing made it grow even wider.

CHAPTER SEVENTEEN

ONE THING ABOUT midwestern America? You could never count on an accurate weather prediction.

Which was how Jackson ended up being down-poured on when rain suddenly sprang up on Saturday morning. He'd brought me back a coffee from Sunrise Brews—and an almond croissant, courtesy of Hemi—so I'd almost felt bad laughing as hard as I had at the sight of him dripping wet in the living room. Almost.

He'd repaid me by picking me up and carrying me into the shower—with my clothes on.

That wasn't to say they'd stayed on for a long time, but it was enough to absolutely drench them. Seeing as I'd also gone through a week's worth of laundry on top of that, it seemed like the perfect day to get some chores done. Vacation rental or not, now that I knew I had a direct connection to the owner, this place was going to be *spotless* by the time we left.

A load of sheets was going in the washing machine in the unfinished basement as I lounged on the couch in a pair of sweats and a Stray Land concert t-shirt, watching the best movie ever made: *Twilight*. It played on mute since Jackson had chosen to utilize my work station at the counter as his preferred writing location for the day.

"You know you can turn the sound on," Jackson said.

My eyes shifted from the TV screen in his direction to find him staring unabashedly at the movie.

"Aren't you supposed to be writing?" I asked in reply.

"Working on it."

I grinned. "It's okay to admit you can't resist Robert Pattinson's charms."

"I don't even know what this is."

My grin disappeared, and I sat up on the couch. "Are you kidding?"

"No…?"

Jackson hardly had a chance before I hurled the plaid, decorative pillow with a few questionable stains on it his way. He ducked just in time, and it soared over the counter, only to knock over the glass of water I'd poured and forgotten.

"Would you look what you did?" my intended target accused, standing from his stool.

"This would've been easily prevented if you hadn't said something so absolutely unbelievable."

He turned back over his shoulder to stare at me before he snatched the hand towel hanging over the oven bar and began to soak up my mess. "I feel like I didn't say anything that out of the ordinary."

"You just admitted you've never seen one of the most culturally significant cinematic masterpieces of the current century," I argued. "You might as well have just confessed to murder."

This time when Jackson turned to me, he was glaring. "Don't you think that's a bit dramatic?"

I shrugged. "I speak only facts."

To his credit, Jackson kept up the Tori You're Crazy look for a while—until his eyes drifted to the TV screen where the movie was still playing on mute.

His expression softened significantly. "Is this…" He lifted a hand to point at the screen while he continued to stare at it contemplatively. "This isn't where that guy is from, is it?"

"That guy?" I repeated.

"The one." When I raised a brow at him, he clarified. "Jordi's guy."

"Jackson Santiago Albrecht," I chastised. "You mean to tell me Alfie Fletcher earned you a refreshed spot on a best-seller list and you couldn't even be bothered to *remember his name?*"

"I did that on my own, thanks. It's called *talent.*"

"I'd throw another pillow at you if I didn't need to dive across the couch to get it," I told him flatly.

Jackson ignored that—aside from pointedly tossing the wet towel he'd used to clean up the result of my last pillow-throwing attempt into the sink—and returned his attention to the movie. His brow furrowed immediately.

"I'm sorry, but is he *sparkling?*" Jackson sounded appalled.

I grinned. "Told you it's iconic."

"I just…" He trailed off again, but hadn't stopped watching. His laptop remained untouched and open to his manuscript on the counter.

My grin widened. "Want to join me?"

That snapped him out of his trance. "Huh?"

I slapped the spot on the couch beside me. "It's all yours if you want it."

For someone who hadn't paid one iota of attention to his manuscript in the last half hour—not that I'd been keeping track—Jackson stared at it with a particularly forlorn expression, as if he felt sorry for casting it aside.

"It won't get mad at you if you take a break," I added.

Jackson cocked his head. "I haven't done shit for this chapter in an hour," he said. Ah, so worse than I'd thought. "And doesn't movie time sound like a bit of a reward?"

I shrugged a shoulder. "Kinda," I agreed. "Why does it matter? Were you planning on cashing in a different reward?"

"I was considering it…"

The way his eyes roamed my body sent a wave of heat through me, but I ignored it, shifting in my seat so my legs were curled up beneath me.

"Well, if what you say about your absolutely dismal progress is true—"

"I didn't say dismal."

"—then maybe it's better you take a break anyway," I finished suggesting. "Sounds like you're stuck, and what kind of person would I be if I let you leave this trip without watching my favorite movie?"

Jackson's eyes widened, his face twisted in something of a mix between curiosity and surprise. "Favorite?"

"Some of us—meaning me—are clearly more cultured than others, and it's beginning to show." I patted the couch again. "C'mon," I encouraged. "You know you want to."

If there was one thing I'd mastered over the years, it was persuasion. I'd gotten the sing-song, teasing tone down perfectly, and combined with my big blue eyes and encouraging smirk, not a lot of people said no when I pulled out my secret weapon.

Laura always told me I was one of the most dangerous people she knew for that reason. Probably because my influence over her usually ended with one more tequila shot than we should have taken.

I knew Jackson, however, was not as easily susceptible to my charms. He'd have no problem telling me to stay quiet and let him work; he'd come join me later if he wanted.

If it really came down to it, I knew there were other ways I'd be able to persuade him. But he was right. We'd created the reward system so he could continue to make progress. So *we* could continue to make progress.

Not that a few hours of classic early-two-thousands cinema would make-or-break that. But it was clear he was trying to hold out.

So much so that he spun and headed the opposite direction.

"I thought we were past the running away thing?" I called out, watching as he headed toward the bedroom, expecting him to disappear within it.

Until he pivoted and went for the sliding pantry door. It creaked as it folded open, and I sat up higher on my knees to get a better view of what he was possibly doing.

"I'm not running away," he said. "I'm seeing if there's popcorn in this house."

"Popcorn?"

He leaned back just enough to come into my view a bit better. "You said this is a life-changing experience?" he asked, and I nodded. "Then I'm doing this right. We're having popcorn, dammit."

I lowered myself back down and couldn't help the smile that formed slowly as Jackson rifled through the sparse, non-perishable contents that had been left behind by previous cabin renters. It only took a few minutes before he let out a muttered, "Success," and held up a packet of microwave popcorn.

"You get that going, and I'll make sure this movie is back at the beginning," I said, then immediately began my search for the remote.

"You're going to watch it again?" Jackson asked. "We can just start where it's at now."

"Oh no. Not a chance." I pulled the remote from between the couch cushions in a much more triumphant manner than

Jackson had with the flattened brown bag of kernels and artificial butter. "You said it yourself—we're doing this right. You're getting all one-hundred-twenty-one minutes of sparkling vampire goodness."

"Tell me you didn't just state the exact run time."

I smiled. "You're in for a real treat, Albrecht. Get ready."

JACKSON TOSSED HIS crumpled paper-towel-turned-napkin onto the coffee table and sat back in the couch, his popcorn bowl in his lap. His eyes still hadn't left where the credits rolled, the next movie suggestions listed at the bottom of the screen.

"Well," I prompted. "What did you think?"

Jackson's jaw tensed and he blinked rapidly at the TV before a huffed laugh escaped him. "I mean, that was… something." His attention finally drifted away from the credits and landed on me. "That earned the honor of being your favorite movie of all time?"

"I'm not sure it's an honor."

Jackson's head cocked in a way that told me I was dead wrong. "You're unbelievably opinionated, Tori."

"That makes two of us," I countered, then reached over to grab a few pieces of Jackson's remaining popcorn. I tossed them into my mouth before I added, "I'm eager to hear more of what you think, since you know I hold it in such high regard."

"I'm not sure that's a good idea," Jackson said. "We just started sharing a room."

"So?"

"So, I don't want to be murdered in my sleep."

I chuckled. "I should have expected nothing less than hatred from you." The way he'd been so intently staring at the screen earlier had given me too much false hope. Maybe he really *had* been that stuck on his manuscript.

What a trooper.

I'd thought I'd be met with some sort of sarcastic remark, but instead, Jackson's forehead scrunched. "What do you mean by that?"

"Huh?"

"Why did you expect me to hate it?"

"Well, I hoped you wouldn't, because now that means I have to watch the next four movies by myself," I admitted. "But... I don't know. You always make fun of my romance books." I nodded at the TV. "This is a romance, too."

Once again, Jackson defied my expectations by turning his face down to his popcorn bowl. He played with a piece absentmindedly as he muttered, "I'm not *against* romance."

"Coulda fooled me." I reached for the remote and began to scroll to the recommended movies. "Do you wanna watch the next one or—"

A warm hand wrapped around mine on the remote, making

me pause my movements. And when I looked up at Jackson again, he was watching me. The confusion from earlier was gone, replaced with something more like…

Shit, did he look upset?

The next thing I knew, the remote was out of my hand and tossed beside his napkin on the table.

"Okay, I get that you didn't like it," I said, "but you could just say you don't want to watch."

Jackson stood in response to that, his height really becoming more noticeable with me still sunk into the ancient couch cushions.

"The laundry should be done," he said. "You go check that, and I'm going to start writing."

A slow grin spread on my lips. "Oh, so do you mean to tell me you were *inspired* by *Twilight*?"

The forehead flick was unexpected, but not uncalled for.

"Not in the slightest," he assured me. "But once I get this god-forsaken scene finished, I'm going to call in my next reward."

"Wasn't this your reward?" I asked, brow scrunched.

Jackson shook his head. "To quote you—the more cultured of the two of us—I believe the word used was *break*, not *reward*. I can still cash one of the latter in today."

My mind drifted back to what he'd said before we started the movie, when he'd looked at me with the same hunger I'd grown so accustomed to.

"The laundry should only take me a little bit to transfer," I said. "I can read while you finish your scene, then we can meet in the bedroom?"

"Nope."

If the forehead flick was unexpected, nothing had prepared me for the moment Jackson lowered, bending at his waist to get more on my eye level. His hands found the back of the couch on either side of my head, trapping me within them. His face stopped no more than two inches from mine. One of us could have twitched and our lips would meet.

What was it with him and constantly putting me in these scenarios? Between this and the wall, I wasn't sure what I liked more.

I wondered how obvious my enjoyment was because Jackson aimed a smug grin at me.

"I know that's what you want," he said. "And believe me, I want it to. But I'm going to pick a different reward once I finish my scene."

"Another lactose-free meal?"

That earned a chuckle, the rumble of it vibrating through me more than I'd thought possible even with our proximity.

He surprised me yet again with a chaste kiss to my forehead before he straightened. I missed the heat he'd radiated as soon as he was gone.

"Not quite," he said. "But since I imagine I might be a few hours, maybe you can watch your next movie, then we can enjoy our leftovers while we watch my selection for the day."

My brows rose. "*Your* selection?"

I tried to imagine what Jackson Albrecht might enjoy watching in his free time and couldn't think of anything aside from World War II documentaries and Lord of the Rings. We'd never discussed our favorite media, but he gave me those vibes.

He chuckled again, as if he could sense my mental anguish. Oh, I bet he loved that he'd stumped me like this.

"You're going to be eating your words," he said, then left me in suspense on the couch.

CHAPTER EIGHTEEN

IT TOOK JACKSON three hours to finish his work. *Three.* During which I was able to complete two loads of laundry, fold it all, and still finish watching my next movie.

Not that I paid any attention to it. My thoughts kept going back to what he could possibly want to watch that would make me take back what I'd said.

"One Italian sausage hoagie sandwich with extra peppers and melted mozzarella," Jackson recited, remembering how I'd made my dinner the night before, and handed me my plate.

"And one with no peppers, extra non-chunky marinara." I said as I took his offering.

He smiled, setting the meal I'd also recalled down on the coffee table before he sat down on the couch beside me with a groan. "Exactly." Jackson turned to me, smile still in place. Growing, actually. "You ready?"

"My anticipation has driven me to the brink of insanity, I think."

He chuckled, and if I hadn't been holding a plate of messy, hot food, I might have reacted more when his hand found my thigh. His other grabbed the remote, and he began navigating the menu like we did this all the time.

I tried to concentrate on Jackson's task rather than his touch. It didn't prove too difficult—especially when he landed on the last possible option I would have ever guessed.

Mostly because I had no idea what the hell it was.

"Get ready to take back everything you said earlier," Jackson said as he selected a show called *Garden of Bleeding Hearts.*

It took a moment to load, but no amount of buffer time would have been enough to prepare me for the semi-animated title sequence complete with a song that wasn't in English. If the actors and unfamiliar text on the screen were any indication, I'd guess this had been produced somewhere in Asia.

"Uh, Jackson," I said after about ten seconds of silent observation.

"Hm?" he responded, and I could tell he was amused.

"What's this?"

"*Garden of Bleeding Hearts.*"

"Believe it or not, I can actually read," I retorted. "But I mean… what is it?"

The opening credits ended in a flourish of hundreds of multicolored animated hearts, which quickly blended into one large red one in the center of the screen. Animated flowers bloomed around it before blood started dripping from it—and that's what we followed into the transition to the opening scene.

Jackson leaned forward to set the remote down, satisfied now that the show was rolling, and picked up his sandwich. "It's a K-Drama. One of the best, actually."

"K-Drama?" I repeated.

"Korean drama," he clarified, even though I hadn't really needed it. My state of shock was rendering me incapable of doing anything but repeating what I'd heard. "They really started to pick up in popularity a few years ago."

"And you decided to watch it?"

"I was in between shows," he said with a shrug. "And the premise sounded intriguing."

"So… you watch these a lot then?"

"Not all the time, but they're definitely in the rotation." Jackson took a bite of his dinner. "There's a K-Drama for anything," he said with his mouth full. "Fantasy, historical, contemporary—it's incredible."

I wanted to keep asking questions—so many questions—but I also realized very quickly that I needed to pay attention. I'd already missed probably half the opening nighttime conversation between what looked like two handsome gardeners because I hadn't been reading the subtitles.

"And is this one historical?" I guessed, given the set and

costumes on screen.

Jackson swallowed his food, but didn't say anything further. He only pointed at the screen.

I couldn't help my gasp when, suddenly, one of the gardener's eyes turned red and he opened his mouth enough to reveal fangs.

His companion didn't stand a chance after that—or so the dramatic music led me to believe. The actual shot didn't show anything more than the first gardener lunging for his prey.

"No way!" I exclaimed, nearly sending my sandwich flying. "This show has vampires?"

"I thought you'd like that. You know, given all the hype over the last year. And the movie today, of course."

Oh boy, had he guessed correctly.

"I thought you didn't like this stuff?"

Jackson side-eyed me. "I write fantasy."

"No, I know that. But I mean—" I gestured to the TV where the scene had shifted into something much brighter. A princess in her castle it looked like. "This is *not* your breed of fantasy."

"Meaning?"

"Meaning this is exactly the sort of thing I'd expect you to make fun of me for enjoying."

Jackson shrugged as his attention went back to the TV. "I like stories with substance. *This* has substance."

"What? And *Twilight* doesn't?"

I was already grinning by the time he cast me another side-eyed stare, thankful he picked up on my sarcasm right away. He shook his head and chuckled before he took another bite of his sandwich.

"Watch and learn," he said, pointing quickly to the screen. "I can't wait for you to see a *real* vampire romance."

"Those are fighting words, Albrecht."

"Get used to it, Wilson. You're gonna be hearing a lot of them once I officially prove you wrong."

He wasn't watching me anymore. Jackson's attention was split between the subtitles and his sandwich, which made it even easier for me to go unnoticed as I kept staring at him. This anomaly of a man who made me so angry one moment, lustful another, and now… this. Whatever it was.

I could almost guarantee no one else had seen this side of Jackson. And it made me smile.

That's, of course, when he decided to look at me again.

"What's got you so happy?" he asked.

I was either starting to get hot flashes about twenty years too early or blushing really hard, given the heat that overcame me.

"I—" I tried, then shook my head, my eyes lowered. "Nothing. Just… this scene is cute."

When I glanced up, watching him from under my lashes to gauge his reaction, he wore a soft smile, too.

His eyes darted in the direction of the TV and back.

"Watch," he said, his voice no longer possessing the challenging, playful tone from before. "You're gonna miss the best parts."

I WASN'T THE biggest fan of losing, as many people in my life could attest to. Many of them were directly related to me or had known me very familiarly for years.

The fact that Jackson had already picked up on that little tidbit and felt comfortable enough to challenge me was dangerous.

Because the grin he aimed at me when the Korean-pop-ballad-accompanied credits started rolling was nothing short of challenging.

I shifted in my seat, finally giving my half-asleep legs some relief after not moving for the last hour, and set my plate on the end table beside me. I'd been so focused that it had stayed in my lap the whole time, even after I finished my sandwich approximately five minutes into the episode.

Jackson grabbed the remote and pressed pause before the next one started, his anticipatory stare boring into me.

I cleared my throat and sat back into the couch. "It was good," I said with a nonchalant shrug.

"Oh, please."

"*My* review of *your* show is right on par with *your* review of *my* movie."

"It's missing something."

"What?"

"The part where you admit I have superior taste."

I didn't even honor him with a verbal reply. Instead, I chose the physical route.

The double middle finger got just the reaction I wanted. Perhaps even a bit more, when Jackson scoffed at me then leaned my direction, dragging me under his arm. A small squeal escaped me. If this man gave me a noogie or put me in a headlock, I swore to god I'd never go down on him again.

But then, amid our laughter, I found myself tucked into his side, hair still intact, head not locked in the crook of his arm. In fact, my head had found quite a comfortable spot on Jackson's shoulder.

"Admit it," he said, squeezing so we were pressed even closer together. I wiggled the arm that was trapped between us free and rested it on his chest.

"You're gonna have to try harder than that if you want me to—"

I squealed again when he pulled me again, harder, until I was practically on his lap.

"Okay, okay!" I conceded. "You might have better taste. But in fairness, you haven't seen *Eclipse* yet."

"And I'm not going to because I've already gotten what I wanted." He pressed a kiss to the top of my head. "You really did like it, though?"

"A lot more than I thought I would," I admitted. "I mean,

how the heck can Taeyeon say no? YeJoon has literal hypnotic abilities."

"Well, for starters, he's staff and she's a princess, so it's actually very easy for her to say no." Jackson chuckled when I pinched him. Logic wasn't allowed when talking about fantasy stories. He should know that. "But he can't use them on her, either."

"What?" I turned just enough to look up at him from my place on his chest. "Why?"

"Looks like you're going to have to keep watching to find out," he taunted.

I groaned and turned to the TV again. Jackson's chuckle sounded louder than it probably was, what with my ear pressed against him, but I relished it all the same.

"I hope it rains tomorrow," I mumbled. "Then I won't feel bad about binge watching."

"You can watch it with the sound on," Jackson added. "I know you'll be reading the subtitles anyway, but I'm used to having K-Dramas on as background noise while I work."

"They don't bother you?"

Jackson shrugged at the same time his hand found my hair, his fingers playing absentmindedly with my curls.

"I use them as inspiration. The stories really are beautiful when you pay attention, and hearing about the kinds of things I'm writing helps put me in the right mindset. Besides, I normally put on the dub while I'm working."

"I didn't realize you were writing a vampire romance."

"I'm not, but… never say never, I suppose. There's definitely a market for it."

We left the unspoken implication of that statement hanging, but I could tell Jackson was distracted now. Honestly, it was the first time I'd thought about the possibility of this trip ending poorly for him in a few days. As far as I could tell, he'd also let reality fall to the wayside. Apparently, it was lurking a little closer than I'd realized.

"That's one thing I noticed you're missing," I said, trying to change the subject.

"For what?"

I turned up to him again. "Your books. They have almost no romance. And if they do, it's just kinda in the background."

"You've read my books?"

"I've been trying to," I said. "I didn't bring them here, though, since I thought that might be… I don't know. Weird, I guess? Uncomfortable."

"I suppose." His fingers drifted from my hair to my arm, stroking the skin that was left bare by my t-shirt.

"So, if you use these shows for inspiration, why leave the romance out?"

His hand stilled for a moment before the rhythm picked back up and Jackson said, "I've never believed I was qualified to write about it."

"Why not?"

Jackson shrugged. "Every creative writing professor I ever had told us to write what we know. Obviously, I don't know anything about medieval warriors or dragons, but any of the real stuff…" He trailed off, as if thinking about how he wanted to explain himself properly. "I've always worried people would be able to tell I didn't know what I was talking about in that regard."

"What regard?"

"About being in love."

I was about to keep asking my short questions, but what he'd said suddenly clicked.

"Wait," I said, sitting up a bit. "You mean to tell me you've *never* been in love?"

"Not that I'm aware of, no."

It was such a Jackson answer that I couldn't think of anything to say back for a few seconds.

"No middle school crush?" He shook his head. "No weird celebrity infatuation?" Another shake of his head. "An obsession with a particular porn star?"

"I—" His brow furrowed. "No?"

"Well, you have to get off somehow." Jackson lifted a brow, and I clarified, "Other than… you know." I gestured between us.

"And I have to be in love with someone to do that?"

The insinuation was enough to bring heat to my cheeks.

"No, but I've heard it makes it more enjoyable."

"So, I take it you've found yourself in a similar predicament?"

"I—" Now I'd been caught. "I've been in love before."

At least I thought I had. It was the most I'd ever felt for any guy I'd been sleeping with, that was for sure. Freddie Hart. My sophomore year of college. I could still remember the exact cologne he wore—*Dior* Sauvage—and how he would always make sure we didn't just make it about the sex. I got to *know* Freddie.

The other guys I'd found myself tangled up with had always been more to the point. Meet up. Fuck. Go home. No strings or complications.

Maybe that had been the right move because the moment I found out Freddie had gotten himself a girlfriend—one he'd apparently been talking to while we'd been in our little arrangement—it broke me. More than I'd thought it would. More than any of the others, that was for damn sure.

Second best, yet again.

"Boyfriend?" Jackson asked.

I shook my head and smiled wistfully, hoping it hid the hurt of the memories. "No. Just a... a thing." I lowered my eyes before I asked, "Have you had a girlfriend?"

"A couple," Jackson admitted.

"And you never loved any of them?"

"If I had, I'd still be with them."

Touché. "So that's why relationships exist in your books, but not at the forefront."

"Exactly," he confirmed. "I know people fall in love, so their happiness exists in my world. My main characters… they just don't know what it is to fall in love because *I* don't know." He paused, his hand stilling once again in my arm. "I'm actually trying it out in this newest book, though."

"Seriously?" He nodded. "And what made you decide now's the time?"

"I've started to feel more confident about it. I've been put in more scenarios for it over the last year. The experience, that is."

"Ugh, right?" I groaned. "Jordi and Alfie are disgustingly in love. It's adorable."

I expected Jackson to say something along the lines of, "They drove away paying customers," or "They should have saved it for the bedroom, not my book signing," but he shocked me instead by saying. "Yeah. Jordi and Alfie."

It was such a short response that I almost wanted to press more, but refrained. I wasn't going to open the door to bashing on my best friend that Jackson tolerated, at best, and her new beau. The restraint he was showing already was a vast improvement from what I could have expected a few months ago. A few weeks ago, even.

Maybe this trip wouldn't be a *total* failure after all. Slow and steady and all that.

"Well, I think your readers will be excited," I said instead. "Everyone loves a little romance. And I mean *everyone*," I tacked on, scratching my nails on his chest.

"What's that supposed to mean?"

"It means maybe you should stop flapping your lips and press play on the next episode, Albrecht. I'm not sure I can wait for tomorrow to see what happens."

Thankfully, he didn't argue. Instead, he tightened his arm around me and picked up the remote with the other, keeping me close as the opening credits started up again.

CHAPTER NINETEEN

"HERE I WAS thinking you two had up and left town without saying goodbye."

Jackson held open the door to Ziggy's, and I ducked under his arm, entering the bar to the tune of classic rock and a bit more conversation than usual. Still, Rosie had somehow managed to clock us as soon as we opened the door.

The immediate awareness of her patrons made me smile.

"We didn't visit for, like, two days," I said.

"That's two days too many," Rosie countered as Jackson and I took up our usual seats at the bar.

It was then that I took notice of the other end where the regular guys sat. The conversation I'd heard upon entering wasn't only from a few new groups, as I'd expected, but also an expanded crew.

Jackson must have seen it, too, because he asked, "Get some

new friends while we were away?"

"Not new," Rosie explained. "Just not invited as frequently. Or they don't want to come, which is—" She shrugged in an *It's Whatever* way. "I don't blame the guys for wanting some time away to do whatever it is you men do when the missus isn't around."

"Wives, I take it?" I asked.

"One wife, one girlfriend," Rosie corrected with a nod. It was then directed toward the group in question. "Gus has been seeing Rhonda for a bit now. I don't think either one wants to settle down again, though. Don't blame 'em. One marriage is more than enough."

"Speaking from experience?" I realized I didn't know a thing about Rosie, but if she could question me about my love life, I sure as hell earned the right to question her about hers.

"I am." Rosie shucked her rag over her shoulder and placed her hands on her hips, her gray bob bouncing above her shoulders. "Married a wonderful man for ten years then called it quits."

"If he was so wonderful, why'd you get divorced?" Jackson asked, and I might have reprimanded him for the blunt question if I wasn't curious, too.

Rosie grinned and leaned forward on the bar top, crossing her arms on the surface.

"Take it from me, kids," she said. "Nothing is worse than feeling like you're in second place in a marriage."

"He cheated on you?" Jackson's eyes were wide.

"Rosie, I don't know if that's what I'd consider wonderful," I added.

"Oh, no! No, no, no! I meant what I said. Christopher was wonderful. Still is, actually. I see him from time to time around here when he visits. He's out in Green Bay now, but we kept in contact." She tapped her chest three times with her index finger. "*I* was putting *him* in second place. He never complained—he was way too nice to do that—but I was definitely putting more time and effort into this place, especially once my dad passed. I started to feel bad, so I made the move that I knew he never would."

"And is it… better?" Jackson asked, sounding skeptical.

"*Loads*," Rosie said, and I could tell she meant it wholeheartedly. "He stayed here in Timberland Creek for a bit then moved to Madison, met a nice woman, re-married and had a sweet little family. I got to stay here and man the ship," she said, gesturing to the entirety of the restaurant. "It's exactly what we both wanted but could have never found together."

"That's really nice," I said, a small smile curling my lips. "And it's great there was no bad blood." I needed a third hand to count all my parents' friends that had gotten divorced under horrible circumstances. At least half had gotten wine-drunk in my childhood home's kitchen, bitching and moaning to my mom about how horrible the male species is, telling Laura and I how we could never trust a guy, how we were better off building success on our own than falling for the lies of a man.

The advice ended up being absolutely useless for Laura, who came out when she was seventeen. But I'd always kept it in the back of my mind. Not that I didn't think I could sufficiently support myself without a man's help; I was doing perfectly fine so far. But it was hard to listen to my mom's friends when I saw the happy couple that was my parents.

Finding a companion in life wasn't my primary focus, but it was definitely cooking on the back burner. Still present, just not getting my full attention quite yet.

Instead of prying further into Rosie's opinion on the matter, I nodded toward the other group. "And the woman with Marty is Mary, I'm guessing?"

She was pretty. A middle-aged woman with straight brown hair down to her chest. She was wearing a plain black shirt with jeans, but had accessorized with some of the loudest clay jewelry I'd ever seen in my life.

"How much exploring have you done without me?" Jackson asked.

"Marty told me about her," I replied, then nudged him. "You can thank Mary for those Italian sausage sandwiches."

At that, Jackson's eyes widened again with interest, and he said, "Rosie, please send that woman another round of whatever she's drinking on me."

I knew Jackson and I had become more familiar with one another—especially after cuddling and watching K-dramas together, which I still wasn't one-hundred-percent certain how I'd ended up wrapped in his arms for three hours until the cuddling had turned into other activities—but the nudge and gentle tilt of my head so it rested on his shoulder came from somewhere I didn't know existed. Some ultra-comfortable one. That didn't take into consideration how onlookers might interpret it.

Until Rosie's grin grew and her eyes narrowed in a very knowing way.

"You've got it, sugar," she said to Jackson, but her eyes remained on me until she turned to fulfill the request.

"She reminds me of you."

The comment threw me off-guard, especially since Jackson had picked up a menu from the holder and had begun to flip through it—as if we both didn't already know our orders by heart at this point. I'd thought he'd been paying exactly zero attention to me, but apparently not.

I lifted my head. "Rosie?" I asked, and Jackson nodded. "Why?"

He gave a one-shoulder shrug. "I feel like that's something you would do."

"Give up men for work?" Obviously, our pillow talk hadn't strayed into the topic of career aspirations yet because that was so far from what I intended to do it was almost laughable.

Even if the majority of them sucked, men still gave me more pleasure than my desk job ever had.

"No, but maybe I could see you getting pissed off enough for that, too," he said, finally side-eying me.

"Don't worry, Albrecht," I said. "You're giving me way too many orgasms for me to consider dropping you."

Jackson gave me a sly grin. "And if the orgasms stop?"

I shrugged. "I'll schedule a performance review for next month."

He chuckled, scanning the menu before he shut it again. I watched him from the corner of my eye as he leaned back in his chair and stretched his arms back over his head. The Purdue University shirt he was wearing—I was beginning to think it was the only casual piece of clothing he'd packed—hugged his flexed biceps and lifted just enough for me to catch a fleeting glimpse of the happy trail that disappeared into the waist of his jeans.

"I was talking more about the getting divorced thing," he said when he came back down.

"I don't even know how to respond to that."

"Not in a bad way," he clarified, clearly realizing how the comment had come across. "In the way where you won't settle. Or let anyone else settle."

"Oh."

He raised a skeptical brow. "Do you not agree?"

"I mean, not totally," I admitted. "I think I'd probably settle, but to an extent, you know? Like, if the guy is a piece of shit I'd get out, but if he's a guy like Christopher... Yeah, I'd probably stay married."

"Even if you're not happy anymore?"

"That's the part where you're wrong," I said, nudging him again. "I wouldn't get married in the first place if I thought I wouldn't be happy in the long-run."

"And you can just tell that from the get-go, huh?"

"What do you mean?"

"Has everyone you've ever been with shown you all their red flags right away or something?"

"No." I huffed a laugh. "Hell no."

"Then how do you know you won't start disliking something about them ten years down the road?"

"I don't. But I'm a pretty good judge of character."

"And you still kept me around?" Jackson asked, sounding almost disbelieving.

Couldn't say I blamed him, honestly. But hearing him talk that way about himself—assuming he was someone I wouldn't want to spend time with in any capacity—made my heart hurt a little.

"Orgasms, remember?"

Thankfully, that made him brighten a bit before he said, "You deserve them," and nudged me back. I don't think he intended for me to hear when he muttered, "You deserve a lot."

I might have asked him about it if two drinks weren't plopped down in front of us at just that moment.

Not just two drinks.

Two shots.

"Oh, Rosie," I groaned, my head lolling to the side in dread at seeing the two small glasses of amber liquid. "Not again. I'm still recovering from the last time."

Rosie held up her hands. "I swear this one wasn't me."

"Then who…?"

Jackson, who'd been following Rosie and I's conversation, his eyes traveling between us when we spoke, turned the same time I did to look down the bar.

The group at the end immediately fell into a cacophony of hooting, hollering, and clapping, all of them encouraging us to accept their offering. Mary lifted her fresh drink in cheers before she sipped what looked like an old fashioned—Wisconsin-style, of course.

Some of the other sparse off-season visitors that had trickled in that evening were now watching, too.

"I don't think we have a choice in this one, Wilson," Jackson mumbled out the side of his mouth, leaning towards me enough for his arm to press flush against mine. "We have an audience."

"Such a man of the people, are you, Albrecht?" I teased.

"Every one of them is a potential book sale. I'm just thinking strategically."

I chuckled at that then reached for my shot glass.

"Then bottoms up," I said. Jackson followed my lead. Our glasses met with a soft clink. "To five more sales."

I almost couldn't hear Jackson's chuckle over the increased cheering as we tossed the drinks back.

"HIT ME WITH your best shot!" I sing-screamed with Mary and Rhonda, our arms slung around each other's shoulders.

How the jukebox at Ziggy's had escaped my attention during previous visits was a mystery, but now that I knew it was there, it was over. At least until I went through the approximately fifty songs that ranged from Rat Pack classics to soft rock of the early two-thousands. But I was pretty sure I could listen to women-led rock all night.

The guys didn't seem to mind, either, as us ladies sang Pat Benatar's (arguably) best song for the third time in the last half hour. They were too busy trying to teach Jackson about the history of Wisconsin sports. I wouldn't be surprised if he revealed to me later that he was simply humoring the older men, since they seemed pretty entertained, breaking off into their own tangents from time to time to argue who the best quarterback of the Packers was or if the Bucks would take home another NBA championship anytime soon or if Timberland Creek's very own contribution to the National Football League would make the Pro Bowl that year.

Rosie held out a bottle of vodka to me, and I leaned in, using the neck as a microphone. Thank god for everyone else in the bar that it wasn't actually one. No one but the group of regulars needed to be subjected to my off-pitch singing. At least I had Rhonda to help counteract it, should anyone hear. She was incredible.

"Ope!" I said, head popping up when I realized the song had ended, and reached out to get another quarter—

Only to find the pile I'd cashed in had been depleted.

"Oh no." I pouted as I sat back down on my barstool. "I'm out."

"Gus, you got change?" Rhonda asked.

"Marty will have some if he doesn't!" Mary supplied.

"I've only got a few dimes and a nickel," Ray said, showing us the handful of his loose change.

The other two men didn't come up with much else. Gus, for whatever reason, had a paperclip in his pocket, along with a bottlecap that surprised me a lot less.

Then it was in front of me. The key to continuing my jam session with my new townie friends.

Just as I reached for it, the quarter was pulled away.

"Hey!" I said, twisting in my stool to find Jackson snickering, the quarter still pinched between his thumb and index finger. "Jackson, I need that!"

"If you want the music to keep playing," he said, "*I* get to pick the next song."

"Or I could just ask Rosie to hit play on whatever music system she uses."

But the traitor shook her head when I looked pleadingly at her. "I'm a little intrigued by what he'll pick," she said.

Jackson dropped the quarter and caught it in his fist with a lot more coordination than I'd expected from someone who claimed to have never played sports.

"I'll be back," he announced, then wandered toward the jukebox.

A few minutes later, the familiar intro of *Hungry Heart* by Bruce Springsteen started playing.

"Oh!" Mary was ecstatic. She set down her drink and popped out of her barstool. "I love this song!"

"One of the best," Rhonda agreed, and placed her hand on Gus's. "C'mon, old man. Time to treat your woman to a dance."

"How about you ladies continue the party?" Gus tried, but his girlfriend wasn't taking it.

"Nuh uh. You're getting your butt out of this seat and dancing. You too, Marty."

"What about me?" Ray asked.

"You think I'm leaving you out?" Rosie chimed in. Then she rang the bell by the kitchen window. "I'm taking five, Walter! Watch the front, would you?"

She didn't wait for a confirmation before she lifted the wooden flap on the bar that allowed her to exit. That was all it took for the other women to get the courage to drag their partners from their seats, too. I smiled at Gus and Marty's griping that quickly disappeared as they saw how excited Rhonda and Mary were to get them to cooperate. With the men's frequent visits to Ziggy's, I wondered how much time the couples spent together. If their jobs—a painter and local theater actor, respectively, for Mary and Rhonda—allowed much time at all.

I took a sip of my old fashioned—these Wisconsinites were onto something with this modified version—as I watched them take up their dancing positions. A few of the other patrons had been inspired, too, going out into the middle of the floor with their kids or partners to join the fun.

It was so simple. So innocent. So small-town that I felt like I'd suddenly been transported into a scene from a Hallmark movie.

And that's when I saw Jackson across the room, waving me over.

I pointed at myself, as if I didn't already know I was the target of his summoning. When he nodded, I did it again. That earned a shake of his head and a more exaggerated sweep of his arm as he tried to get me to leave my seat.

His already existing smile only grew the closer I got to him.

"I thought you'd never make it over here," he said.

"I thought I was imagining things," I retorted. "I never pegged you for a Springsteen fan."

"You never pegged me as a K-drama enthusiast either."

He was right. There were a lot of things about Jackson that

were surprising me in the best way lately.

Like when he extended his hand to me.

I stared at the offering, unblinking, until Jackson said, "I don't bite."

I grinned. "Liar."

He rolled his eyes, but amended, "I don't bite *in public*."

That made me chuckle, but the smile that came with it faded again as my eyes resettled on his upturned palm. "But… what are you doing?"

His eyes slid to the side, in the direction where the others were still swaying—or twirling and dipping in an over-enthusiastic manner in Rosie and Ray's case—to the rhythm of the song. "Inviting you to dance?"

"You dance?"

"Not often," he admitted. "But I've been known to bust some moves on a wedding dance floor or two after a few drinks."

I smiled as I tried to picture Jackson on a dance floor in any sort of social setting. It was such a normal comment—one I would have made myself or could imagine just about any other person I talked to saying.

Yet Jackson saying it had once again bridged that gap that I'd created in my mind when it came to him. The one that made him Author Jackson instead of Just Jackson.

It was crazy to think that I'd gone so many years without knowing this side of him existed. The one that was secretly funny and somewhat shy and sentimental.

I liked it.

And I imagined I'd like what came after I placed my palm in his, too.

So, I did.

Jackson's hand curled around mine, and though we'd never danced together before, we moved naturally, his hand finding my waist, mine pressing flat against his chest. We'd been this close more times than I could count at this point, usually without clothes on. But the way he held me against him, swaying to the steady beat of the song…

"I would try to show you some of those moves I was talking about, but my feet are stuck to the floor."

I snorted, my forehead resting on his chest to hide my reaction before I realized I didn't care. Jackson's smile was as wide as mine, his chuckle vibrating in his chest, when I finally let him see my face.

"And here I was, only accepting your invite so I could see said moves," I teased.

"Maybe I'll get Rosie a mop before we leave. And a new burger recipe."

"Memaw has to have one, right?"

"Right there with her pot pie." His smile widened, as if he hadn't expected me to remember that little bit of information and was happy I had. "Think we'd get a cut of the sale?"

I scoffed. "Can anything just be fun with you? No business

talk," I added, flicking his chest.

He grabbed my hand to prevent further harm, and in a surprising turn of events, brought my knuckles up to his lips to kiss. I couldn't stop my attention from straying just past Jackson, to where the older women were watching us, somehow all positioned within their own dances so they could gossip. When I narrowed my eyes at the leader of the bunch—Rosie, obviously—she winked.

"Something going on back there?" Jackson asked.

My attention snapped right back to him. "No, why?"

"You're making funny faces."

"I'm just upset I'm not getting the full *Dancing With the Stars* treatment during our dance here."

"I promise when I finally accept the offer to be on the show, I'll come back and we can try again."

My eyebrows skyrocketed. "You've been asked to be on *Dancing With the Stars?*"

"Fuck no," Jackson said. "Even I'm not conceited enough to think I'd earn that invite. That's for actual celebrities. Not authors. People who an audience will vote for, and whatever."

There it was again. That talk like he wasn't important. That break in the exterior-facing ego I'd always thought was so impenetrable.

My sight flitted past Jackson again, and when I saw the others were still distracted, I took my chance. He seemed just as surprised as I was in my decision to give him a quick kiss, but it had felt like the right thing to do.

A little crazy. Especially in public. But right.

"I'd vote for you. Every damn week, as many times as possible."

For a second, I thought he might return the gesture and lean down to kiss me again. He did, technically. But his lips landed on the top of my head instead. It didn't stop the butterflies from going any less wild in my stomach, though.

He smiled down at me when he pulled back. "That means more than you know."

CHAPTER TWENTY

ONE THING I'D never get used to in Timberland Creek? Having people twenty years my senior—minimum—being able to rally harder than me.

One thing I'd never get used to anywhere? *Jackson S. Albrecht* being able to rally harder than me.

Staying out until close—which was whenever Rosie deemed it, which was *always* late—dancing at Ziggy's hadn't been in my bingo card for the day. I'd decided by ten that I was ready for bed, but seeing Jackson having so much fun… I hadn't been able to bring myself to even hint that I was ready to hit the hay.

The townies had welcomed him—us—and we'd spent hours laughing and dancing and shooting the shit, as if we'd known them for two decades, not going on two weeks.

Watching as the guys wrapped their arms around Jackson's shoulders, pulling him into conversations, singing badly along to classic rock, was something I hadn't known I'd needed to see. But in that moment, my heart could have melted at witnessing such genuine happiness.

We'd been to event after event together. Starr-hosted parties. Conventions. Indie bookstore signings. Many a time, Jackson and I had been thrown into social settings where we'd been forced to interact in some capacity. Not once had I seen him welcomed into a group the way the locals of Timberland Creek were welcoming him. But, then again, I'd never seen Jackson put in any effort.

Maybe those cheesy romance movies were onto something. Maybe small towns could warm even the most stone-cold of hearts.

Not that I'd thought Jackson's heart was cold. I hadn't thought that for some time now.

Especially not after we'd stumbled through the front door, drunk on giddiness—and in my case, semi-severe sleep deprivation—as much as we were drunk from the alcohol we'd consumed. Not as he'd wrapped me in his arms the same way he had during our first dance and pulled me flush against him. Not as him cupping my face turned into him pushing my hair back so nothing got in his way as he kissed me. And most definitely not as we'd traveled clumsily and blindly, refusing to break away from one another, to the bedroom.

My back arched as I stretched the sleep and soreness from my body, knowing Jackson wasn't beside me any longer. A quick glance as the twin bed next to mine told me he wasn't there either.

For someone who didn't socialize much, the guy was a champion. I'd give him that much.

I groaned as I reached for the vintage bedside table to retrieve my phone. Ten-thirty. And five email notifications, two missed calls, and a few stray texts.

Shit. It was fucking Monday.

One more thing about small towns that I'd never get used to? Somehow time ceased to exist. These people operated on their own rules—as proven by Rosie's open-till-we're-shut mindset. And as much as I loved being able to get lost and forget about responsibilities for a second, it made reality kicking me in the ass that much harder.

I wasn't even sure I was properly dressed by the time I burst out of the bedroom, expecting to find Jackson in the kitchen or living room—he only went up to the loft when he *really* needed to concentrate nowadays—but aside from the lingering scent of coffee, there was no sign of him.

Hm. Maybe he'd gone to Sunrise. And if he had, I hoped he brought me back a coffee. Lord knew I needed it to fight off the delayed Sunday scaries that were currently plaguing me.

The last thing I wanted to do was find out whatever Alexis needed help with. Or see why Iris had called at seven-thirty. Or why Brandon in sales had added a meeting to my calendar to—

"Not at all."

My head swiveled.

Jackson.

There weren't many places for him to hide, yet I still couldn't find where his voice had come from.

"No, I don't think so."

It took me way too long to realize he wasn't in the house. He was outside the front door. A quick glimpse of him through the small curtained window as he passed by gave him away. But he didn't come into the house. Instead, he continued to linger just outside, his steps crunching on the gravel of the driveway.

His next pass by showed me the tray of coffees in one hand—bless him—and his phone held up to his ear with the other.

He probably thought I was still asleep.

If I hadn't heard him say, "No, it's been the most wonderful time of my life," next, I might have texted him to let him know he didn't need to worry about being noisy.

But I didn't.

Because I was a nosy bitch.

Whoever he was talking to, it was someone he felt comfortable opening up around. And as the person responsible for getting him to do just that on this trip, this was important intel. This could be the moment that made this whole trip successful, where I learned exactly how to make sure Just Jackson was available all day, every day. Or at least that's what I was telling myself as I crept closer to the front door to eavesdrop.

Even through the barrier, I could hear his chuckle as he said, "Mom. Seriously? That's a little dramatic. And that's coming from me."

His mom. She'd called him once before on this trip, too.

I couldn't help smiling a little at the idea of them having weekly check-ins.

"Yeah, that's her," he said, then paused while he waited for a response. "She's stunning." Another pause and a chuckle. "Are you kidding? She's way out of my league."

I couldn't stop myself from peeking through the window, just enough where I could see him, but he couldn't see me. Based on the face Jackson was making, I could almost guarantee he was getting some sort of Mom Speech about how he's an absolute catch, but he wasn't buying it.

They were talking about… about a woman?

"I'm glad *you* think I'm handsome, Mom, but unfortunately that doesn't earn me a whole lot of points in the dating department. I don't remember if she's said anything. No, it's all still relatively new. I'm not sure. We haven't talked about that."

My legs stopped working, and I slumped back against the door.

This wasn't just any woman. This was a woman he was having *conversations* with. The important ones, even during what he claimed was a new relationship.

And he hadn't brought her up at all? Not once. Not in this

whole trip while we'd been—

I felt sick. Was I… was I the other woman? Was I unwittingly coming between Jackson and whoever it was he was seeing? No matter how many flaws he had, I couldn't see him as a cheater. Not even a little. And yet…

Maybe they weren't exclusive. Maybe… maybe she wouldn't let them be. There was nothing wrong with having a little fun—finding a little pleasure—while things were being worked out.

But that excuse sounded even flimsier than the one I'd given myself about why I was sitting here against the door listening in to begin with.

I severely regretted that decision the longer I remained here.

Because the longer I sat here, the more I was learning about how I was being Freddie Hart-ed all over again.

"I'm not sure what she thinks. We've…" Jackson sighed. "We've known each other for so long, so it's been interesting. Not in a bad way, but I can tell there's still some kinks to figure out." He paused for a longer time than he had before. "I don't know what I'll do if that happens. At this point, I'm not sure I could handle it."

I jumped when the screen door rattled, but it didn't open. Jackson was leaning back onto it.

"It's not love. Not yet. But… but it could be, I think," I heard him admit.

And that was the breaking point.

I sprang to my feet and flung the door open.

"Shit."

Jackson jumped away from the door, the tray of coffees and his phone going flying as he stared wide-eyed at me.

"Tori," he said.

My eyes shifted to where his phone lay among the puddles of coffee on the driveway and back. "You gonna get that?"

That seemed to remind him he'd been on a call mere seconds ago.

"Mom, I have to go," he said as he hastily brought the phone back to his ear. "I'll call you later. Love you."

He ended the call without waiting for any sort of response on the other end, his focus already back on me.

"You're awake," he said.

"Yeah. I overslept."

"I felt bad waking you up," he said. "I was going to bring you coffee, but—" He gestured to the spilled drinks. "I can go get more if you really want one. Or you can join?"

He knew I'd heard him. He had to know. Yet here he was, acting completely normal. And I was too much of a coward to admit that I had, in fact, been eavesdropping.

No. That wasn't why I was being a coward. It was because last night I'd had one of the best nights of my life in the arms of this man, both at Ziggy's and in bed. And if I told him I'd heard him admit he was falling in love with another woman, that would end. Point blank.

No more dancing in sticky dive bars. No more watching K-

Dramas while cuddling on the couch. No more falling asleep in his arms. And no more glimpses of Just Jackson.

"I have a meeting with Rahm and Marcus soon," I said. It was in two hours, but he didn't need to know that. "Maybe you go on your own."

Jackson stared at me for the most uncomfortable moment we'd shared in a long time before he finally snapped out of his trance and nodded.

"Yeah," he said, then cleared his throat. "Yeah. For sure. I'll probably grab my laptop then. Get some writing done while I'm at Sunrise."

"Sounds good. I can… meet you there after?"

He nodded again. "I'd like that."

After one more hesitant smile, he shuffled past me into the cabin, his hand brushing my hip on the way. Even such simple contact was enough to make my breath stop.

Two could play this ignorance game. Unfortunately, I was competitive as hell and very much not ready to lose Just Jackson. Not as I was just getting to know him.

CHAPTER TWENTY-ONE

"SO, HOW ARE things going in the great Wisconsin wilderness?" Rahm asked with a grin, clearly aiming for a joke.

I forced a smile, playing along. "It's been good. I'm getting used to cheese at every meal and everything."

Thankfully, my boss laughed at that. Even Marcus cracked a smile in his little box on the virtual call.

"That's wonderful to hear, but aside from your new dairy-heavy diet, what can you report?"

Classic Rahm, not letting the casual conversation last too long.

"Well, I'm pretty sure Jackson is close to finishing his manuscript," I said. "He's been very motivated lately." For reasons they would never know, of course.

"That's great," Marcus said. "Any idea where it's sitting? How much is actually left?"

"He hasn't said specifically, but he's in town at a coffee shop working on it right now. If I were to guess, one act maybe? Less?"

Marcus let loose a low whistle, while Rahm said, "Sounds like you're working miracles up there, Victoria."

"I wouldn't say miracles, sir."

"No, I do suppose there's a bigger challenge than this particular author actually writing. He's never had a problem with that, has he, Marcus?"

"Not at all. So long as Jackson is signed with you, you'll never have to worry about running out of publishable works."

I couldn't help grinning at the subtle pitch. And given Rahm's expression, which came across even in a virtual format, it looked like it might have done its job.

But only if I gave the report the two men were hoping for as well.

"Jackson's attitude has definitely shifted in the last few weeks," I said. "Even more so than the last time we spoke."

"Really?" Rahm asked.

I nodded. "I can stand to be in the same room as him for up to a whole hour now."

Thankfully that joke landed, too. I never knew what to expect on these calls, but I needed to hide my nerves somehow. Sarcasm seemed as good a strategy as any.

"Please tell me it's a little longer than just an hour, Tori," Marcus said.

"It is. I swear. And I've noticed he's grown quite a fan-base in the town, too. A lot of the locals are recognizing him at this point in our stay."

"That's promising," Rahm said, his brows raised as if he'd been expecting me to hop on this call and say I was near the point of throwing Jackson in the lake and all the locals wanted to run him out of town. "Very promising, actually."

"I expected nothing less from you, Tori," Marcus said with a smile. "If anyone could turn Jackson around, it was you."

"Yes, indeed," Rahm agreed, a little less convincingly than I'd hoped. "But that does bring us to the point of this particular conversation, then, doesn't it? We're nearing the end of the second week, after all."

"The rental owner said we could extend to four, if needed," Marcus reminded us. "I spoke with her prior to the stay starting."

I didn't bother saying I had an in with the owner's family now, too. Something told me Marty and Mary would convince Quinn to let us stay here as long as possible.

"We agreed when this all started that we would start with two weeks. The necessity of a third—and any other subsequent weeks—would be determined by this group, no?"

"That's correct." Marcus's hesitation came through loud and clear.

"Given what Victoria has told us, I'm not sure if any additional time is needed. Despite your aversion to me using the word, I'm going to reiterate that what she's accomplished in only two weeks is rather miraculous."

Praise from Rahm Singh wasn't given out willy-nilly. Earning anything that felt even remotely like a compliment was a rare experience for Starr employees. So, hearing him say I was performing miracles should have left me elated.

Except I knew what performing miracles actually meant.

"I don't disagree," Marcus said.

"We're on the same page, then? Victoria and Jackson no longer need to be on this restorative writing retreat?"

I really hoped the little virtual box I was in didn't show the color drain from my face as dramatically as I felt it.

"Well, actually," I interrupted. Rahm's eyes shifted, probably from giving Marcus's box a digital death glare. I swallowed, not loving that they still weren't exactly screaming *cheery*. "W-we're technically into our second week. I'm not sure what the refund policy is for cancellations?"

"Non-existent," Marcus confirmed. "They might as well stay the full week otherwise we lose out on a couple thousand dollars."

Rahm's following silence was enough to make me worry. For a corporation like Starr, a couple thousand dollars wasn't much. They could make that back on day one of a successful release. Hell, on day one of a Jackson S. Albrecht release. But I knew Rahm was thinking short-term. And right now, thousands sounded intimidating for the budget sheets.

"If we stay the rest of the week," I butted in again, "I could make even more progress. If I'm performing miracles, as you say, Jackson could come back a saint."

It had to work. It absolutely had to. I wasn't ready to leave this cabin and Timberland Creek and my housemate and the scary nighttime creatures and—

"Fine." All my tension eased out of me at that one word. "But come Friday, this little experiment is done. Whatever progress Jackson has made—both personally and in his work—is it."

"That's fair," Marcus agreed. "Tori? You think a few more days will be good enough?"

I nodded, my thoughts already drifting a million different places, before I managed to squeak out a soft, "Yeah. A few days. That's good."

I DIDN'T CARE about Alexis's problems setting up a paid social campaign for a new release or the thirty emails waiting, unread, in my inbox when I ended the call with Marcus and Rahm.

No, what I cared about was finding Jackson because I was not going to sit with this news by myself.

It was already Monday. That meant we only had four more days before our time was up and we'd go home. When that line between Author Jackson and Just Jackson would become finite again. Bolded even.

Fuck the real world.

Fuck living in different states.

Fuck having a job where everyone I worked with saw him as

some sort of villain.

Fuck feeling like I couldn't tell anyone I was sleeping with him for that same exact reason.

And *super* fuck knowing that as soon as we left this place, Jackson would return to whatever woman he was falling in love with back home.

That was all I could think about as I got closer to town. The half mile had felt like nothing, I'd been so lost in my thoughts. And by the time I pushed open the door to Sunrise Brews, I was convinced I'd simply teleported there.

"I was wondering when you'd show up," Hemi greeted from behind the counter. "The usual?"

"Yes, please. Thanks, Hemi."

That was all that needed to be said, thankfully, because I paid the café owner no further mind. Instead, I beelined for Jackson's table in the front of the shop.

He was already waiting for me, his attention no longer on his open laptop. I didn't think he'd typed a single word since I'd entered the café. But then again, I could have blacked out the sound of his keyboard clacking the same way I'd blacked out my entire walk.

The chair screeched on the wood floor as I pulled it back and took a hasty seat.

"Are you done working for the day?" Jackson asked.

"We're not getting an extension," I said. There was no point in delaying the announcement. "We leave on Friday."

Jackson's eyes drifted back to his screen and his upper lip

puffed out as he ran his tongue along his teeth. Buying time. At least I wasn't the only one at a loss of what to say.

Of course, we both knew the extended time hadn't been a given, but going into this, I never would have guessed it would have been so… easy. I wondered if Jackson thought the same, now that both our assumptions had been proven wrong.

At least he would be going back to his girl with a better attitude.

My fists curled in my lap at the thought of someone else reaping all the benefits of my work. The soft smiles. The K-Drama nights. The definitely-not-*Dancing-With-the-Stars*-worthy dancing. The coffee runs where he knew my order without asking.

I didn't think it was possible, but I hated someone I didn't even know.

"Four days," he finally said. Then his head tilted from side to side in a contemplative way. "Three and a half at this point."

"Yup."

He lifted his eyes to me again. "You gave me a glowing review, it sounds like."

"I—" My fists uncurled. "It would have been impossible for me not to," I told him, my voice hardly above a whisper.

His throat bobbed when he swallowed, his jaw tense, like he was on the verge of saying something, but holding himself back.

"I'd better get to work then."

That wasn't what I'd expected, but it was better than silence.

"How much do you have left in the manuscript?"

Maybe I'd been misreading his reactions. What I thought was sadness over leaving might have actually been worry about not having enough of his book finished. This was a double-ended challenge, after all: stop being an asshole *and* write a best-seller.

As much as I felt overwhelmed trying to help him, Jackson had it so much worse.

"I think I'll be able to finish it," he said. "Or I'll come very close to it."

"I wouldn't worry about it too much. I'm sure what you have already is brilliant."

I meant it. He was good. Everything about him, I was realizing, was good in a way that was almost infuriating. Like everything he'd ever let me see before this trip had been a complete and utter lie.

Well, outside the bedroom, at least. His performance there was more than consistent.

His soft smile in response made my chest tighten. Why, for the love of all that was good in the world, did it keep doing that lately? Didn't it know it needed to stop? Like, soon.

"You're going soft on me, Wilson. You're dishing out too many compliments," Jackson teased.

"Tori."

We both turned when Hemi called my name, letting me know my drink was ready. She set it on the counter, but didn't wait for me to go grab it like she usually did. Instead, she kept herself busy cleaning her espresso machine, clearly giving us some space.

I pushed back my chair and stood, my stomach doing a weird flip.

"I don't say anything I don't mean, Albrecht," I reminded him, then nodded at his laptop. "I'll leave you to your writing. Text me when you're done?"

"Yeah," he said, giving me another one of those infuriating, heart-jumping smiles.

I left him with, "Don't forget you still have a few rewards left to cash in," before I walked over to the counter to grab my coffee.

"Don't worry," Hemi said when I started futzing with my belt bag to retrieve my card. "It's on the house."

I stopped, hand still inside the pocket. "Hemi, I can't do that."

"You can, and you will." She swatted at the air. "Don't you dare take any money out."

It was a small gesture, but after the day I'd had, it was almost enough to bring tears to my eyes. I wondered if Hemi noticed because she gave me one small smile, her face softening before she turned around to get back to work.

At least one of us could run from the emotions. Or straight up pretend they didn't exist.

"You know," Hemi said, her back still to me, "I was beginning to forget you two weren't from around here. You fit right into this little town."

"Yeah," I said, my voice quieter than I expected. I cast one last look at Jackson over my shoulder. He was already hunched over his keyboard, focused like the world outside didn't exist. If only I had something like that to distract me from this growing ache in my chest. "I was beginning to forget too."

CHAPTER TWENTY-TWO

I WASN'T EVEN entirely sure Ziggy's was open when I walked through the front door, its squeaking hinges enough to notify Rosie and the two barbacks she was talking with of my arrival.

No music was playing. No regulars were seated at the other end of the massive wrapping bar. The TVs were off.

And when Rosie's brows lifted and she said, "Tori," like she hadn't expected me, I knew I probably wasn't supposed to be there.

"I'm sorry," I said, stopping in my tracks, halfway to the barstools I realized I was headed toward out of habit. "The door was unlocked. I can just—"

"No, no, sugar. Take a seat." She patted the counter in front of my usual spot, then turned to one of the barbacks. "Finish stocking in the kitchen. That new shipment of condiments came in. Oh, and Terry finally dropped off a crate of fresh pickles. I'll be back in a second to help, 'kay?"

I settled into my seat as the staff disappeared into the back.

"You have a lot of help around here?" I asked, realizing I hadn't seen more than Rosie and maybe one or two other people tending the restaurant.

"More so in the busy season. Off season I can manage on my own." She nodded toward where the two guys had just gone. "Those fellas help me out during the days. Heavy lifting and what not." As soon as she finished speaking, she leveled me with a Rosie Stare. "I'm guessing you didn't come here to talk about my employee roster?"

"Nope."

"And you've got one of Hemi's drinks so you don't need one of mine."

"Well, we'll see."

"Oh no." Rosie leaned forward on the bar, resting on crossed arms. "What's wrong, honey?"

"We're leaving at the end of the week. Jackson and me."

"I thought you kids were here for a month?"

"That's what we originally thought. It was… it's a strange set of circumstances that brought us here to begin with. But long story short, my boss doesn't think we need any extensions."

"That's good isn't it?" The brightness I was used to from Rosie had returned a bit. "Means you did everything right?"

"I guess."

"You seem upset for someone who just succeeded in what

they set out to do."

I took a sip of my coffee to give myself a moment to think of what I could say next. I liked Rosie, and I trusted her, but she didn't need to hear *all* my grievances. "It… I thought I'd have more time, is all."

"For?"

"To be here."

A slow smile spread across Rosie's lips at my admittance. "It grows on you, doesn't it, city girl?"

"What?"

"The small-town life."

"I don't have anything against small towns," I told her. "Hell, I'll take listening to chipmunks being eaten by owls over non-stop sirens going down my street any day."

Come to think of it, I hadn't heard a single siren—or any sound that was common outside my Oak Park apartment, for that matter—since I'd gotten here. There had been nothing but peace and quiet.

And the occasional woodland creature murder, but like I said, I was getting used to those.

Knowing there was a big, warm presence beside me at night to protect me helped.

I swallowed, not wanting to think about how that would be gone, too, in a matter of days.

"Earth to Tori."

I snapped out of the daze I'd fallen into when a hand waved

in front of my face. Rosie looked even more worried than she had when I first walked through the door.

"I love Timberland Creek as much as the next old lady," she said. "But something tells me it's not just leaving this town that's got you upset."

I knew what she was trying to get me to admit. Not in a nosy way; more in a way to get me to stop lying to myself. But I couldn't do that. Not now. Not knowing that, in four days, it wouldn't matter what I thought I might be feeling. Jackson would be back in Indiana, and I'd be back in Chicago.

There was no chance. Even if we kept up what we'd been doing, I couldn't, in good conscience, continue whatever this was we'd gotten ourselves into. I was already struggling as it was, knowing I'd be tossed aside soon.

Good thing I had more than one thing bothering me. There was no way Rosie wouldn't call me on my bullshit if I said nothing was wrong.

"I'm supposed to be working right now," I told her instead.

The following look of confusion should have been expected. "Do you want to head out?"

"No." I set my coffee cup on the counter. "Nope," I repeated, popping the P. "There's not a single part of me that wants to go back to that cabin and sit behind a computer. Look!"

Rosie reared back when I shoved my phone in her face, the lit-up screen in view. One notification after another popped up.

"It never stops," I said. "They always need me."

"Isn't that supposed to be a… good thing? Means you're good at what you do. People rely on you. Trust you."

"Yeah, I guess. But then shouldn't I—I don't know. Shouldn't it feel more rewarding?" Rosie startled when I tossed my phone onto the counter. "I should be excited to wake up and deal with this bullshit every day."

"And instead, you're sitting here complaining to a sixty-eight-year-old bar owner who's never worked an office job a day in her life?"

"Exactly."

When my brain registered the sarcasm—way too late, I might add; a true tell to my stress—I looked up to find Rosie chuckling.

"Don't worry, honey," she said before I could formulate any sort of apology. "If you think I got into this business without knowing I'd hear all sorts of grievances, you'd be mistaken. I used to joke with my old man—back when he ran this place— that he should charge extra for therapy sessions."

"Not a bad idea," I said.

Rosie shrugged. "I'm a business woman."

"So, did you always want to take over Ziggy's or is that what you wanted to do?"

"Be a corporate monkey, you mean?" When I nodded, she shrugged again. "That's what I would tell people. I think for a bit it was lawyer. Then it changed to doctor. Teacher was a big thing for a few years, but you know how it is when you're a kid."

"I told people I wanted to be a princess until I was a solid sixteen-years-old."

My companion threw her head back and laughed at that. "That doesn't shock me one bit, missy."

"When did you finally settle on taking over the family business?"

"Somewhere between my sister moving across the country, my brother going to prison, and my parents getting too old to keep up the hard work."

My eyes widened beyond my control. Tact had never been one of my strong suits. But over the years, Rosie must have gotten used to similar responses because she hardly reacted.

"Rosie… shit. That's a lot." Then the realization of the situation dawned, I stared at her in disbelief. "You've dealt with all that and you're letting me sit here and complain about my perfectly okay job?"

"We've all got our stories," she replied. "I'm sure you've got some trauma in there, too, we just haven't gotten to the point where you want to share it with me yet. I have a feeling the job wouldn't be so bad if you didn't."

Damn. Maybe I *should* pay Rosie for therapy. That was a better evaluation than any of the psychiatrists I'd seen in Chicago had ever given me.

"Since you're not usually one to stay quiet, I'm going to

assume I hit the nail on the head there," Rosie continued. "And you don't need to tell me anything you don't want to, sweetie, but I'm gonna give you some advice.

"I didn't want to own this bar. Not even a little. I loved helping my parents out, but I never saw myself here long-term. It wasn't until I tried out a few other jobs—retail mostly, but that's a small town for you—that I found out this gig isn't half bad.

"I'm not saying go home and quit your job. But I'm also here to remind you that you're young. There's still plenty of time to figure out what you want to do in life. And who knows—maybe this is just a rough patch. I still have plenty of bad days at this place, even if it's where I know I'm supposed to be. Hell, just a few weeks ago, Ray broke a stein that's been in this place since it was founded. Knocked it right off the shelf when he went in for a toothpick of all things."

"And you still danced with him last night?" I teased.

"You betcha. Just so I could step on his toes every chance I got."

A much-needed smile spread across my lips. I could add Rosie to the list of reasons why leaving Timberland Creek would be so difficult. All of the people here, honestly.

You fit right into this little town.

I took a sip of my coffee, fighting against the tightening in my throat.

"I'm glad we met, Rosie," I finally said. It had taken too long to speak, but Rosie hadn't pushed me. She'd just waited as I digested everything. And hell was it a lot.

"I'm glad we met, too, sweetheart. And, hey." She reached halfway across the bar to lightly tap my hand. "You're not too far away. A few hours right? There's nothing stopping you from coming back for a visit now and then. I'm sure I speak for plenty of people in this town when I say my door is always open to you. And your author friend, of course."

"He's going to be so happy that's how you remember him."

"Hard to forget when that's how he introduces himself," Rosie retorted, and I chuckled. "Has he liked it up here?"

"I think so." Honestly, I wasn't sure I'd heard Jackson voice his opinion of the town. If he had, it was when we'd first arrived, and I took anything he said at that time with a grain of salt. Most of what either of us had said in those first few days had been out of spite.

"I should put him in contact with Quinny Nelson. Marty and Mary's girl," Rosie clarified, and I nodded. "She might be able to set him up with a place."

"What for?"

"We get all sorts of artsy folks around here. Painters, mostly—like Mary. But we could use an author or two."

"What? Are you recruiting for the town now?" I joked. "Gotta hit your creative population quota?"

"No, no. We've got plenty of creatives around here. It's a nice, calm place to concentrate, you know? They can get a lot done."

"I can bring it up to Jackson," I offered. "I mean, he wrote almost a whole book while we've been up here." Plus, anywhere had to be better than Indiana.

His lactose intolerance might not be into the idea, but his productivity sure would be. Dietary adjustments would be a very small sacrifice to make once Starr no-doubt offered him his contract extension when we got back.

"Only downside is that the nearest bookstore is in Green Bay."

"So, I was right," I said.

"About what?"

"When we first got here, I did a little exploring. Wanted to know how we'd survive, and all that."

"Naturally," Rosie said, nodding.

"Saw pretty much everything we needed except a bookstore," I concluded. "Isn't that, like, small town requirement number one?"

"That's my other quota I'm working towards, actually. Been emailing with Hallmark to see what's needed to be a *real* small town. Not whatever we are now because, yes—you're correct. There's no bookstore."

"How do you all survive?"

"The Internet?"

Duh, Tori. Timberland Creek might have less than one-thousand people in it, but those people weren't living in the

Stone Age.

"The postal service works the same way it does here as it does in Chicago, hun," Rosie added with a smile. "But I will say, I miss walking into a store to pick out my next read. It was a shame when Prose & Cons closed a few years back."

"What happened to it?"

Rosie shrugged. "The same thing that happens to all of our businesses that go under. Not enough traffic in the busy season to help survive the off season."

It didn't help that brick-and-mortar stores were closing left and right around the country due to cheaper, more convenient options online. While avid readers like myself—and apparently Rosie—liked the good old-fashioned trip to the bookshop, most people were looking for the best deal.

Stores just couldn't compete with the big corporations. Especially when books themselves cost more and more every year as printing costs continued to increase.

I could, unfortunately, count on both hands how many indies I'd worked with while at Starr that were no longer in operation.

"But you know what they say, right?" Rosie continued. "After every storm is a rainbow. If they wouldn't have closed, we wouldn't have Sunrise Brews. Seems like Hemi has proven just as beneficial for our little visiting writer extraordinaire, eh?"

My hands wrapped unconsciously around my cup. "Yeah," I agreed. "This town is lucky to have all of you. Truly. I don't think we would have had nearly as great an experience on this little forced retreat if we'd been placed anywhere else."

Rosie's lower lip jutted out in a pout, and a second later she huffed a laugh, her eyes going up to the ceiling.

"Well, shoot," she said. "Now you're gonna make me cry."

She snagged a cocktail napkin and dabbed away tears that had yet to fall. I struggled to keep my own at bay, having barely held it together after leaving Sunrise as it was. With all the emotions the last few hours had caused, I wasn't sure they'd ever stop if they started. So better to not let them start to begin with.

Besides, Jackson would call me out on any signs of it. That was one conversation I wanted to steer *way* clear of.

"I know you two probably have a lot to get done the next few days," Rosie said, her voice a bit more strained than it had been before. "But don't be strangers, okay? And don't you dare think about leaving without saying goodbye."

"We'd never," I assured her. "And it's like you said. We can visit."

"You swear?"

"Of course."

I didn't know how or when, but I hoped I wasn't telling a lie.

CHAPTER TWENTY-THREE

JACKSON HAD GONE quiet. Aside from the times we were forced to interact—in the shared bathroom, in our bedroom, while eating the dinners I either prepared or brought back from town—he hardly paid me any mind.

I tried not to take it too personally because when we did talk, it was wonderful. But I could see his stress in the tension of his shoulders, the bags under his eyes. When he'd come back from Sunrise the day I'd let him know our extension had been denied, he'd been the most frazzled I'd seen him during the whole trip.

That had been almost forty-eight hours ago. We didn't have much time left as it was, but even so, I was beginning to worry.

Still, I didn't bother him. I kept to myself, working or reading or going on walks, to allow him whatever privacy I could. Rahm had already told me I'd performed my miracle. No longer did I worry about what would happen to me when I made it back to the Starr offices.

Jackson, however, still had something to prove. That wouldn't happen if he didn't turn in a manuscript.

The countdown didn't help the already high-pressure situation.

Every so often I'd glance back over my shoulder, peeking through the window, to watch him type away, hunched over his keyboard at the kitchen counter. I'd given up my space when I realized work wasn't going to happen. I wasn't able to concentrate. I'd blame it on a bad signal if anyone asked, but my motivation to do anything except sit outside and enjoy the last bits of the Wisconsin-wilderness air was essentially zero.

Jackson really should have been the one out here. The fresh air would have done him some good. He'd been cooped up for days now, either in the loft or at Sunrise. At least the latter gave him more glimpses of natural light. That was part of why I'd suggested he come down from his cave. I was pretty sure all the work I'd done on this trip would be reversed with a few more hours of solitary confinement.

So when the front door creaked open and Jackson showed up in the doorway, it was safe to say I was pretty shocked.

"Switching venues?" I asked, sitting up a bit in my Adirondack chair so I could see him better.

"I'm almost done," he announced. "Just the epilogue is left."

"What the—" My book shut with a *slap*, and I pushed myself fully out of the chair to stand just as Jackson stepped outside. "You wrote a whole book?"

"Almost," he confirmed, then smirked. "Wasn't that the point of this trip?"

I didn't give him the satisfaction of a verbal response and instead opted for smacking him lightly on the shoulder with my current read.

That might have been the wrong choice because his hands grabbed onto my arms, keeping me close even when I'd intended to pull back.

The moment I'd told him we wouldn't be staying here past Friday was about the same time we'd stopped being intimate. I'd tried to chalk it up to Jackson needing to focus; he'd been upfront from the beginning about seeing what we were doing as a distraction. But a part of me couldn't help wondering if he was trying to distance himself. Remind himself that this was fun, but couldn't last. He had someone else to go back to when we left Timberland Creek.

And I'd be left in the dust yet again.

Now, I couldn't stop the way my heart leapt or the heat that naturally pooled in my core whenever Jackson came into close proximity. Even when we were shuffling around each other in the bathroom, trying to share the same sink for our bedtime routines, or in the kitchen when we tried to prepare our meals, the most innocent, accidental brushes of his skin against mine elicited reactions that wouldn't normally happen.

When he went to Sunrise, I snuck some much-needed quality time with my vibrator in. Thankfully, no more intrusions had happened, but I couldn't help my thoughts from straying in the same direction they'd gone in the early days of our trip. Wishing it was him giving me satisfaction instead of a battery-operated wand of silicon.

He was doing the smart thing, though—reinstating this distance between us, slowly but surely.

Plenty of people I was perfectly platonic with grabbed my arms, after all.

Those same people, however, didn't slowly slide their hands down them to hold onto my hands. The one not holding the book, at least.

My eyes strayed from his face to watch where he oh-so-gently grabbed hold of my fingers, opening the fist I hadn't realized I'd formed to lace our hands together.

"I wanted to call in another reward."

It was nearly impossible to hide my surprise over his request. He hadn't so much as mentioned our reward system since he'd started furiously writing a few days ago. Clearly, he'd made progress in that time. So, it made me wonder why he was only just doing anything now.

One last hurrah, maybe? Get it out of our system once and for all.

"Oh yeah?" I replied, my voice taking on the seductive drawl I usually adopted when we flirted with each other.

"I want to take you to dinner."

If I'd been surprised before, it had increased ten-fold now.

I reared back. "What?"

"I want to take you to dinner," Jackson repeated. "A nice one. Not Ziggy's. And not on Starr's dime either. It's on me."

A dinner. No local bar rats or Rosie. Just the two of us. Like…

"Like a date?" I asked.

"If you want to call it that."

Holy shit.

"I, uh—I'm not sure I packed anything nice enough for a date," I said.

"That's okay. You'll look great in whatever you wear."

It was the most basic of compliments, but my heart still skipped all the same.

"Did you have a restaurant in mind?" No matter what reassurances he fed me, I was *not* someone who went anywhere underdressed.

"I asked Hemi for a few recommendations and she told me about The Flame," Jackson said. If I remembered correctly, that was the supper club in town.

Definitely not a place I could get away with athleisure.

Which also meant it would not be a cheap date. This man meant business.

"It's *your* reward," I reminded him. "I feel like I should be treating *you* to this nice dinner, not the other way around."

"This is what I want," Jackson assured me. "And trust me, it's definitely a reward for me."

My brow furrowed, but Jackson's expression didn't waver. As much as I hoped I'd find a crack in the façade, leveling him with the same kind of stare that even Laura broke for, he held firm.

He *really* wanted to do this.

"Okay then," I conceded. He dropped my hand after I squeezed his twice. "Looks like I'm going to have to go shopping."

"I told you, you don't have to—"

"Ah, ah, ah."

I shoved my book against his chest, and once his hands went up to hold it, I dipped inside the front door to snag my wallet and sunglasses.

"Have you ever known me to look anything less than spectacular?" I asked, slipping my sunglasses on.

Jackson chuckled. "Of course not."

"Exactly. And besides, this is your last reward before we leave. I'm making sure it's a damn good one."

A slow smile spread across his lips. "I know you will."

For a moment, I thought he might say more, but when he stayed quiet, I lifted my glasses again and headed out to town.

We had one more night out. And I was about to make it the

best damn date Jackson had ever experienced—even if it was just a reward.

Because *I* needed this to be the best damn date, too, if only so it would distract me from our impending end.

AFTER CALLING IN reinforcements—also known as bursting into Ziggy's, demanding Rosie join me on a shopping spree, then subsequently going into Sunrise to coerce Hemi into letting us borrow her new part-time twenty-something-year-old barista, Harper, for fashion advice—I somehow managed to find a dress.

As I stood in the bedroom, examining myself as best I could in the mirror above the dresser, I still wasn't sure I was sold on it.

I smoothed my hands down over the orange fabric, trying to convince myself the girl I only knew as my part-time caffeine supplier hadn't been lying to me.

"That's your color," Harper had said immediately when I'd come out of the curtained dressing room at one of the little boutiques in town. One that Harper, conveniently, worked at while not occupied at Sunrise. Hence why Rosie had gone to her for assistance. "Holy shit, I wish I could pull that off. Your curves are immaculate."

It was those curves, not so much the color, that had me

worried.

I was confident. No one would argue that. But I'd also gone my entire thirty-two years knowing my figure wasn't the one most men would find appealing. They'd choose a size two over my size sixteen, nine times out of ten. Which was why the fashion industry didn't usually cater to me, either.

The fact that I'd found anything in my size amazed me. The fact that it had actually worked out surprised me even more.

I kept replaying Harper's compliments in my head as I tried to push the self-conscious thoughts away.

Why the hell was I so worried anyway? It was Jackson. He'd already assured me he wouldn't have cared if I wore leggings and a t-shirt. He'd seen me in worse, that was for sure. This dress was leagues above what I'd been wearing this whole trip.

"Fuck," I muttered as I lifted myself onto my tip-toes, twisted to the side, and sucked in my stomach. Or tried to. It didn't go much of anywhere, even with my shapewear.

"Fuck," I said again and lowered back to the ground.

Rosie had thought I looked good. Harper had thought I looked good. I thought I looked good—for the most part.

It was the idea of a stupid man—a stupid man who wouldn't even be a blip in my life outside of work in a matter of two days—thinking I looked good that was worrying me so much.

The nerves wouldn't go away until I showed him the outfit. It was now or never, I supposed. Our reservation was coming up soon anyway. I couldn't hide in the bedroom forever.

Jackson was standing in the living room, his back to me, when I finally came out of hiding. Unlike me, the man had packed nothing but polos and button ups—if I wasn't counting the Purdue shirt that doubled as pajamas. He'd chosen something I hadn't seen him wear yet for the dinner, though. A black button-down shirt paired with some dark-wash Levi's.

Naturally, my eyes drifted to where the denim hugged his ass. But it was a difficult decision, picking between that view and the way the shirt clung to his arms. The way he was fidgeting with the buttons at the end of his sleeve stretched the fabric taut.

The old house let him know he wasn't alone anymore the second I took a step on the squeaky floor.

Jackson turned, and at first his wide eyes were still filled with something like panic. Like he was the one who was worried about how he looked, as if he weren't completely polished twenty-four-seven.

The moment they registered me, though, they softened.

If I'd been self-conscious before, it amplified as Jackson gave me a once-over, his jaw hanging open the tiniest bit. Then again. Then again. As if he were trying to memorize the image of me.

I tucked my hair behind my ear, only for the curls to win and it pop right back out in front.

"Is this too much?" I asked. "Rosie said it would be okay, but—"

"No!" I froze at Jackson's sudden outburst, my eyes widening. He cleared his throat before repeating, "No," much softer. "It's perfect. It's… wow."

It was a rare moment when a man reacted in such a way when they saw me. Then again, it was a rare moment for me to get done up so nice to go out. Not that Jackson was unaccustomed to it; he saw me in business attire all the time at events and meetings.

This was different. This was me dressing for myself, not to meet some silly corporate standard.

Apparently, it did the trick.

Maybe I'd have to start trusting that when people told me I looked good, I actually did. A shocking concept, I know.

"Are you just gonna stand there gaping?" I teased when Jackson neglected to move.

I genuinely believed he hadn't realized what he'd been doing when he cleared his throat again and straightened his posture.

Jackson offered his elbow to me. "Are you ready, milady?" he asked, putting on a bad English accent.

I couldn't help but laugh as I accepted. "Indeed."

He smiled. "The Camry awaits."

CHAPTER TWENTY-FOUR

I'D NEVER BEEN to a supper club before, so I hadn't known what to expect when we arrived at The Flame. I'd guessed correctly when it came to the low lighting, uniformed wait staff, and candlelit-and-white-clothed tables.

I had *not* guessed that Jackson and I would be the youngest people here by at least two decades, nor that it would smell faintly like cigarette smoke.

"Do you think they have a smoking section?" I asked Jackson as soon as our waiter walked away to put in our order of a glass of cabernet and scotch, neat.

"Doubtful," he said, coughing into the crook of his arm. "It's probably left over from the seventies. You know—the last time it looks like this place had work done."

I chuckled. He wasn't wrong. If the dark-green carpeting was any indication, the owners clearly weren't avid HGTV watchers. Not that I was a big fan of the current all-neutral trend myself. At least this place had some charm to it.

The conversation gave me the perfect excuse to scope out a bit more of the dining room. We were one of four total tables sat. A group of four gentlemen. An older couple. A single man enjoying a steak. After my conversation with Rosie a few days ago, I wondered what these people did in Timberland Creek. Or if, perhaps, I was wrong about them being locals and they were simply rolling through, like Jackson and me.

I didn't have much time to contemplate it, though, before our server came back with our drinks. He set the wine down in front of me and the scotch in front of my companion.

"Do you folks think you're ready to order or would you like a bit more time?" he asked.

"We'll take a few minutes," Jackson said.

I smiled politely at the man before he walked away. When my eyes settled on Jackson again, he had his drink lifted.

"To a wonderful trip," he said.

I raised my glass in response. "And to holding out two full weeks without killing one another."

"I was never planning on killing you," he replied as our glasses met with a soft *clink*.

"Yeah, well, you also started this trip saying you wouldn't fuck me, so…"

If he'd chosen anything but a sipping drink, it might have come back out his nose. Instead, Jackson hunched over and did the more gentlemanly thing of spitting it back into the cup before nearly choking.

"I—didn't—" he tried between coughs. "Seductress," is what he finally ended on.

I shrugged and took a much more composed sip of my wine, using the glass to hide my smirk, though I wasn't sure it did much good.

"So," I started again when I set my glass down. "Your final reward. Is it everything you hoped for?"

"It's just getting started."

"You're one of those people who will totally hate this whole ordeal if your steak isn't cooked perfectly, aren't you?"

"I would never," Jackson said. When I leveled him with a stare, he amended, "But if I say medium well and it comes out obviously medium rare, I won't hesitate to send it back."

"And there he is," I said through a laugh.

It was supposed to be a joke, but Jackson's face fell. "What does that mean?"

"Just… I don't know. That I'm not used to that kind of behavior from you anymore, I guess."

"You did a good job," he complimented, softly. Hesitant to admit it out loud.

"No." Jackson looked up from his drink. "No, I'm starting to think you've always been good," I said. "I'm just a little confused why you wanted to hide it. Could have saved us from this whole trip in the first place."

"Do you wish this trip wouldn't have happened?" This time, he sounded scared. Like his curiosity had won, but he didn't actually want to hear my answer.

I shook my head. "I'm very happy this trip happened."

And I was. So much so that the reality of our impending departure date made me nauseous.

When Jackson didn't say anything else, I fired back, "Do *you* wish this trip hadn't happened?"

My eyes tracked his movements as he picked up his glass, swirling it in a gentle motion so the light amber liquid inside flowed in a circle. "That's a bit of a loaded question."

"Is it?" Felt like a simple yes or no to me.

Jackson nodded, his eyes still trained on the movement of his drink, before they finally lifted to me. "I think you know I hated the idea at first," he said.

"Yeah, because I'm a seductress."

"Which is why those first few days were so rough—to put it nicely." Jackson grinned, his eyes narrowed on me, to which I replied with a proud grin of my own and a nonchalant shrug. Ah, the days when he'd tried to hold off from being around me. Good times.

His lips flattened again, though, and his gaze returned to his drink. "I told you I liked having you around. You were just... more of a distraction than I'd anticipated."

"Okay, then it seems like the answer isn't so loaded after all," I challenged.

"It's not only about you. There's..." He trailed off, swallowing. I'd gotten so used to him opening up with me, letting Just Jackson through, that I'd forgotten we *weren't* that close. There were things he still kept from me—that he probably kept from a lot of people.

"You don't need to talk about it if you don't want to," I said, trying to save him the stress.

"It's—no. I'm—shit." Jackson set down his glass and leaned forward on crossed arms. "It's complicated."

"That's why I'm giving you an out, my dude."

"I *want* to tell you." He said it with a conviction I hadn't expected. "I'm just… bad at it. Emotional stuff."

"Perfect. So am I." I leaned back in my seat, wine glass in hand. "Lay it on me."

Jackson raised a brow. "You… want to hear it?"

"Duh." I took a sip then motioned for him to get on with it. "I might even give you the honor of hearing some of my own emotional trauma if you're lucky."

Jackson wasn't stupid. He knew exactly what I was presenting him with: a chance to get inside my head. The problem worked both ways. He hadn't been open with me, so I, in turn, hadn't been open with him. It was only now that we were breaching the conversation that we were both realizing it.

Two people could fuck and partake in superficial pillow talk as much as they wanted. But at the end of the day, Jackson and I had always been the people to run—him more than me, though I wasn't without total blame—as soon as things started to sound too serious. One of us would find an excuse to leave the other's hotel room, busy ourself with something around the cabin, claim we needed to go work, straight-up bolt without any excuse at all. It always ended the same way.

But after two weeks of near non-stop interaction… this sort of conversation was inevitable. I mean, he admitted he watched K-Dramas in his spare time. What could be more vulnerable than that?

"You remember how I mentioned that foster brother of mine? Sam?" When I nodded, Jackson continued with, "Him leaving really fucked up my family. Mom most of all."

Oh shit. He was going *deep*.

Chalk this up as one of the times I felt guilty about joking about trauma. Having a dark sense of humor was a blessing and curse.

"You said he left as soon as he turned eighteen?" I asked, trying to recall the little details I'd been given beforehand.

Jackson nodded. "The *day* he turned eighteen. Didn't give any warning. Just came downstairs in the morning with his one suitcase and a bunch of garbage bags filled with his stuff, argued for a bit then stormed out the door and got in some beat-up old truck. Never saw him again." He ran his hand down his face, his eyes now distant, as if he were back in his childhood home watching it all happen rather than sitting across the table from me.

"Mom had a cake ready for him," Jackson continued. "We were all standing there waiting to sing happy birthday, and instead we got into a shouting match where he told us we were, essentially, all pieces of shit. He'd never wanted to be a part of our family. He didn't need us anymore. All the usual bullshit kids spew."

I nodded as if I had any idea what that was like. The worst argument Laura and I had ever gotten in was about a stolen sweater—which turned out to be misplaced in the back of my closet behind the hamper; whoops. And my parents were angels sent to Earth as far as I was concerned. Even if they weren't, the idea of telling anyone who put in the energy to make sure I was raised well and provided for…

It was unfathomable.

"I'll never—no matter how long I live—forget the look on Mom's face when Sam called her a psycho bitch," Jackson said. "All she ever wanted was for him to be happy—for both of us to be happy. And if you ask me, I won the Mom Lottery. The fact that Sam didn't see that… that he took all her kindness for granted…" He shook his head, eyes cast down at the table. "It wasn't *her* fault she couldn't conceive any more kids. So, she tried to make sure someone else's kid was well-loved instead."

"She sounds like an amazing woman," I offered. "Truly. And it seems like you're really close with her."

"I am," Jackson said. "I have to be. Not because I don't want to. I know some people think talking to their mom all the time is a chore. But I genuinely enjoy it. And for a while…" He paused again, and I let him take his time, watching as he took a sip of his drink. "For a bit there it was just us. Her and Dad got divorced about a year after Sam left, and I've always been on my own. We depended on each other, and the last thing I wanted was for her to be disappointed again.

"That's why I work so hard on my writing," Jackson explained. "Everyone always gave Mom shit because her one kid left and the other was an English and creative writing major. So, I tried to prove them wrong."

"Sounds to me like you did." Also sounded like his mom needed better friends, but that wasn't my advice to offer.

"Yeah, the best-seller thing usually shuts people up," Jackson agreed. "Especially when it's happened six times. But that's what sucks about stuff like that. As soon as they find out I'm not getting my contract renewed, none of that will matter."

"Don't say that," I interjected. "You're gonna get that contract renewal, Jackson. I know it."

"But that leads me back to your original question." Shit. I'd forgotten how this whole conversation had started. "Me coming here meant I had failed—myself and my mom. I didn't want her to hear about this and think another one of her kids had failed her."

That… made a surprising amount of sense. No wonder he'd been so livid about everything that had happened since the original meeting. Why he'd worked tirelessly for two weeks to make sure he came out of this trip with yet another best-seller. It hadn't been for his pride or ego, as I—and probably a whole lot of other people—had originally thought. He was doing it so his mom would be proud. Not even of him. No, he just wanted her to feel like *she'd* accomplished something as a mother.

It was so endearing I almost wanted to cry.

Instead, I leaned forward in my chair again, placing my glass on the table.

"I get it," I admitted. "The whole feeling-like-a-failure thing."

Jackson's head tilted, and he watched me with narrowed, suspicious eyes. "I feel like you're just saying that to make me feel better about myself."

I let out a huffed laugh. "Please. If there's one thing I try my best to refrain from doing, it's boosting your self-esteem."

"True," Jackson agreed. "But you don't give me much reason to believe you fail at things often."

"Fake it 'til you make it, baby," I said, earning a smile from my companion, albeit a small one. "Best life philosophy I've ever adopted."

"Teach me your ways."

"That's why I'm here, isn't it?"

"I guess it is."

My eyes fell to the table setting in front of me, and I absently started playing with the dessert spoon that wasn't rolled in the napkin with the rest of the cutlery.

"I'm… I'm scared to leave."

Genuine curiosity crossed Jackson's face. "Why?"

I shrugged. "I know Rahm said we didn't need that extension, but I'm… nervous? It sounds stupid, but I feel like everything lately has been good until it really comes down to discussing it. Then, all of a sudden, it's not good enough."

"I promise to be on my best behavior, if that helps."

I lifted my gaze to Jackson again to find him sitting there with a look of utmost determination. If I was going down, he was apparently going down with me, but it wouldn't happen without a fight. Or at least without proof that he was not, in fact, the asshole everyone thought him to be.

"It has nothing to do with you," I told him. "I… just ever since Lynn left, I feel like I'm being compared to her. I mean, it makes sense since we're in the same role."

"Sure, but Lynn was, what? Twenty years older than you? She's been in this industry for decades."

"Yeah."

"So, comparing you to her is like comparing apples to oranges."

"*You* want to tell that to Rahm?" I asked with a raised brow. When Jackson dutifully found the hem of the table cloth to play with, I had my answer.

"Long story short, I'm not looking forward to going back and being second best to a person who doesn't even work at Starr anymore," I said then took a sip of wine. "I'm sick of being second."

In friendships. In relationships. In work.

It was exhausting, mostly because everyone expected me to be so bright and bubbly all the time. The Fat, Funny Friend, as some drunken frat bro once told me in college. I'd tried to tell myself it didn't mean anything; it was the cheap vodka talking. But I'd still gone home and cried myself to sleep that night.

Much like Jackson would never forget his mom's reaction when his foster brother left, I'd never forget that statement. It would forever linger in my subconscious, no matter how many therapists told me to give myself more credit than that.

Easier said than done.

"For what it's worth," Jackson said. I hadn't realized I'd been spacing out until I heard his voice. "The people who make you feel that way are absolute shitheads."

The strangled laugh escaped beyond my control, partly because it still amazed me to hear Jackson talk so casually.

The other part was because, whether he knew if I was aware or not, he was a portion of the problem. We'd leave here, and he'd go back to his girl while I went back to the life I'd lived before Timberland Creek.

Except Jackson wouldn't be a part of it anymore.

I gave him a small smile to hide my real emotions as I lifted my glass.

"Thank you for inviting me to dinner," I said. "It's nice to pretend I'm someone's first choice, for once, even if I know I'm the only choice right now."

"Tori, I—"

"To your renewed contract and unending success," I cut him off.

For a second, I wondered if Jackson would accept the toast. He stared at me, his face pained. It was like he was fighting every ounce of will power in his body not to finish whatever he was trying to say before I'd stopped him. I didn't need to hear it. Everyone's sentiments were always the same.

Then, he lifted his scotch.

"To success."

CHAPTER TWENTY-FIVE

WHO KNEW THAT supper clubs were high-key pretty good? Pricey. But the chicken I'd consumed was up there for one of the top ten best meats I'd ever eaten.

And even better: Jackson's steak had been cooked to such perfection that he'd actually moaned while eating it.

"I'll never be able to find another meal like that in all of Indiana," he said as he held open the front door of the cabin for me.

I ducked under his arm and snuck inside before I said. "Indiana? Dude, I live in *Chicago*, and I'm worried I'll never be happy with chicken again."

"Do you think Rosie has connections?" Jackson asked as we made our way through the living room, the kitchen, and into the bedroom. Glad we were on the same uncommunicated page about going to bed. I'd be out in a matter of minutes after all the food and wine. "I'd be willing to have meals shipped."

"You going to be able to cook the steak as well as that chef did?" I challenged, tossing my purse into my bed. "Or risk heating up already-cooked meat to make it less perfect?"

"I'm a decent chef. I'd be willing to learn."

"Well, if you ever figure it out, make sure to let me—"

I stopped myself. No, Tori. There wouldn't be any of him letting you know. If anything, Other Girl would be the first to know when Jackson learned how to cook meat at a five-star-restaurant level.

Jackson emptied his pockets onto the dresser like he did every night, as he asked, "Let you what?"

I looked up to find him watching me in the mirror's reflection.

"Nothing," I said. "Never mind."

After all the deep conversations at dinner, he didn't seem to mind passing on another one.

"I'm gonna use the restroom," he announced. "Do you need anything in there?"

"No, it's all you." When he continued to watch me suspiciously, I took a spare hair tie off my bedside table and flung it at him. "Go, you weirdo. I'll just do my skincare after you're done."

Looking equal parts amused and curious, he did as I'd instructed. When the door shut, I followed the lead getting ready for bed.

Only I couldn't get very far because the zipper on the side of my dress got stuck at the seam that ran across my chest.

"Shit," I muttered as I tugged again.

Nothing. The thing wouldn't budge. I swear, these seams were put on dresses by designers with vendettas against people with boobs bigger than a C-cup. As if it was our fault we'd been blessed with curves of all kinds.

It took Jackson ten minutes before he finally emerged from the bathroom again, dressed in his usual distressed t-shirt and plaid pajama pants.

"Finally," I said through a sigh, rising from the seat I'd taken on my bed. I'd given up on standing after about two very-impatient minutes.

Jackson's pace slowed and understandable confusion dawned. "I… sorry? My toothpaste is almost out, so it took a bit longer to—"

He stopped speaking as soon as I placed myself in front of him, bent slightly to the side to reveal where I'd started to unzip the dress.

"Help," I said. "Please."

Jackson grinned. "And here I thought I was in trouble."

"Not unless you rip the dress."

He chuckled, but then his hands were on me, one on my hip to keep me steady, the other on the zipper. It took three good tugs for him to finally get it past the seam, after which it slid down with ease.

So did the strap when Jackson pushed it gingerly off my shoulder.

His lips met the skin the orange fabric had just been hiding.

Their touch was so light that goosebumps instantly covered my body.

It had only been a couple of days since we'd touched like this, but I knew one thing for sure: my body craved him. It wanted whatever he was willing to offer me more than anything.

But I needed to cut off the addiction before it got even worse. My supply would be gone in a matter of days as it was. Might as well get used to the feeling of the loss now. What was the point in torturing myself with something I could never have? Should have never had to begin with. He belonged to someone else.

"Jackson," I said, half breathless, wanting him to keep kissing my shoulder, my neck, my jaw. But he couldn't. *We* couldn't. "Jackson. No—stop."

I spun with enough speed to shake his hands off where he'd placed them on my hips and took a step back.

"What are you doing?" I asked.

His confusion—and was that a little bit of hurt I saw from my rejection?—was more than evident. "Trying to kiss you?"

"Why?"

"Because I want to, and I thought you liked it?" He said it like someone who'd just been surprised with a pop quiz.

I shook my head. "I can't."

Jackson's mouth opened, and a small noise escaped before he shut it again, his eyes widening. "Shit, are you on your period? I should have asked. I'm sorry. I—"

"Jackson. Wha—no, I'm not on my period. I—" I huffed out

a laugh. "You're going home to another woman."

It wouldn't have surprised me if his eyes came right out of his head, they were opened so wide. "I'm *what?*"

"Don't play dumb," I accused. "I heard you on the phone with your mom."

"With my—" He seemed to have genuinely forgotten the little jump-scare I'd given him a few days ago, but as soon as his memory started working again, Jackson grinned. "You *did* hear me."

"Duh." The single syllable came out of me with all the gusto of a bratty teenager. "Which is why we can't do this. I refuse to be the other woman."

Jackson's entire body eased as his tension faded, and in a voice as soft as the kisses he'd just been gifting me said, "You don't want to be second best."

My throat tightened immediately, my eyes stinging with the tease of tears. Why the hell did he have to be a man who actually listened? Let alone a man who picked up on moments where my confessed insecurities were in play.

But instead of fighting back, the most I could manage was a strangled, "Yes."

For someone who dealt with words a whole lot, now would have been a wonderful time for him to use them. I would have taken anything at that point, even if it was him telling me point-blank that I was right. That would be easier than standing there, watching him go from hurt to confused and back again, over and over and over.

At least I wasn't alone in those feelings, I supposed.

"I… I don't know what to say," Jackson finally admitted.

"Then don't say anything," I replied, swiping at my eyes as best I could without smearing my make up. "Let's just—I'll go use the bathroom and we can go to bed and survive this last day and forget this ever—"

"No, wait."

He grabbed my wrist as I tried to sneak past, wanting desperately to be within the confines of the bathroom so I could finally let my damn tears fall. It was becoming harder and harder to hold them in, the longer we stood there.

"Jackson, let me go."

"Listen to me first," he pleaded.

"There's nothing left to say. Just let me go so I can—"

"I don't know what to say because I can't imagine why you would ever think there's anyone I'm even remotely interested in more than you."

Thank god my dress was unzipped because my airways couldn't have handled any more restrictions after hearing that.

"You—huh?" I squeaked out.

Jackson grinned, his hand trailing from my wrist to my hand. I watched openly as he intertwined our fingers together, just like he had the night we'd danced or this morning. With so much ease. So naturally. As if he'd been imagining how he would do it for days, weeks, months and had finally gotten the chance.

"The woman I was speaking about with my mom? That was

you, Tori," Jackson clarified. "She's asked about you anytime she's called during this whole trip. The time you decided to eavesdrop just so happened to be the time I finally let her ask me more than one question before I cut her off."

"Why?"

"Because I didn't want you hearing me talk about you and think—"

"No," I interrupted. "Why… me?"

I couldn't help thinking back to that conversation and some of the snippets I'd heard.

She's stunning.

She's way out of my league.

It's not love. Not yet. But it could be.

"Why *not* you?" Jackson said back.

Fair. "When?"

"The first time I saw you. I'd already been working with Starr when you came to the company. That first meeting you joined…" He shook his head, as if he still couldn't believe the reality of his memory. "I thought you were the most beautiful woman I'd ever seen."

I tried to remember that meeting, too. Had I even realized who Jackson was? I'd started with the romance division, and switched into fantasy… shit—it had to have been at least five years ago now. That's how long ago the meeting in question would have taken place, if it really was right after I'd switched imprints.

This little crush of his had been going on for *years*.

Holy flying fudge nuggets.

"Why didn't you say something?"

"I was terrified. I'm not exactly smooth with the ladies."

"I don't know about that," I argued, the first hint of a smile forming on my lips.

Jackson chuckled and brought my knuckles to his lips, kissing each one before he added, "I also fucked up by opening my fat mouth and quickly learned you weren't going to take any shit. Figured I'd lost all chances then and there."

"You were probably right."

"Which leads me to ask…" His free hand found my waist and pulled me closer. "Why did you ask me to sleep with you?"

"Truthfully?" I asked, and he nodded. "I was lonely and you were there. Plus, I might have found you annoying, but I never thought you were unattractive."

"I'm noticing some past tense in there."

"You've grown on me. A lot."

"That was the plan."

I tilted my chin up to better meet his eyes. "The plan?"

"My rewards? Haven't you noticed how none of them were what I'm sure you were intending when you offered them?"

"I—"

My argument died on my lips because I'd be damned—he was right. Cooking dinner. Watching movies and K-Dramas. Even tonight's outing.

I thought for sure when I proposed the reward system, he'd look at it the same way I had been: as an excuse to continue sleeping with each other. Instead, he'd—

"You were planning dates the whole time," I concluded.

"I admit tonight's was the most obvious, but, yes." Jackson leaned down and pressed a kiss to my forehead. My temple. "All I wanted to do was spend time with you, Tori. You could tell me the sex stops now, and I'd be okay with that as long as you're still willing to spend time with me."

I raised an accusatory brow.

"Okay, I'd be kind of upset. The sex is amazing," he amended, and I let out a strangled chuckle. "But I'm serious. I'm sure you heard me say this already, but I… I'm falling in love with you. You come first, Tori Wilson. Always."

One blink was all it took for the tears to finally spill over.

That one statement—he had no idea how much it meant to me. No matter how hard I tried to put it into words, it wouldn't suffice. No one—not once—had ever said that to me, let alone made me feel like they meant it with one-hundred-percent sincerity.

Because I knew Jackson didn't waste his words. What he'd just told me? It was the whole-hearted truth.

Jackson's hands moved to my face, holding it on either side while his thumbs brushed over my cheeks, wiping away my tears.

"I figured you probably wouldn't be happy to hear all this," he said. "But please don't cry."

"Not happy to—?"

Oh, this idiot. This wonderful idiot.

Jackson clearly wasn't expecting it when I lifted myself onto my toes and brought my lips to his. His whole body went tense, but I didn't stop. Not until he loosened again and the hands that had just wiped away my tears found their way around my waist, holding me close.

"I don't want you to talk like that anymore, got it?" I said when I pulled away. My hands went up to his face, forcing him to look at me as I added, "I don't care what anyone says. You are an incredible person, Jackson Stanley Albrecht. And I'm so lucky to be your first choice."

Jackson's eyes widened and he blinked twice. "That's… that's it."

"Huh?"

"You got it," he said. His hands slid up my hips to the slight dip in my sides. "My middle name."

"Jackson Stanley Albrecht," I repeated, and he nodded. "I told you I'd figure it out eventually."

He grinned. "I would have told you eventually, Victoria Elizabeth Wilson. I plan to tell you all my secrets."

I knew he meant it, too, when his lips crashed into mine.

I'd meant every word I'd said as well. Tori from a year ago would have never believed it, but I could see myself falling in love with Jackson the same way he claimed he was falling in love with me. I had been for months, I realized. I'd just confused it with another four-letter L word.

While that part of our relationship was wonderful—as Jackson had also been kind enough to point out—it was the smaller memories that played in my head as he kissed me.

The soft touches.

The quiet cuddles.

The way he handled my fire.

The stolen glances.

The shy smiles and quiet laughter.

There was a reason he'd allowed me to see those parts of himself. I'd just forced myself into thinking they couldn't possibly be only for me. Because no one had saved anything just for me. Except Jackson.

The strap of my dress slid off my shoulder again, and this time I didn't stop it. Nor did I stop it when Jackson repeated the action with its twin, allowing the fabric to pool at my feet.

We were a mess—roaming, kissing, touching any inch of skin we could find on one another. It became much easier for me when Jackson unbuttoned his shirt and shrugged it off, leaving it on top of my dress as we stumbled back toward my bed.

It was like clockwork, both of us working from muscle memory and all the times we'd done this before: positioning ourselves on the mattress, Jackson settling between my legs, my own wrapping around him, wanting to keep him as close to me as possible.

The only thing that was missing, I realized after a few seconds, was the feel of his lips on me, trailing down my body like he so often did.

Instead, I opened my lust-heavy eyelids to find him staring down at me.

Jackson's hand cupped my cheek then moved back, clearing the mess of curls that had fallen onto my face in our hurry. Now, there was nothing of that usual eagerness in his expression.

"I can't believe anyone ever made you believe you are anything less than perfect," he whispered.

And that was it. If any reservations remained, they'd been erased with that one statement. That look of pure adoration in Jackson's eyes.

I loved this man. Undoubtedly and unabashedly.

My hands found their way into the hair at the back of Jackson's head, pulling him down so I could kiss him. It was clear he'd lost his sense of urgency, his kisses softer, his caresses slower. I had too. All I wanted to do now—possibly forever— was be near him.

And when we finally discarded our remaining clothes and he slid himself into me, we took up that same pace we'd set, content to relish in the time we had left together in whatever way possible.

CHAPTER TWENTY-SIX

I WAS WARM, and it wasn't because of the sun-shining, birds-chirping kind of picturesque Disney-Princess morning that was heating the bedroom.

Nope. It was because of the man-sized space heater that was wrapped around me.

To think he'd looked at me like I was crazy for suggesting creating a mega-bed for our penultimate night's sleeping arrangements. I wasn't normally a cuddler, but after what I could confidently say was the best sex I'd ever had, I wasn't letting Jackson get away so easily.

Hence mega-bed: our twin beds pushed together and covered with a spare queen sheet I'd found in the bathroom linen closet to make sure they didn't separate. We'd used two of his belts at the headboard and footboards of the beds to help, too.

I knew he'd gotten over his initial hesitations the moment his arm tightened around me and his face burrowed into my neck.

"Good morning." Jackson's sleepy voice was just about the sexiest thing I'd ever heard. Why had I waited until now to figure that out?

"How did you know I was awake?" I asked, turning slightly to allow him to kiss my cheek. My ass *might* have also pressed a little bit harder into his crotch.

Seemed like he was just as excited to wake up next to me as I was to wake up next to him.

"Seductress," he rasped, and I chuckled. "You might think you're quiet when you sneak out of hotel rooms, but you always make a little noise right when you wake up."

"Oh yeah?"

"Mhm." Jackson placed another kiss on my shoulder, my neck. "A little moan."

"Sexy," I teased.

"Very," he agreed, then pulled me tighter, forcing me to turn onto my back.

His lips were on mine as soon as he could reach them, giving me one of the same, languid kisses we'd shared the night before.

Whoever decided rough sex was best—well, they were onto something, for sure. But more people needed to talk up the sensual kind, too. This shit was amazing.

"You have any big plans today?" I asked when he pulled back.

"I think I have to finish writing a best-seller."

"Sounds lame."

Jackson shrugged his shoulder that wasn't pressed to the mattress. "It's either that or face the wrath of the woman sent here to babysit me."

"Can't fuck with those crazy bitches, man."

Clearly, that wasn't what he'd been expecting. Jackson's head dipped in an attempt to shield his face, as if I couldn't hear his soft laughter. The break in character made me smile.

"She's not that bad," he said when he regained some composure.

"Really?"

"Yeah." His lips met my forehead before he continued, "She's fun." A kiss on my temple. "And hilarious." A kiss on my cheek. Then against my lips, "And fucking beautiful."

"She sounds pretty understanding," I mumbled against his mouth, my hand beginning its decent down Jackson's body. "She might even be willing to let you get started a little later?"

As soon as my hand wrapped around his semi-hard length through his briefs, I'd expected him to accept my offer. But instead, Jackson surprised me by saying, "I think she has to work."

"She has some sick days to use up," I replied, stroking him.

"No, no, no."

I laughed as Jackson removed my hand and pinned it above my head. He rolled over me, hovering just enough so he could meet my eyes. Still, it didn't stop his erection from pressing into my stomach.

My eyes darted down to catch a glimpse of it. Jackson chuckled.

"You're insatiable," he teased.

"Or you're just irresistible," I shot back.

The vibrations of his quiet laughter hit me everywhere our bodies touched.

Jackson didn't fall for my tricks, though, and instead bent to kiss my nose. "I should have told you I had a crush on you a long time ago," he said before he rolled off me and the bed altogether.

I sat up, pulling the sheet with me to cover my chest. "Aw, c'mon," I said with a pout as he went about the room to start getting ready for the day. "Just think of all the time we have to make up for because you didn't. All the fun."

He smiled back at me over his shoulder while he buttoned his jeans. When he was done, he snagged a shirt off the top of his open suitcase, and the happiness brought on from the previous night and this morning dimmed.

Those suitcases would be packed tonight. We'd leave tomorrow. All this was coming to an end just as it was beginning.

"Hey."

My concentration had been so intent on the luggage that I hadn't realized Jackson had come back to stand beside the bed. He leaned forward, propping himself up on his hands, his face inches from mine.

"We'll have our time," he whispered, as if reading my thoughts. "And I still have an epilogue to write. That means one more reward, remember?"

I tried my best to smile as I nodded.

Jackson kissed me again, quicker this time, as if he knew anything longer would be too tempting.

When he left the bedroom, casting me another smile before he did, I laid back down with a groan.

I'D TAKEN UP the couch for work, while Jackson sat at the kitchen counter. It was for the better that neither of us was looking directly at the other. Who knew what would have happened if we had? Not work, that was for sure.

And the theory proved correct when, two hours after we first sat down in our respective spots, a shadow loomed over me.

My vision strayed from my screen, settled on the two legs in front of me, and traveled up to find Jackson standing there.

"It's done."

"Care to clarify?"

He shook his head, smiling at my playful bullshit, before he grabbed my laptop and moved it to the coffee table. The man had great foresight because the moment he took a seat beside me, I snuggled under his arm.

"My book," he said, holding me tight against his side.

"He's a drafting machine, ladies and gents."

"And I believe he has one more reward left to cash in."

My fingers crawled across his chest, towards the buttons of his polo shirt. "And does he have anything in mind?" I asked, my voice sultry as I teased the top button.

"I've got a few ideas."

"Yeah?"

"Mhm…"

I'd been waiting hours for Jackson to lean down and kiss me, and just when I thought I'd get my wish, he paused.

"*Garden of Bleeding Hearts*?" he whispered mere centimeters from my lips.

The fucking tease.

But he'd said the one thing that might have been better than sex. Or tied with it, at the very least.

I smiled. "I'll pop some popcorn."

IT WAS SAFE to say I was hooked. English-language TV shows were bound to lose a single viewer because this? It was good. Damn good. Possibly-better-than-*Crimson-Curse* good, as far as vampire-related shows were concerned.

I knew Jackson had watched it through at least once, but it was hard to tell what re-watch this was, given he was just as enthralled as I was, the both of us cuddled together on the couch as YeJoon battled the vampire slayer vying for Taeyeon's hand in marriage.

I swore if those two didn't end up together by the end of the show—which, following typical K-Drama fashion, would tragically only have one season, or so Jackson believed—I would riot. I'd fly to Korea and demand that my vampire and princess find eternal happiness, or so help me—

A creative, fictional threat never came to me. The show I'd been so intently watching immediately became background noise when Jackson nuzzled his face into my neck.

"What are you doing?" I asked, tilting my head just enough so he could get better access. And thank god I did because the moment he began sucking at the point where my neck met my jaw—

"I've already seen this," he mumbled against my skin.

"It's your reward."

"I keep getting distracted."

"By what?" I teased.

Jackson's head popped up, his eyes already unbelievably clouded over by lust. "You keep reaching for popcorn."

"And?"

"And it's a little too close for comfort."

I'd give him that. The bowl *was* situated in his lap.

"You should have taken me up on my offer this morning," I said as Jackson got back to work on my neck. His hand went up to the opposite side of my jaw, his fingers tangling in my hair to make sure I remained angled just the way he wanted me. "Aren't you hungry for a little snack, too?"

I grabbed hold of the bowl and jostled it on his lap.

A low groan escaped him, the vibration of it tingling my skin. As if that wasn't enough to absolutely turn me on, his hand shifted again, grabbing me under my jaw, his gaze meeting mine. The sheer possessiveness of it all made wetness pool between my legs.

"I'm very hungry," Jackson said, his voice low and seductive. "Just not for popcorn."

There was no time for my brain to form a coherent response—not that I'd believed I would have been able to anyway—before he kissed me, hard and desperate. Not at all like the kisses we'd shared over the last twenty-four hours.

This. This was the Jackson I was used to. The one that worshipped me with his hands, his lips, his tongue. The descent he was making down my body hinted that he was preparing to do just that right now.

The popcorn bowl clattered to the floor, its contents spilled, when Jackson slid off the couch and onto his knees. He gazed up at me, our eyes never breaking from one another as he reached for the band of my lounge pants. His hands hooked inside, grabbing hold of not only them but my panties.

I wiggled as he pulled them down and off me, but still he never stopped staring directly at me. He was obviously horny as hell, but there was something else there in the way he looked at me. That, even in these rough, hurried moments we shared, I realized had always been there. An adoration. A look that made me believe he truly thought he was the luckiest man alive to get to see me this way. In *any* way.

My lips curled in and my whole body reacted when he kissed just above where I was aching for him.

"I fucking love this pussy," he said, then ran a finger through the slick folds. "Tell me it's mine."

"It's yours," I told him. Fuck, if he didn't do more than tease me soon, I'd combust.

He kissed the same spot as before, his eyes on mine. "Promise?"

"Yes. Jackson—*fuck*, just—"

My plea died in my throat the moment he found my clit. He suckled it into his mouth before his tongue circled it, working me in a way that was pure magic.

My hips bucked off the couch. My hand tangled in Jackson's perfect hair, keeping him where he was. Not that he looked like he had any intention of stopping. Especially not when he slipped two fingers inside my slickness.

There was no way I'd ever be able to have sex with anyone else again in my life. Not after knowing what it was like to have Jackson. It wasn't as though I'd want to anyway. No one made me feel as cherished, as sated, as loved as he did when we were together.

I risked leaning forward just enough to grab my shirt and lift it over my head, leaving me bare. I'd never been so satisfied with my choice to not put on a bra that morning. My hands found my breasts, pinching the peaked nipples, trying to create as much sensation as possible. *Needing* to create the sensation. There weren't enough hands available to touch me everywhere

I wanted to be touched. I sure as shit wasn't going to let Jackson stop what he was doing to assist.

His expertise of my body showed within minutes. I moaned, my back arching off the couch as I came. And by the time I settled, my body content, but still craving more, Jackson was nearly undressed.

I wasted no time.

Still trembling, I made my way off the couch and onto my knees before him.

"I can't believe this cock belongs to me," I said, taking him in my hand and licking up the underside of his length.

Jackson bit his bottom lip, then ground out, "Not even asking permission to claim it?"

"No," I said, looking up at him with a playful grin. "I know it's mine."

His chuckle shifted into a groan as I took him into my mouth. My hand worked his shaft while I focused on his tip, all the while watching him from under my lashes. Nothing but pure pleasure was etched on his face, and knowing I was the cause made me all the more excited to keep going.

Jackson's hand found my hair, and his hips began to move. Forward and back, forward and back—fucking my mouth slow and deep until I was gagging, my eyes watering.

He pulled back, allowing me a reprieve, and just as I was about to go back in for more, he stopped me.

"You're gonna make me come before I get inside you," he said, half breathless.

I smiled, proud of my work, as Jackson helped me to my feet. His arms wrapped around me as soon as I was standing, and he bent down to kiss me. It almost distracted me enough that I didn't realize how he was moving us. Where I'd be positioned.

"I, um—" I broke away when Jackson lowered himself onto the couch. "I can go on the bottom."

"I want you to ride me, Tori." Jackson spoke so matter-of-factly that I almost felt like challenging him would be impossible.

Almost.

I swallowed, focusing on his length rather than his face. It would be so easy to climb into his lap and take him, but— "Wouldn't you like some good, old-fashioned missionary?"

"We can do that too." Jackson reached for my hand, urging me forward. "I'll fuck you however you want me to."

A nervous laugh escaped me as soon as our lips met, but I still didn't do as he asked.

"Missionary then?" I tried again.

"Tori... is something wrong?" He wasn't asking me to get what he wanted, the way so many men would. There was genuine concern in his voice, his eyes. "I thought you liked being on top?

He was right. I actually *loved* being on top. It gave me the control to make sure I found my pleasure. Of course, that wasn't usually an issue with Jackson, but it had been with plenty of other guys who couldn't have given a rat's ass if I finished or not.

But despite that, I preferred being on the bottom. It was easier to hide that way, with the other person covering me. In the dark it didn't matter so much, but here in the daylight, every one of my flaws would be on display.

Each roll in my stomach.

The extra dip in my hips.

Hell, even the cellulite and stretch marks on my thighs, depending on the position.

Every reason why one man or another had claimed I wasn't as desirable as other women.

I'd be bearing all of them to Jackson.

"I do like it, it's just—I—" My sights drifted to the window. "It's never been this light while we…"

I didn't bother finishing the thought. I knew Jackson had gotten the gist as soon as his eyes softened—then hardened right back up again.

He was pissed. Not at me, but at the idea someone had planted such awful thoughts in my head.

"Tori, I meant what I said last night." He stood, both his hands going up to my face. "Look at me," he said when I tried my best to not meet his eyes, even with his attempts to get me to do so.

"Victoria Elizabeth Wilson, I could kill anyone that made you believe you are anything less than beautiful," he whispered.

"No, you won't," I argued, my voice even quieter. "You wouldn't even kill that spider at that signing in Omaha."

"It was a pretty big spider, you have to admit."

"You still won't hurt people."

"I'd use very strong language to threaten them, though."

I couldn't help laughing. It thankfully brought some lightness back to Jackson's face.

He leaned down and kissed my forehead.

"You're beautiful, Tori," he said again. "Every inch of you. Head to toe. Your eyes." He kissed the lid of each one. "Your nose." He kissed that too. "Your lips. Your neck. Your chest."

He kept going, naming all the parts of me he loved and kissing each one in turn until he was on his knees, his hands on my hips.

"Your stomach."

My throat tightened when his lips met the skin on the place I'd so long believed made me unsexy.

"Your—"

I tugged at Jackson's arm and brought him back up to his feet. The man truly would have kept at it. He would have laid down on the floor and kissed my feet if it meant proving the sincerity of his words.

But I didn't let him. Instead, I guided him back down onto his seat on the couch—and I got on top, straddling him.

"Tori, we really don't have to—"

"I want to," I said then kissed him. "You earned it."

His stare made me feel like he was waiting for me to change my mind, and he only broke when I lowered myself onto his waiting length.

"Fuck," Jackson moaned, hands going to my hips the same

time his head fell back. "I'll never get used to it. How good you feel around my cock."

Likewise. In this position, he filled me so completely. With just the first roll of my hips, I was already on edge. Jackson might have been too, if his tightened hold on me was any indication.

"Just like that," he ground out. "Fuck—yes. Ride my cock just like that."

I leaned forward, using the new angle to pick up the pace of my movements, rolling my hips, lifting and lowering myself, all in an attempt to build up to release.

"*Jackson*," I moaned, my mouth against his ear.

I lowered my head further, never ceasing my movements, as I bit his earlobe, licked up his neck. He reciprocated by moving his hands from my waist to my breasts, kneading them before he brought one of my pebbled nipples into his mouth.

"Fucking perfect," he recited when he released it with a *pop*.

"I'm gonna—" I sucked my lower lip between my teeth when he moved onto my other tit. "Jackson, I'm gonna come."

"Hold on." The look of pure dejection that crossed his face when he realized he needed to stop sucking my nipple was incredible. "Hold on just a little longer."

"*Jackson*," I repeated. *Pleaded.* Hopefully he got the hint that that might not be possible.

"Fuck."

His renewed hold on my hips was so tight that I had no choice but to stop moving on my own. Instead, he pounded into me, fast and frenzied as he tried to chase the same release I was about to experience.

"Jackson, I—"

We were flipped before I could finish speaking, my chest on the couch, ass in the air, Jackson behind me. He hadn't even lost his pace in the process, his cock still driving into me, filling me in the most luxurious way.

My hands clutched the arm of the couch. When I turned my head to the side, it was just enough to catch a glimpse of Jackson, his forehead coated in a sheen of sweat. His whole body, actually.

"*Jackson.*"

I couldn't take it anymore. I was going to—

"Surprise! Is anybody ho—ly shit!"

I clenched around Jackson as the orgasm overcame me, my back arched and face pressed into the couch cushion. I was seeing stars; the whole room bright with—more daylight?

"*Fuck.*"

A feeling of emptiness overcame me when Jackson pulled out, and for a moment, I couldn't tell if he was cussing from the sex or from the surprise guest I found when I lifted my head just enough to see the front door.

It might have been a little bit of both, since beads of warm liquid landed on my lower back seconds later.

I was too stunned to think about covering myself, but I wasn't sure it mattered. Marcus had both his hands firmly over his eyes anyway.

"Shit."

I turned just in time to see Jackson grab a decorative pillow from the couch. He placed it on my ass, angling it so he could attempt to hide his dick from view, too. As best he could, anyway.

"I—" he began. "Wow, Marcus. Hi."

When Jackson tried to wave at his agent, the pillow fell, toppling to the floor atop our discarded popcorn and clothing. He reached for it, but almost joined it. Instead, Jackson opted to use his hands for coverage as he scurried to find something else to hide my naked bits from view.

This could not be worse.

Or so I thought until I heard the creaking, and the next thing I knew, Jackson and I were dropping as the bottom of the couch hit the floor.

Now it could not be worse.

Marcus's hands were still over his eyes, but I didn't need to see those to know he was absolutely fuming.

"What the fuck," he seethed, "is going on here?"

Jackson and I didn't respond. We both turned to each other, our expressions communicating our identical thought loud and clear.

Our deadline was here.

CHAPTER TWENTY-SEVEN

WE HADN'T SAID goodbye.

That thought had dominated my mind during the entire agonizing drive home on Thursday evening—we hadn't even gotten a full last day at the cabin—and it hadn't left me since. Four days later, sitting at my desk, the same thought looped, relentless.

I'd promised Rosie we'd say goodbye. But who knew when—or if—I'd get back to Timberland Creek to make good on that promise? God, I wanted to. One day back at work, and I'd already fantasized about smashing my face into the keyboard at least three times.

I'd been in the office for two hours.

A nice walk to Sunrise Brews sounded perfect right about now. The chain store coffee I'd gotten on the way in just hadn't hit the same, and now I was paying the consequences—among other things.

My eyes flickered to the doorway as a gaggle of employees passed. My team knew I'd been back since Friday. They'd figured it out during a call when my background was distinctly *not* a cabin in the northern wilderness.

I'd been encouraged not to go to the office. Marcus had been there on Friday. Jackson told me he'd been asked to go in, too, but I'd never heard the outcome. We'd barely spoken outside of the occasional check-in texts. I ignored his FaceTime on Saturday, already overwhelmed by Laura's questions about my early return and unwilling to take on anything more.

His goodnight text, complete with the kissing face emoji, made me regret that.

At least he hadn't opened our conversation with "I didn't get my contract renewed," which I took as a good sign. Maybe while Marcus had been mad—read: livid—he still wouldn't sever ties completely. There was still hope for Jackson.

Maybe even for me.

Maybe all of this would blow over. People would forget. We'd move on, make boatloads of money off Jackson's next book, and everyone would live happily ever after. I mean, I hadn't even heard from Rahm since I'd gotten back. Maybe Marcus hadn't told him about—

My phone buzzed as an email hit my inbox.

TO: Victoria Wilson "vwilson@starrpm.com"
FROM: Rahm Singh "rsingh@starrpm.com"

Victoria,

Come to my office.

Rahm

It could've been a Slack. Instead, it was a nightmare-inducing email where I'd still read the implied but non-existent *now* in my head.

I should have written my will when I'd had the chance. Someone needed to cherish my signed and special edition book collection when I was gone.

Too late now.

The walk from my office to Rahm's wasn't long, but each step stretched into eternity. By the time I reached his door, my legs felt heavy, like I was dragging weights behind me. His nameplate glinted in the dull office light, mocking me.

Do it. March to your death, it said.

I rolled my eyes, muttering, "Fuck off," under my breath.

Shit, I was *really* going nuts after the last few days.

I took a deep breath. It was now or never.

My knock echoed down the hall like a drumbeat of doom.

"Come in."

I turned the knob, opening the door with a deliberate slowness. Each inch felt like stalling for a few more seconds of control, my polite smile already frozen on my face. First glance: Rahm behind his desk, stoic as ever. Second glance: Ann from HR. *Shit.*

"Rahm." I nodded at him before glancing at her, dialing my tone up a notch. "And Ann! Long time no see."

Ann returned my smile, but hers was the kind you gave right before delivering bad news—hands folded, every inch of her screaming 'official business.'

This wasn't good.

"Victoria, take a seat," Rahm said. His voice was calm, but the tension in the air was suffocating.

Not wanting to push my luck, I hurried into the seat beside Ann. I cast her another soft smile. Maybe if she felt bad for me, she'd show me mercy. Rahm sure as shit didn't look like *he* had any intentions of doing that.

Rahm leaned back, fingers steepled. If he had a cat, he'd look like the Indian version of the Godfather. "How was your trip?"

Oh, he was good.

"It was wonderful," I replied. "Nothing like some crisp, Wisconsin air to lift the spirits."

"And Jackson?" He raised an eyebrow. "I met with him last week, and his improvements were evident. Even finished his manuscript, I was told."

"He did." I tried to keep my voice even, but the tension wound itself tighter in my chest.

"And all in only two weeks." Rahm clucked his tongue. "I knew he could draft quickly. He's proven that skill in the past.

But as for his sudden shift in attitude—it's incredible. It was like a new person walked into my office."

"That was the goal, sir," I said.

"Ann and I are so curious how you managed it."

I cast a sidelong glance at the HR manager before I told Rahm, "That question makes me believe you've probably already heard."

The stare he leveled at me after I spoke further proved that.

Rahm sat forward in his chair again. "Did you know that it is against Starr Publishing and Media's policy for employees to fraternize with the talent?"

My brow furrowed and I stammered, "I—what—no, I—where does it say that?"

I turned to Ann, but her head was down, her focus on her twiddling thumbs in her lap.

"The fact of the matter is that, especially in your role, what has happened between you and Mr. Albrecht can be seen as favoritism," Rahm continued. "If word gets out to our other authors that you've broken policy—"

"A policy you still haven't shown me."

"—it makes us look bad. Like we can't control our employees."

"First," I said, leaning forward in my chair, a finger lifted. I didn't think I'd ever used such a stern tone with Rahm before, and it was clear he hadn't expected it either. "I might work here, but you do *not* control me. What I do in my personal time is my business and my business only."

"That trip was expensed on the company's dime, Victoria, so, respectfully, we do have the right to question you on what was done there," Rahm fought back. "Marcus tells me the incident occurred in the middle of the day. Is it safe to assume that was what you were up to when you should have been doing your job?"

I couldn't think of any argument for that. One look at my computer history and both Rahm and Ann would see my time online was close to nil towards the end of the trip.

Even Ann finally looked up when Rahm shook his head and mumbled, "Unbelievable," under his breath.

"Okay," the HR manager said. "I think we need to calm down a bit."

"I told Lynn you weren't ready for this role," Rahm said. I couldn't stop my eyes from widening, but it was still more subtle than Ann's jaw dropping. "And here we are, less than a year later—less than *six months* later—and you're already making cataclysmic mistakes."

"That's what you wanted, right?" I challenged. "For me to fuck up?"

The member of the HR team in the room probably had something to do with it, but Rahm actually had the audacity to appear offended. "Excuse me?"

"You wanted me to fail," I said. "Ever since I was promoted, I've been held to this… this *insane* standard. That's probably why you sent me on that stupid trip in the first place. No one thought Jackson Albrecht could be a decent human being, so let's give it to Tori along with a subtle threat that she'll lose her job if she fails."

"What?" Ann asked, aghast.

"I didn't—" Rahm started, casting her a glance before his expression hardened on me again. "This has nothing to do with why you were assigned the task of this trip, Victoria. From what I remember, *you* were the one that suggested it. Now, it seems we know why."

"No. Marcus suggested it," I argued, my tone flat, tired. "At least *he* had confidence that I'd be able to do it."

"The fact remains that you broke policy even if you did succeed at the task at hand."

"Again, I've yet to see this policy." I crossed my arms over my chest and turned to Ann. "Is it in the employee handbook?"

"I'll have to check, but—"

"I'll give you the choice, Victoria," Rahm continued, blatantly changing the subject back.

Asshat.

It was incredible that the employees of Starr had put up with him for so long. That the rest of the Board of Directors allowed him to continue his work here. I'd never deny that the man was smart as hell, but that didn't make up for the misogynistic tendencies and blatant abuse of power he displayed. I mean, heck—no one else could get away with talking to an employee like this with a member of HR present.

If I didn't need to pay rent so desperately, I might have walked out by now. Instead, I tilted my head to the side, mouth in a tight line, as I waited for his stipulation.

"We haven't offered Jackson S. Albrecht a contract for his new series," Rahm announced, and my heart dropped.

Was that why he hadn't said anything? Had he been dropped and was too embarrassed to let me know?

"After some deliberation, Marcus and I came to the conclusion that we would talk with you before any decisions were made." Rahm's tone made it sound like that hadn't been his idea. Another favoritism point for Marcus. "Now that you have officially confirmed the situation, I will present you with the two options we settled on."

I swallowed, trying to keep my face as even-keeled as possible. No way was I letting this asshole know I was nervous.

"You can either continue seeing Mr. Albrecht, but one—or both of you—will no longer be associated with Starr," Rahm said. I glanced at Ann to see if she'd picked up on the threat this time, but she hadn't moved. I wondered if she'd been briefed of these decisions beforehand.

Not that the entire situation didn't warrant HR's participation, but me potentially deciding to terminate my employment with Starr definitely did.

But as I'd already calculated, unemployment wasn't an option at the moment.

"What's the alternative?" I asked.

"You end whatever relationship you've developed with Mr. Albrecht," he stated. "And you will be taken off all projects related to his career with Starr."

"But he gets his contract?"

Rahm shrugged. "Marcus and I still have some details to discuss, but yes. It does look like Starr would be able to offer him a contract for a new trilogy."

Any nerves that had plagued me seconds ago turned into excitement. He'd done it. Jackson was getting his contract—probably. Rahm wasn't one to build up hope, though, so the fact that he'd spoken positively at all was a good sign.

If I wasn't so pissed off, I might have actually jumped out of my chair at the news. Instead, I remained seated there, the only sign that I'd heard Rahm at all being the faintest hint of a smile at the corners of my lips.

No way was I letting that man think for one second that he'd done something to make me happy. That smile was for Jackson and Jackson only.

Which really left me with one choice.

MY PHONE STARTED ringing just as I stepped off the train at the Oak Park Metra station.

Jackson.

He'd tried to call me two other times while I was at the office, but I'd sent him to voicemail then followed up with some vague text about being busy at work.

Now, well after the end of the day, there was no excuse why I couldn't talk with him. I *should* talk with him. Sure, we hadn't established any clear titles for one another while at the cabin, but those last two days alone made it pretty obvious where we stood.

We'd admitted we were falling in love with each other—out loud, at least. Internally… internally, I knew I'd already fallen. It had been a long, slow process to get there, but it had happened.

And now I was being a coward because I knew the conversation I was about to have would hurt me more than it would hurt Jackson.

"Hey," I answered, my voice already threatening to break.

"Hey," Jackson echoed. I couldn't take how happy he sounded. "How was the first day back?"

"Oh, you know. It was a day."

"How was Alexis?" he asked in a teasing tone.

"She stayed away, thank god." Truly. I didn't think I could have handled all of her problems on top of everything else.

But something told me it was the *everything else* that had been the reason for her keeping her distance. Over the last year, I'd learned that office gossip spread like wildfire within Starr.

The marketing team had single-handedly provided almost a year's worth of entertainment for the company. Probably even more reason why Rahm had been so livid. He was sick of our bullshit.

Jackson chuckled, and I heard something clatter on the other line. Pots and pans, maybe? It *was* nearing seven in the evening in Indiana.

"Did you… you know."

"Get reprimanded?" I guessed.

"Yeah." His playfulness was gone. Now, nothing but nerves accompanied his words.

I finished my descent down the stairs from the train platform and stepped out of the rush of fellow commuters. They continued on their way, back to their homes, their families, none the wiser that the woman some of them had bumped into in their hurry was on the brink of tears.

And here I'd been, thinking I was on the path to that same sort of happy ending. That's how I knew what I felt was real, though. I was willing to sacrifice it all to make sure that Jackson was happy instead. If he didn't get this contract… I couldn't imagine the devastation he'd face.

"Rahm wasn't cheery, I'll say that much."

"Shit, Tori." There was more activity on his side of the call, and I guessed it was probably an attempt to buy time when he added, "You… you still have your job, right?"

I shut my eyes, trying to fight the burning in them. The act caused tears to slip down my cheeks. "Yeah. I do."

"Good. I swear, I would have driven to Chicago and wrung that asshole's neck if he'd decided to—"

"Jackson."

All the noise on his end stopped. Even if I couldn't see him, I could imagine him standing in a kitchen that I'd never even gotten the chance to visit, in an apartment I'd never gotten to sleepover in. I hadn't realized how much I wanted that—to see where he lived, his routines in his own space, how he'd decorated. More of those little insights into Just Jackson that I'd grown so addicted to on our trip.

He still hadn't said anything, which didn't surprise me either. My tone hadn't exactly been hopeful.

"I can't see you anymore," I said.

More silent tears fell as I waited for his answer.

"Like… for work?" he asked. "That makes sense. I didn't expect them to let us after—"

"No." My face scrunched in pain as I tried to keep my sob at bay. "Jackson, we… whatever we started has to end."

Another pause before, "But… why?"

My free hand went up over my mouth to stifle the pained noise that escaped me. I knew I was a coward for having this conversation over the phone, but I didn't think I'd be able to handle it in person. Not hearing him like this. God, he sounded so dejected.

"I want you to get your contract," I whispered. It was all I could manage. "You *need* to get your contract."

"Tori, did they give you an ultimatum?" I startled at the loud *bang* on the other line, like he'd knocked something over or slammed his hand on the counter. "I swear, next time I see that fucker I'm going to—"

"You're not going to do anything but accept the offer that's presented to you," I interrupted, mustering as much sternness as I could.

"It's not fair, Tori," Jackson argued. He made a noise, and I knew he was shoving his fingers back through his hair. "They can't tell us how to live our lives."

"They see it as a conflict of interest. Favoritism," I recited, rolling my eyes as I recalled the feeble excuses I'd been given. "Something about a fraternization policy."

"Then how about they remove you from my marketing team, not out of my fucking life?" There was another crash. "Fuck!"

I knew, despite being on the receiving end of his statements, I wasn't the target of his anger. The same emotions had overcome me that very same morning as I'd been presented with the choices. There was no easy way out. One way or another, one—or both—of us was going to end up screwed.

At least this way, we both got something we wanted—even if I'd definitely drawn the short straw.

"You're going to accept the contract," I repeated. "And you're going to publish that best-seller I just watched you write, and you're going to kick ass in this industry."

"And what about you?" Jackson challenged. "What are you getting out of it?"

"I get to keep my job."

Jackson let out a huffed laugh. "Yeah—working for an absolute fuckwad."

I couldn't help the little smile that formed. My penchant for creative insults had rubbed off on him.

"I've dealt with Rahm for a long time. I can keep dealing with him. But as long as we're both with Starr, we... it won't work."

Jackson went quiet again—for so long that I pulled my phone

away from my ear to make sure he was still there. He was—or so the increasing call time told me.

"I—" he finally said, then groaned again. "Fuck. Tori, I love you. I don't want to do this without you."

And there they were. The three words I'd wanted to hear so terribly. Except they were coming at the worst possible time.

"I love you too, Jackson," I whispered back. "Which is exactly why I made this choice. Your career is everything to you. I wasn't going to be the reason you lost it."

Even if it broke me in the process.

CHAPTER TWENTY-EIGHT

BROKE ME, IT did.

I thought I'd been a mess after Freddie and I ended. I was wrong. No previous heartbreak would have prepared me for the pain I faced the moment Jackson and I hung up the phone. I'd slumped down on the ground at the freaking Metra station and cried for an hour before I finally composed myself again.

Part of it, I was sure, was due to frustration from the day as a whole, but most of it came from knowing that was it. It took less than a year for Jackson and I to meet our end—if I could even call it that. We'd hardly had a beginning.

My bedroom became my sanctuary as soon as I'd gotten home. No way was I letting Laura see me post-cry. She'd have shown no mercy with her interrogation as to why I was coming home from work late and in a state of severe distress. Even Bianca might have shown some rare concern. She was more of a bystander when it came to Wilson sister problems, unless, of course, it was Laura with the problem. Girlfriend came before girlfriend's sister, for sure.

Even a week later, I'd managed to evade them. Mostly because the only time I left my sanctuary was to go to work, go to the bathroom, or make some sort of girl dinner. Real meals sounded hard and take-out was so damn expensive, especially after I'd gotten used to the ten-dollar entrees at Ziggy's.

I shoveled another spoonful of peppermint ice cream—found in the back of the freezer from Christmastime—into my mouth. More layers than probably necessary for spring in Chicago covered me, but nothing brought a girl comfort like fuzzy socks and her favorite oversized sweatshirt.

And the next episode of a K-Drama.

Some might have considered it a rare form of self-torture, but they were the only form of entertainment that felt even remotely tolerable. Plus, I couldn't go on living without learning what became of Taeyeon and YeJoon.

They got their fictional happy ending. It only took one day into my self-isolation to find that out.

Now, I was four more series deep into my newest obsession. All fantasy. All romantic subplots. Enjoyed in the darkness of my bedroom.

God, when had I gotten so pathetic?

Maybe it was all the vampire content I'd been consuming, but I actually hissed when the overhead light in my bedroom lit up.

"No big lights," I whined and shielded my eyes.

My request was not granted. Instead, the floor creaked and a soft *click* was followed by enhanced brightness. A lamp. I lifted my eyelids just enough to see a blurry outline of Laura standing at the foot of my bed.

"Looks like no lights in general, actually," she said. "Have you seen the sun lately, Dracula?"

"Not funny."

"Cain Luther?"

It was easy to narrow my eyes at my sister since they were hardly open to begin with. "What do you want?"

"I'm doing a wellness check." Laura plopped down on the end of my bed, tucking her legs under herself, crisscross applesauce style. "B mentioned not seeing you today, so when she picks up on that kinda stuff, you know it's legit."

"I'm honored," I replied, not sounding the least bit sincere.

Laura gave me a look before she glanced back over her shoulder at my TV. "What is this?" Her brow scrunched when she undoubtedly noticed the subtitles.

"A K-Drama."

"You watch those?"

"It's a new development."

"Something to do with your work trip?"

I lifted a brow, my eyes still somewhat narrowed. Wow, I really *had* trapped myself in the dark for a long time if it was taking this long to readjust. "Why would it have anything to do with my trip?"

Laura shrugged. "I don't know. You've been acting all weird since you got back."

My response to that was eating more ice cream. I should have known she'd catch on. Us Wilson girls were basically private investigators. Nothing got past us.

Except maybe the affections of an author that went unreciprocated for multiple years, and only when they finally were, it was determined that they couldn't be, sending the receiver of said affection into a spiral.

But other than that, we were spot-on for everything.

"Was the he-devil really that bad?" she asked.

"No."

"Ya know, when I stopped hearing from you so often, I thought about driving up there." Laura reached toward me, taking my spoon from my hand and dipping it into the ice cream pint. With her mouth full, she continued, "Figured he might have murdered you in your sleep or something. Or you'd murdered him." She paused, thinking, then pointed the spoon at me. "That one actually would make more sense from what I've been told."

Clearly, she hadn't been told nearly enough. I had no one to blame but myself for that. Here I was, mourning a relationship I'd been too chicken-shit to tell my own sister about. If it was any other person, she would have been the first one I told. The minute we slept together, Laura would have gotten a phone call—and she would have picked up, no matter the hour, because that's the kind of sister she was. We would have talked for hours, and she would have listened to every gory detail, and all of this could have been avoided.

But I hadn't. I'd kept Jackson a secret. Painted him as this villain I'd always thought he was. Now, no one would understand why I was so upset to have lost him. To everyone else in my life, he was the *he-devil*, as Laura had so kindly called him.

I could still try, I supposed.

I reached for my remote and hit pause on my show. I'd need to do some major rewinding later.

"I… I'm going through a bit of a breakup," I admitted, so quietly that I hoped Laura didn't hear.

She did.

My sister dropped the spoon and choked on her ice cream before letting out a sputtered, "*What?*" through her coughing. Then she pummeled my legs over my blanket. "Victoria Elizabeth Wilson, does the sibling code mean *nothing* to you? What the fuck! Why didn't you tell me? Who is he? Do I know him?"

"You know *of* him." That was for sure. The statement also saved me from further wrath for not telling her who it was. I could tell she was deep in thought trying to figure it out.

"Is it that barista at that café you always go to? Man-bun guy?" This time, the hit to my knee was much more playful, a proud smirk lighting my sister's face. "Get it girl. He's super cute, you know—if you're straight."

"It's not him," I said, then slumped lower, trying to hide

under the blankets. "It's… Jackson."

Laura's eyes were as big as saucers, but she didn't say anything. That was actually scarier.

"So… yeah," I said, filling the silence. "Surprise."

"You mean… the he-devil?" Laura finally managed.

"Please stop calling him that."

"Holy shit, you're not kidding." She repositioned herself so she was sitting on her knees, hands on her thighs, attention fully on me. "Since when?"

"Since the convention tour last year."

"You've been dating someone for almost *a year*?" Laura sounded absolutely flabbergasted. Probably because she hadn't figured it out for herself in all that time.

"Not dating," I clarified. "We… we were hooking up. A let-steam-off thing, you know? And then we were sent on this trip and… well, it escalated a bit."

"I'll say." Her lips trilled as she let out a breath. "Damn."

"I didn't tell you at first because I didn't think it would be more than a one-time thing," I confessed. "But then it kept happening and I was in too deep and—" I sighed. "You know how it is when the dick is just *that* good."

Laura tilted her head. "Tor, the exactly one guy I've slept with helped me realize penises aren't for me."

"Right." The one downside to my only sister being gay? She'd never understand the alluring yet fatal rarity of finding a great dick.

"But I mean, good for you for finding one you like even if

the guy is only half-decent?"

"He's better than half-decent." *Half-decent* was an insult, right up there on the caliber of *he-devil*. "He's… charming. And he listens—like, actually listens. Not that fake listening shit guys pull to get you to shut up. He smells nice and can cook and is super accomplished and has a good relationship with his family—or his mom, at least. His family's a bit broken. He's an awful dancer, but will do it anyway. And he's so vulnerable. God, it's so bad, Lo—the shit he's had to deal with. That's why he's such an ass," I said, poking her with each word to punctuate my statement. "It's a shield. And as soon as that goes down it's like—bam! New, incredible person."

And I'd let him go. Just like that.

It took a minute for me to realize I'd zoned out, lost in the daze of memories from the last few weeks—before that, even. Laura's lack of expected commentary was part of the reason it had taken so long.

"I know I suck for not telling you," I whispered.

"You don't suck," Laura replied. Then her face softened. "You've got it bad."

"Yeah." It had been a few days, but all the talk of Jackson brought around some fresh tears. One fell down my cheek when I blinked.

"Oh, Tor."

Laura was curled up beside me in an instant, wrapping me in a hug I hadn't realized I'd desperately been craving.

"It's so stupid," I said, sniffling. "He's just a guy."

"Yeah, but it sounds like he's a guy you might… you know."

"Love?"

"You said it, not me."

I nodded as best I could with my head on my sister's shoulder. "I do. Or I was starting to. We didn't really have a chance to let it go very far."

"Why did you guys end things if it sounds like it was going so well?"

"Starr."

"Excuse me?" Laura tapped my back, and I lifted my head to meet her gaze. "Did you just say your *job* is the reason why you broke up?"

"There's some policy that says employees can't date." Turns out it was actually a thing. Ann had pulled the page where it was listed out of the employee handbook and left it highlighted on my desk.

"He's not an employee, is he?"

"No, he's talent, which is apparently worse according to my boss."

"Have I ever told you I hate corporate America?"

I managed a small smile. "A few times."

"Well, who knows." Laura offered a comforting smile of her own as she wiped my tears away with her sleeve. "No one says you have to stay at Starr forever. I know you love the book stuff and all that, but if you ever leave, then you'll be free to date, right?"

She was right on both accounts. I'd never expected to have a crazy-long tenure at Starr, but it would be hard to find another job that would allow me to be surrounded by books if I left. At least in Chicago. New York could be an option; they were the hub of all the major publishers. But I was pushing it as it was when it came to cost of living.

Who was to say Jackson wouldn't have moved on by the time I found something new anyway?

I was about to argue when my phone buzzed. I might have let it sit there if it hadn't continued.

Who the heck was calling me at nearly nine at night?

Laura must have been curious, too, because she glanced around me to see my phone on the nightstand. She grew visibly confused.

"Okay, how many secret suitors do you freaking have?" she asked.

"None. What are you—?"

But I saw what she was talking about as soon as I turned around to grab my phone.

Marcus was calling me.

CHAPTER TWENTY-NINE

I MADE LAURA leave before I picked up Marcus's call. By the time she actually listened, I'd missed it.

"I was just leaving you a voicemail," he said by way of greeting when I called him back.

"Sorry, pesky roommate slash sister."

"Probably still better than nosy teenager children."

I grinned, despite the nerves beginning to swirl in my gut. Marcus and I hadn't spoken since he'd caught Jackson and I at the cabin. "Can't speak to that yet."

"You'll learn one day."

"Did you call me to talk about children or…?"

"No, no—just getting distracted," he said. "Sorry for the late-night call, but I wanted to check in."

This was… not normal. Sure, Marcus and I talked a fair amount, but not to the point where he would normally call me up on a random weekday night.

"I'm fine." I meant it as a statement, but the inflection snuck in at the end, making it sound more like a question. "And you?"

"Can't complain, but, hey—you haven't happened to talk to Jackson recently have you?"

I swallowed. "Uh, no. It's been a little bit." Apparently, Jackson's agent hadn't been made aware of recent developments, and I didn't plan on being the person who told him. "Why?"

"We met with the board at Starr today. About that contract for the new series?"

"Right. Yeah."

"We missed you at the meeting, first off."

Not what I expected to hear, given my last experiences with both the men he was implying missed me. "I'm still doing a lot of catching up. From when we were gone."

"Uh huh." Marcus's smirk came across loud and clear through the phone. "Well, regardless, I thought you should know that the editorial team at Starr offered to buy the rights to the book. Only as a trilogy, which is less than what we were hoping, but it was still a pretty good offer. Bigger than his last one."

My heart leapt into my throat. "That's wonderful. Congrats."

"Yeah, that offer came in last week, actually. Today, we went in to talk things over—you know, the nitty gritty of it all."

"Sure."

"Jackson turned it down."

I sat up like a zombie come back to life, so quick the

movement almost caused my phone to fly out of my hand. "What?"

"Wow. So, you actually didn't know."

"Of course I didn't know. Why would I know?" My hand ran up my forehead, into my hair. "Jesus…" I muttered more to myself than to Marcus. "So that's it? Is he done?"

"No, he's not done," Marcus said, easing a big chunk of the weight in my chest. "I'm going to continue to represent him, but we're going indie. Probably self-publishing, but we'll see if a smaller press would be willing to pick him up. We still believe this book has a great deal of potential in the market, especially with the new style choices Jackson made."

"New style choices?"

Marcus was quiet for a second. Then, "I wasn't going to bring this up, but… did you two do any talking while you were up at that cabin?"

"We weren't constantly having sex, if that's what you're implying," I responded, a hint of an edge in my tone. "We did a lot of talking."

"And Jackson never brought up what he was working on?"

"He gave me updates on his progress."

"But he didn't tell you about the content of his book?"

"I—no?"

Marcus went quiet, and in the silence, I could hear what sounded like a keyboard clacking.

"Check your email," he instructed after a few minutes.

I pulled my phone away from my ear and tapped the speaker

button before I went into my mail app. Right there at the top was a brand-new message from Marcus with the subject line "CONFIDENTIAL: Jackson S. Albrecht – Echoes of the Eldertide Book 1." He'd included an attachment, and I realized what it was as soon as I opened it.

"Am I legally allowed to have this?" I asked as I scrolled through the first chapter of Jackson's most recent manuscript.

"Technically, I make that call, so yeah. It's all yours. The first five chapters, anyway. That's all I have. We used it for the pitch."

"I… I don't know if Jackson will want me to read this," I admitted.

"Maybe not, but I think it's important you do. It might make his decision make a little more sense." Marcus chuckled, and I could just imagine him shaking his head like he had during so many other conversations. "It's no wonder why you're so shocked he didn't accept the offer."

"What's that supposed to mean?"

Once again, I could hear Marcus's smile as he said, "Read the chapters, Tori. Then you'll get it."

IT TOOK ME an hour to make it through the document, and that was mostly due to me pausing to mutter, "Holy shit," to myself approximately every five minutes.

The book was brilliant. Only five chapters in, and I already had half a mind to email Marcus back, pleading with him to find a way to get me the rest.

To think it had only taken Jackson a handful of weeks to create this. I knew this portion had likely been written before we'd left for our trip, but if the rest of the book followed its lead, I understood why Starr had offered him such a great deal to obtain the rights.

But I saw what Marcus meant—why this one was so different from the rest of Jackson's books.

He'd included a romantic subplot. And not just any romantic subplot. One with a beautiful, golden-haired maiden with whom the main character believed he never stood a chance.

The conflict was, obviously, a multitude of fantastical reasons, but I saw it for what it was. I might have missed it had Jackson not opened up to me the way he had, admitted so many of his secrets.

The main character—that was him. And the love interest… she was me. Curves and all.

I'd waited most of my life to see women who looked like me be represented in books, but never in my life did I think I'd actually see *me*. Tori Wilson. My image forever immortalized on these pages.

And the way he spoke about me…

I'd paused at that, too, in order to let the welling tears pass. It was always nerve-wracking reading romance written by men. Too many supple, bouncing breasts and what not. But this—it was like that adoring look he always gifted me had been translated directly onto the page.

Seeing this, it was clear why Marcus had been so dumbfounded by my shock. It didn't take a rocket scientist to rationalize Jackson's decision.

It was also how I knew he meant every damn word he'd ever said to me—or about me, if the manuscript was to be considered.

I swiped out of the document and typed out a quick now I get it text to Marcus.

It was half past ten at this point, so I didn't expect him to respond, but my phone lit up with a new call.

"Thought you might," Marcus greeted.

"It was impossible not to." I sighed and ran my hand down my face. "Jackson's still technically under contract with Starr for the last *Bandits of the Forsaken* book?"

"Mhm. That'll take at least a year—maybe two—to put out." I suppressed my groan to keep this call a little professional. I *hated* the fraternization policy. "We have another meeting tomorrow to go over the details."

That little tidbit of information had me perking up instantly. "You're both still in town?"

"I'm always in town," Marcus reminded me. "But yes— Jackson's here too. I think he's planning on leaving after the meeting."

There it was. My chance. "What time is it at?"

CHAPTER THIRTY

RECEPTIONIST SAM WOULDN'T stop staring at me.

I cast her a nervous smile, my foot tapping impatiently on the tile floor of our building's lobby. A stray Starr employee would pass through from time to time—crossing to another part of the office or returning from a coffee run—and each time, my heart lurched. It was never the person I wanted to come through the lobby.

"Do you have a guest coming in for a meeting, Tori?" Sam finally asked.

I glanced fleetingly at her, not wanting to accidentally miss Jackson or Marcus if they did finally come through. I'd tried to coordinate my trip to the lobby with the meeting time Marcus had given me on the phone last night, but apparently, I hadn't done a great job of that. One look at the digital clock behind Sam's reception desk told me it was already ten minutes past the time it was supposed to end. Not an uncommon occurrence around here, but on a day where I was so on-edge, it was definitely a bit more annoying than usual.

"No," I replied.

That clearly made her confusion regarding my presence in her space grow. This wasn't exactly a place where many people lingered. Though over the last year, she should have gotten plenty used to the unexpected activity.

I peered at the clock again as I clutched my phone tighter in my hand. Only one minute had passed.

Had the meeting ended early? I hadn't let Marcus know my reason for asking about their schedule. They could have left the building without me even knowing. I could have been standing here like an idiot for the last fifteen minutes only to—

The glass doors that led to the office space opened, and this time my heart jumped for good reason.

Jackson and Marcus had their heads down, engaged in conversation, as they entered the lobby. Both of them had their bags in hand, hinting that this was it; they wouldn't be coming back. At least not for some time. As Marcus had said, the process to publish Jackson's last book under contract with Starr would be a long and tedious one.

But I didn't want to wait. I needed to talk to him now. Even just this first glimpse—the first since we'd left the cabin—had me dying to run across the room and throw myself at Jackson.

I wouldn't, of course. We had an audience—one member of which was already probably pretty traumatized by what he'd previously seen. And the office was the last place I should show any public displays of affection. Rahm had eyes and ears all over.

Turns out, I didn't need to. Jackson's eyes lifted from where he'd been watching his footsteps and instantly landed on me. As if he'd known I would be there, waiting.

He stopped, and Marcus followed suit soon after, their conversation coming to a lull.

Sam's eyes darted between us. Yup. The girl was definitely getting some good entertainment lately, courtesy of the Starr marketing department.

My mouth gaped, and my chest rose and fell with heavy breaths. No matter how hard I wanted to, I couldn't seem to get any words to come out. I'd planned to say so much, even going as far as to rehearse in my office all morning leading up to this moment. But my brain was broken now that Jackson was actually in front of me.

He looked good. Polished as always, his brown hair neatly tamed with gel, his white button-down shirt tucked perfectly into wrinkle-free trousers. Even his loafers seemed to have an extra shine to them, but maybe that was just my imagination. I figured he could have shown up in his grey sweatpants and Purdue University shirt and I still would have gawked.

"Tori."

My name on his lips brought me back to reality, but it still didn't entirely fix me.

"Hi," was all I managed to whisper.

"Wha—" He cast a nervous glance back towards the offices from which he'd just come. For the first time, I wondered if Rahm was nearby. "What are you doing here?"

I realized I didn't give a flying fuck what Rahm Singh thought.

I took a few cautious steps toward him. "I work here."

"I know that, but—" This time his eyes shifted to Marcus who gave an encouraging nod. "Won't you get in trouble?"

"It doesn't matter," I said.

I was standing in front of him now, my head tilted back just a little in order to see his face. Marcus took a few steps back, but I didn't miss the smile growing on his lips.

"I read your manuscript."

Jackson's brow scrunched. "I thought you were taken off all my projects?"

"Not *Bandits of the Forsaken*," I clarified.

This time when he looked back at Marcus, his eyes were narrowed a bit and his voice was less enthusiastic as he said, "I see."

Marcus's smile only grew. A true conspirator.

"Jackson." His eyes slid back to me at the sound of his name. I swallowed. "Why didn't you take the contract offer?"

He pivoted, not even trying to hide his shock, as he asked his agent, "Who's side are you on here?"

Marcus shrugged. "I'm a neutral bystander, doing what's best for both parties."

"Hey," I whispered, reaching out to grab his arm. "Seriously, why? You're giving up something huge here."

Jackson stared at where we touched, then his eyes slowly lifted to my face—along with one of his hands. His messenger bag slipped off his shoulder and fell to the ground before the other joined.

"You're seriously asking me that?"

"Yeah, I am," I said. "After all you told me… why would you give that opportunity up?"

"I can make my mom proud in other ways," he said. "I've already built up enough of a readership to where I don't think I need Starr's backing anymore. Besides." His thumbs brushed soothing strokes over my cheeks. "I don't care what you think you know. A publishing contract is nothing in comparison to having a chance with you."

"Holy shit."

Jackson's sight strayed past my shoulder, and I turned around to find Sam gaping wide-eyed at us. As soon as the attention found her, though, she shrank back, a blush growing on her cheeks.

"Sorry," she apologized. "Carry on."

I could have sworn I heard a quiet, "This is better than *Love Island*," as Jackson and I found each other again.

"What if I told you I wasn't worth that kind of sacrifice?" I challenged.

"I'd tell you that's bullshit and you're wrong," he retorted. "Then I'd tell you that I can't imagine a woman like you coming second to my career."

I swallowed my building emotions. "You sure about that?"

"Positive." He spoke so matter-of-factly that I had no choice but to believe him.

"What's your family gonna say when you tell them?"

"Something tells me they'll be okay with the decision," Jackson said, then grinned. "Mom's become much more interested in grandbabies than books as it is."

I chuckled. "Oh yeah?"

"Mhm." His thumbs brushed over my cheeks again. "Not that grandbabies are a requirement."

"I like babies," I said.

"So do I."

I lifted onto my toes, my neck stretched so my lips were only within an inch of his. "Sounds like we might have a solution to your problem, then."

Jackson's hands drifted down to where my head met my neck, angling me so we were within centimeters of one another now. His breath was hot against my mouth as he said, "That's a big commitment, Wilson."

Our lips brushed one another as I said, "You're worth it, Albrecht."

And then we were unapologetically kissing right there in the lobby of Starr Publishing and Media's office. My arms snaked around his neck, and his hands drifted down, pressing flat against my back to keep me close. Not that I had plans of backing away. A tornado would have ripped through the building, and I never would have stopped clinging to Jackson.

"What's this?"

Turns out, I wasn't scared of a tornado, but Rahm Singh's voice was enough to have Jackson and I pulling back from one another, albeit slowly.

The Publishing Board Director eyed Marcus furiously as he strode past, but that was nothing compared to what Jackson and I received the moment he stood before us.

"I thought I made myself clear, Victoria," Rahm seethed. "There is to be no more contact between you and Mr. Albrecht."

Jackson shifted so he stood beside me, his hand never leaving the small of my back. I could feel the tension in it, and when I looked up, he appeared ready to explode.

"I'm done with Starr," he said. "I didn't accept the contract."

"I'm well aware of that, Mr. Albrecht. Thank you." I narrowed my eyes at Rahm's tone. He was speaking to Jackson like he was a child. "But should I remind you of the details of the meeting we just held? Your last book won't be coming out for another fourteen months."

My heart dropped. I knew that stupid final book would become an obstacle.

"Until that book is published, you are still under contract with Starr," Rahm finished, as if Jackson and I couldn't piece that together for ourselves. "Which means the fraternization policy still stands." He turned his attention to me. "Although blatant disregard for authority opens up a whole different discussion."

Jackson's hand pressed harder into my back, and for a moment, I thought it was because he was pissed. It probably was, in part, but then I realized I was worse. My whole body shook with rage, my fists clenched at my sides.

Fuck. This. Dude.

"Don't worry, I've thought of a solution that will fix all of this," I said, my voice dripping with ice. "I quit."

Whatever Rahm was expecting, it wasn't that. In fairness, I hadn't either, but there was no turning back now.

"W-what do you mean you quit, Victoria?" he repeated, sounding genuinely nervous for the first time in his life.

"She doesn't seem too bad now, does she?" Jackson taunted.

Rahm's eyes shifted to him before they landed on me again. "If you leave, just know you'll never be able to come back."

There he was with more threats, except this time, I saw them for what they were: a feeble attempt to maintain his power. That was the thing. Rahm had never had that with me. Not really. I'd been someone who challenged him. Lynn, while a powerful business woman in her own right, had been raised in an era of respecting the corporate hierarchy. Me, on the other hand? I'd never been afraid to speak my mind.

Rahm didn't like that trait in a woman. Rahm didn't like that at all. Anyone who could make his control crumble was a threat, so he offered some of his own in retaliation.

The days of him using that strategy with me, though, were over.

"Fine. I'll find something else," I said with a shrug. "Don't know if you're aware, but my boyfriend happens to be a pretty big name in publishing. I'm sure he can help out."

Jackson's arm moved from around my waist to my shoulders.

He pulled me closer against his side, and when I looked up, he was grinning down at me.

Boyfriend had definitely been the right choice of words.

"Because I'm nice," I continued, "I'll write up a formal two-weeks' notice. And trust me, you'll want me around that much longer. You have *no* idea what you're getting into with Alexis's training."

Rahm's eyes widened momentarily with worry, but he didn't say anything further. I'd just cut loose from my puppet master. There was nothing left for him to do.

"Sounds like a celebratory lunch is in order, don't you think?" Marcus spoke up. He stepped beside Rahm and clapped a casual hand on the man's shoulder. "Tori, care to join Jackson and I?"

"She can't leave. She's still an employee here until—"

"I'd love to," I interrupted with a smile. "Let me go grab my purse."

"No need," Marcus said, waving my statement away with a few flicks of his wrist. "It's on Starr."

I grinned. "Even better."

"Now you just wait a minute—" Rahm tried calling as the three of us made our way to the front door.

"Good luck finding someone else to fill this position," I called back over my shoulder. "Hopefully they exceed your freakishly high expectations."

And for good measure, I tossed up my middle finger as Jackson and I strode through the front doors, Marcus following behind us, none of us bothering to look back.

"Bold move, Wilson," Jackson said, shifting his hold around my shoulders.

"I'll say," Marcus agreed. "What do you have in mind for a new job?"

"I can help," Jackson said quickly. He glanced back at Marcus. "We both can. Between the two of us, we know plenty of connections in publishing."

I smiled, knowing that they would do just that if I asked.

But I didn't plan to.

Laura was right. Corporate America fucking sucked.

"It's okay," I said, then tilted my head back to look up at Jackson. "I think I'm going to try something a little different this time."

FOURTEEN MONTHS LATER

"WE'RE ALL SET. You ready to let in the stampede?"

I nodded and smiled at Hemi. "Let's do this."

She winked back at me over her shoulder before she switched the lock on the front door of Sunrise Brews from closed to open. She'd hardly taken a step back before the throngs of fantasy readers came through the door, eager to get their hands on the latest Jackson S. Albrecht novel at the first-ever Turning Pages Bookstore signing event.

"Slow down. Everyone's going to get their book," Rosie called out, trying to create some order.

Harper was here too, brought in specifically for the event by Hemi. I knew we'd need a little bit of help, given Turning Pages wasn't even in its own space yet. I was still working up to that, using part of Hemi's space until I could save enough of my modest earnings from shifts at Sunrise Brews and Ziggy's to buy my own storefront in downtown Timberland Creek.

I'd called Rosie—or rather Ziggy's since I didn't have her personal number—as soon as I'd walked out of Starr for the last time. To say she was surprised to hear from me was an understatement. If not for Quinn Nelson's confirmation that we had, in fact, checked out of the cabin, the townies might have believed Jackson and I were dead.

They'd really been looking forward to that goodbye.

But it was also Quinn Nelson who'd saved us from explaining ourselves. Turns out people liked it when you said, sure—we might have left without goodbye, but we're making up for it by moving back full-time.

Within three months, she had the cabin privately on the market, Jackson and I put in our offer, I sublet my portion of the lease in Oak Park, and we moved up to middle-of-nowhere Wisconsin.

Except now, it wasn't the middle of nowhere. Timberland Creek was officially home, and feeling more and more like it every day.

I made my way through the crowd to the back of the café, where Jackson sat at a table filled with copies of his latest book. As soon as the reader presented a pre-paid ticket to the signing, he took one off the stack, smiling and chatting with each attendee of the event.

I couldn't help smiling too. He'd come such a long way from those first few signings I'd worked with him.

"Hey."

Rosie slid up beside me and wrapped her arm around my shoulders. I wrapped one of my own around her back, and rested my head on her shoulder—our usual side-hug. Sure, she was technically my boss now, but more than anything she'd become my friend.

"I'm proud of you, sweetie," she whispered. "Proud of both of you."

"I promise I'll take an extra shift or two to make up for you coming here." It was the height of the busy season in Timberland Creek, and this event had taken away two key players from the operation of the always-packed Ziggy's.

"Ach," Rosie scoffed. "Don't worry about that. This is worth it. We have a new celebrity in town now."

I chuckled as my eyes drifted back to Jackson. He was taking a selfie with a reader dressed as a particular blonde maiden.

He'd ended up self-publishing that book after all.

It had instantly hit the top of the indie charts with readers and critics alike agreeing that it was a shame Jackson S. Albrecht hadn't written romance before; he was a natural.

Not that he'd needed reviews to tell him that. I reminded him pretty often myself.

Jackson gave the girl a hug, and she beamed as she left the table with her freshly signed book clutched to her chest. In the brief reprieve between attendees, he found me in the crowd and winked.

I unwrapped my arm from around Rosie and blew a kiss back.

"And to think," Rosie said. "You tried to tell me there was nothing going on between you two kids when we first met."

"Yeah, yeah, yeah," I replied with an eye roll. "We know. We were stupid."

Rosie chuckled. "Nah. You just needed time."

I smiled in response. Maybe she was right, but something told me that wasn't entirely the case.

Jackson and I met each other's waiting eyes again, and he mouthed, "I love you," as he shut the book he'd just signed.

I blushed, heat overcoming me, just like I did every time he reminded me that I'd always come first for him.

Deep down, whether I'd once wanted to admit it or not, Jackson would always be my number one, too.

ACKNOWLEDGEMENTS

I didn't always know that this book (or this series of books, rather) would come to be. The plan had always been to publish *Starstruck* as a standalone and be done. But from the moment I wrote Jackson onto the page during a full manuscript re-write—or maybe more so the time I made him and Tori interact for the first time—I knew another book needed to happen.

As always, I have to thank my parents and brother for their unending support. There have been a lot of books in not a lot of time lately, so thanks for keeping me sane and cheering me on through it all!

Thank you, Jessica, for being a wonderful proofreader and eBook formatter. I'm so grateful to continue to work with you on projects. It's even more fun working with someone I consider a friend!

Thank you, Nicole, for creating the cover illustrations of Tori and Jackson. You truly continue to outdo yourself with your art! Only one set left to go!

Thank you to my friends, family, and work colleagues who continue to show more support than I could ever imagine, even after so many books!

Thank you to the very-real town of Fish Creek, WI, which was the inspiration behind the very-fictional town of Timberland Creek. A special thank you to all the people I've met and businesses I've visited over the nearly thirty years of summer and fall vacations. From Bayside Tavern (Ziggy's) to Blue Horse Café (Sunrise Brews) to Fish Creek Market (Main Street Market), just to name a few that I tried to pay homage to in this book, thank you for making your little town feel like my home away from home.

Thank you to the online writing and bookish communities for your support through the years. Whether you joined recently or before I'd even started publishing, you all continue to give me the courage I need to put my stories out in the world. (You also give me a place to vent with others who "get it", and for that I'm so thankful!)

And last, but certainly not least, thank you, dear reader, for picking up this novel and giving it a chance. By doing so, you are helping me achieve my dream, and I am forever grateful for that!

ABOUT THE AUTHOR

MCKENZIE BURNS is a multi-genre author from Chicago with a passion for writing stories that involve different cultures, witty banter, and women who don't take 'no' for an answer. Her spare time is spent drinking copious amounts of coffee and searching for obscure music.

KEEP LISTENING

Need a little hype music following your read?
Scan the playlist code in your Spotify app to listen to
TORI'S BOSS BITCH PLAYLIST.

STAY CONNECTED

Want to be the first to hear about new releases from McKenzie Burns? Visit her website or follow her on social media!

www.authormckenzieburns.wixsite.com/home

@author_mckenzieburns